The Duke and the King

Book 11 in the Norman Genesis Series
By
Griff Hosker

The Duke and the King

Published by Sword Books Ltd 2019

SWORD
BOOKS

Contents

The Duke and the King i
Prologue 1
Chapter 1 3
Chapter 2 18
Chapter 3 28
Chapter 4 45
Chapter 5 56
Chapter 6 70
Chapter 7 84
Chapter 8 97
Chapter 9 109
Chapter 10 122
Chapter 11 132
Chapter 12 145
Chapter 13 156
Chapter 14 166
Chapter 15 175
Chapter 16 185
Chapter 17 192
Epilogue 202
Norse Calendar 204
Glossary 205
Maps and Illustrations 210
Historical note 211
Other books by Griff Hosker 215

Prologue

I had been Lord Göngu-Hrólfr Rognvaldson. I had been Lord of Rouen and the chief of all the Vikings who lived along the lower Seine. That was before I became a Norman; the first of the Normans. After I had led my men to besiege Paris, King Charles had been forced to seek peace with me. He had given me the land which we held along the banks of the Seine and he had given me a title. He named me Count of Normandy. My men gave me a better one. To them, I was the Duke of Normandy. That meant I did not have to defer to any save the royal family. As I rarely saw any Frankish nobles that was not a problem. I deferred to no one! There was a price to be paid. I had to change my name to Robert. That did not worry me. I had had more names than Loki! No matter what men called me I was still the same warrior I had always been. I was still the most feared Viking.

There was one further price. I had to be baptised and become Christian. Padraig had been the priest who had served me faithfully for many years. He had always said that I had a Christian heart. I was baptised but the dousing with water meant nothing to me. It did not change my heart or that which lay within my giant frame. I had been to the bottom of the sea and lived. I was not afraid of a wetting. In my heart, I was still what they called a pagan. I still believed in the Norns and the Allfather. I was able to reconcile the part of the religion which I was supposed to follow. The Allfather and the One God appeared to me to be the same. When I was in my church in Rouen and the Bishop spoke of God then to me, that was the Allfather. I would never do as Christians were supposed to. I would never turn a cheek. I would neither forgive nor forget a hurt done to me or mine. I took the Frank's coin and I spread it amongst my jarls or, as they were now termed, lords. They ruled my lands for me and I ruled Rouen. My son, William Longsword, knew how I felt. He too had been baptised and he, like me, clung to the old religion.

1

Our old ways did not need a church and we had no priests. If the Christians were foolish enough not to believe in the Norns or witches then that was their loss.

The other price we paid was that I was supposed not to raid the Franks and to control all the Vikings who came to my land. That was not as easy as the King of the Franks made it sound. The Vikings were not a nation. They were a state of mind. There were Norsemen, Danes and Frisians. There were even English Vikings. They did not answer to a king. I had taken gold and made a promise. So long as Charles was King of the Franks then I would keep my word, no matter how hard it was. However, in my heart, I was still the grandson of Hrólfr the Horseman and I was still a Viking.

Chapter 1

It had been some years since King Charles had given me my land. In that time, we had stopped Vikings raiding the land of the Franks and we had, by and large, kept the peace. We had not needed to shed any blood. We merely sent them down to the Loire to raid the Bretons. That kept them far from the land which King Charles ruled. We had not needed to raid because of the booty and treasure we had taken from the Franks. I liked to think that I ruled well. The Vikings amongst my people might have agreed but the Franks did not. I did not rule the Frankish way. I was, supposedly. Christian. I had been baptised. I attended church but another cannot read what is in a man's heart. To me, I still believed in the Allfather. Odin was a better god than the White Christ. He did not turn the other cheek. If I was angered then I punished and I punished in my way. The church did not like my rule. I allowed their churches. I had said that to the Frankish King and I would not be foresworn but they paid taxes like the others who lived in my land. If Padraig had still been alive, he would have known the truth but he had died in Paris. Others had died. Some had been in battle and that saddened me. Of those who had sailed with me from the fjords in Norway only Sámr Oakheart, Bergil Fast Blade and Ragnar the Resolute were still alive. Sven and the others had gone to the Otherworld. All had died with their swords in their hands. I would see them in Valhalla. Haraldr, Harold Mighty Fist, Gandálfr, Bagsecg, Bjorn, Leif and Bjorn the Brave lived still. They now ruled some of my towns but the rest were gone. My son, William Longsword, would rule when I died.

Although I was proud of William, he had faults. Those faults could be laid at my door. I had been preoccupied with strengthening my land when he had been growing up. He could be a little wild. He took many women to bed. When he raided, he brought back slaves and he used them. He did not seem interested in ruling my land. That again was down to me. I had no woman to share my bed. I was married to Normandy. However, he was a good drekar captain. He was a mighty warrior and he could ride. In short, he was as perfect a son as a Viking could wish. However, I knew that he would need to change and I would have to change him. He needed to become a Norman leader. William still raided. He just made certain that he did not raid the Franks of King Charles. All the rest suffered. King Edward of Wessex was not the king his father had been and they brought great riches into my land. Godwin Red Eyes, one of my oathsworn, acted as a foster father when he sailed. He was a good warrior. He had been blinded and Padraig had saved him and given him back his sight. He was as loyal a warrior as any who served me. The Bretons were a threat and we both raided and fought them. I still ruled. My hands were on the steering board of Normandy. They gripped it tightly. William did not wish to usurp me. There were no others who could challenge me. I had absolute power just so long as I didn't attack the Franks. I did not.

Egil Flame Bearer was another who had been my oathsworn. He had been my standard bearer and, like Godwin, had survived Paris. He had changed after that battle. Many of his friends had died. He had been there at the end and I knew that his heart had died a little with Æbbi Bonecrusher and Harold the Bold. He was already married. He had a family. They needed him close to home and I had made him captain of the guard in Rouen. He was happy in that role. He could still fight like a wolf and yet he had a family to raise. With two sons and a daughter, he was changed from the warrior who stood behind me with my banner. He had another purpose in life. He lived the life that his dead oar brothers could not. He was content.

Many men asked why I did not enjoy an easy life as a lord. The simple fact was that I did. As part of the peace, we had agreed I had a child bride, Gisela. She was the daughter of King Charles and she lived with him in Paris. By the time she was ready to be with me, I would have seen almost eighty summers. It was a political marriage. I could enjoy women whenever I chose. In reality, I rarely took a woman to bed. I would not be in marriage again. Poppa, William's mother, had rid me of any desire to be duped a second time. I drank, I hunted, I flew my hawks and I still made war. My mind was as sharp as ever. My lords had taken on Frankish customs. Sven Blue Cheek had never adopted Frankish customs. He had lived as a Viking until the day he died. But even Bergil

Fast Blade now shunned Viking dress. He drank wine and not ale. He had a Frankish wife and their home was little different from any to be found to the west of us. He was still like family to me and when I heard that he was ill I did not hesitate. I took ship and sailed to Caen. My ship was still *'Fafnir'*. Many thought she was too old for me to use and they urged me to build a bigger ship more fitting for the Duke of Normandy. The two of us defied those who thought age made for weakness. I still took the steering board. Erik Leifsson was my captain but his wife had just given birth to another son. I left him in Rouen. It was a short voyage and I enjoyed the thrill of steering once more.

The difference was my crew. Few were true Norse or even Dane. They were like my son and they had some Frankish blood coursing through their veins. That did not matter for in their hearts they were Northmen! The Franks called us Normans and our land Normandy. We were still warriors. They had names like Baldwin and Richard now but when I looked down the centre of the drekar, I still saw faces from the past. Gandálfr's son Mauger The Fierce was typical of the ones who rowed up the river to Caen. He had the same Viking upbringing as his father but none had lived the Viking life of raiding and pillaging. He had his father's colouring but he spoke both Frank and Norse. Our language was changing as were we. My grandfather Hrólfr the Horsemen would have struggled to understand all that Mauger said. He was one of my hearth weru. All ten of them were descended from men who had followed me to this land and all were immensely loyal. Some had fought with us at the siege of Paris when we had won this land but none had the experience their fathers had.

Caen had been the home of Sven Blue Cheek. When he had died, without issue, I had given it to Sámr Oakheart. Sámr had been lord of Bayeux but Caen was the second most important stronghold in my land. Sámr was the man to hold it for me. Bergil lived close by. He lived closer to the Bretons than many of my lords. Sámr Oakheart was a solid lord. If you asked him to hold a town or a bridge then you knew he would. Now, he too was older. He had fought at my side since Norway. He had sons and he had the best of warriors. He too, however, had begun to adopt certain Frankish ways. He dressed like a Frank and he trimmed his hair. He still had a beard. Many young warriors now shaved their faces and trimmed their hair.

"Sámr Oakheart, it is good to see you!"

"Aye lord. We have not raided for some time. My blade aches for Breton blood."

I laughed. Sámr Oakheart had been at Bayeux for many years. He had borne the brunt of Breton attacks.

"Aye, perhaps I will stir this old carcass to chastise them."

"You could do more than that, lord. Frankish warriors do not raid; they invade and make the land of their enemy theirs. Count Gourmaëlon of Brittany is not Alan the Great, my lord. We can eat into his land and retake the Cotentin."

Many of my men felt the same. We had taken Normandy and they wished me to take Brittany too. "You sound like my son. That day may come. As for the rest, we have secure borders?"

He nodded, "We do and the people pay taxes."

"I wish that was true in all of my land. North of the Seine there is discontent."

Sámr nodded, "We always knew there would be. We have fewer lords in that part of the land. It is close to Flanders and we know that Count Arnulf of Flanders stirs up trouble."

"You have heard that here, too?"

"Aye, lord. We have many ships which put in here. The Count of Flanders is ambitious. He has made no secret of the fact that he would like the land which lies to the south of the Somme."

Sámr was a good leader and one of the best friends I had ever had. He was astute. When I looked at him, I just saw a greyer version of the Viking who had fought with me in Paris.

"And Bergil. You are his nearest neighbour, what of him? I heard he was unwell. Some said close to death!"

Sámr laughed, "Dead drunk more like." He became serious. "You know his wife ran off with a Breton lord?"

The words sent a shiver through me. I knew what that could do. My former wife, Poppa, had deceived me with a priest. I shook my head, "I did not know that. What did he do?"

"Took a dive into a jug of wine and did not emerge. If he is unwell it is because he drinks wine and not ale. He rarely stirs from his hall."

I began to become angry. Bergil was like a brother to me. This was not like him. "His sons and daughters?"

"His sons stayed. His daughters fled with their mother. They ran to Nantes."

I nodded. Sámr's wife, Birgitta, handed me a horn of ale, "Perhaps you are right. I should turn my attention to the new Count of Brittany."

"That will not bring back Bergil's wife."

"You think I worry about that? Poppa is in a nunnery and I do not miss her. No, we grow old and fat." I patted my waist. It was growing. "We are Vikings. If we sit and squat then we become Franks! I will see Bergil and give him a kick up the arse. Then we will think about raiding the Bretons."

"By land or sea?"

"Both!"

"Do not forget we have lost many men. Sven Blue Cheek is no longer with us."

"Yet we have many more warriors now than when we took on King Charles! I have my son and I have young warriors. Perhaps this is the time to blood them. The old greybeards like you, Gandálfr and Ragnar the Resolute could watch and advise with me."

He laughed, "Lord Göngu-Hrólfr Rognvaldson, they might call you Robert but that does not make you a Frank. You will stand in the front rank and you will hew heads! As will we! You will not leave us behind to watch. If we go to war then all of us will fight."

Many men have a name that they outgrow. Sámr Oakheart was not one of them. He had been watching my back since we had left Norway and he was still a reassuring presence.

My hearth weru and I borrowed horses and rode to Bergil's hall. As usual, the horse I rode was not big enough and my feet trailed along the ground. It was not a dignified way to travel. Perhaps I was becoming a Frank that I worried about such things. Like most of my lord's homes, Bergil's stronghold was fortified with a raised hall, palisades and ditches. This part of my land was at peace but there were always enemies close enough to make us wary and to need somewhere to defend. This was a new land to my hearth weru. They came from Rouen or north of the Seine. To them, this was a foreign country and they rode close to me. There had been a time when there had been no horse large enough to carry me. That was how I had got my name. I had been called the Strider for my feet touched the ground when I rode a horse. Since then my horse breeders, Erik and Gilles, had managed to breed a new type of horse. They were much bigger than the older type. They were slower but I no longer needed to get anywhere in a hurry. It meant that when we rode my men had to look up at me.

Mauger and William son of Æbbi flanked me. "This is a good country, lord, yet there are many raised halls. Is it dangerous too?"

"Aye William. The Bretons are ever close. When Alan the Great was Duke then we fought many battles here."

Mauger said, "My father told me that he called himself King of Brittany!"

"Aye, he did. He never was and he learned to fear both our horsemen and our shield walls." I laughed, "I remember a time when my warriors did not know how to sit astride a horse and to fight. We had men like Stephen of Andecavis and Alain of Auxerre to fight for us. You young warriors are the future of the clan."

Mauger laughed, "Clan, now that is a word we rarely hear these days, lord."

"And that is sad. The Clan of the Horse was how we called ourselves. When we sailed from Norway there were just a couple of ships with all of our people packed into them. Now we have grown but my heart still yearns for those days when I knew every face and every name." I pointed to the distant walls of Bergil's home. "Once I would see Bergil every day. I have not seen him now since we returned from Paris and I was given Normandy! That is sad and I think we are all weakened by it. We are still few in number. We are surrounded by Franks and Bretons. Most would wish us driven back into the sea."

"They will not do that, lord." He sounded confident but I was not certain. Had I been sent here to stir me from my apathy? Was Bergil's ailment a symptom of something seriously wrong in my land?

We rode the last couple of miles in reflective silence. We were greeted by Bergil's sons, Odo and Robert. They were fine-looking warriors. I was very poor with ages. I could barely tell any man how old was my son. I could not remember when these two had been born. I could not have said which was the elder. When one stepped forward and gave a bow I knew which was the older of the two.

"Duke Robert I am Robert son of Bergil Fast Blade. This is an unexpected honour."

I held my arm out for him to grasp, "We are not Franks to bow and scrape. This is how warriors greet each other." I gripped his arm. He did the same and I was reassured that it was a firm grip. "I hear your father is unwell." They looked at each other and then my hearth weru. I nodded, "Mauger, take the horses to the stable and go to the warrior hall. We will stay here for the night, at least."

"Aye lord."

We were alone. There were no sentries nearby and we could talk. "Now, tell me all and leave nothing out. I want the truth."

"When my mother left us, she seemed to take the heart from our father. He was fond of our sisters." Robert had not said he was fond of their mother. "He ceased riding and spent more time drinking than ruling this land. We were lucky. The border has been quiet. The people are content and the farms prosper. A month since he fell ill. We sent for the priest and he thought that our father was dying. That is when we sent word to you."

I looked at each of them in turn, "And you should have sent to me a long time before he became ill. Did you think it was right for him to drink himself into an early death?"

"No, lord, but you are a Duke and have a large land to rule."

I shook my head. When we had been a clan this would not have happened. "Take me to him and then leave us. My men and I will stay. I will speak to him. You are now both men. We will go to war soon with the Bretons. If your father cannot then I expect you to lead his men."

"Go to war? The Bretons have been at peace. Why stir them?"

"Because, Odo, son of Bergil Fast Blade, we are still Vikings. We cannot fight the Franks. Your father has sunk into a pit of despair. We are warriors and a true warrior has no time for such self-indulgence. Your father's ailment has been sent to stir me from my comfortable life. Come. Time is wasting!"

Bergil's hall was not Viking, it was Frank. I saw the wall hangings his wife had placed upon the wall. There were metal goblets on the table and not horns. A priest was emerging from Bergil's chamber. One thing I did like about the White Christ was his healers. We had volva but the priests who knew how to heal had saved many of our people. I respected them.

"This is Father Geoffrey, our healer."

"Tell me, Father, will my lord live?"

The priest smiled, "Duke Robert, the words men speak of you are true. You are a plain-spoken man. If Lord Bergil eats more and drinks much less then he might still live. If he continues as he has been then we will bury him inside a month."

I liked this priest, "And your honesty does you credit." I turned to Bergil's sons. "And you two will ensure that he obeys the priest's commands." I saw the look of apprehension on their faces. I laughed. "Do not worry, your father will heed my words. Now leave me. I will deal with this. Leave a servant outside the door so that I may send for food."

I entered and was shocked by what I saw. Bergil was a bloated version of the man I had known. His face looked to be twice the size I remembered. His eyes were bloodshot and puffy. I took in the empty jug of wine. Some had spilt upon his sheets. It looked as though he had bled in battle. He was not fighting men. He was fighting himself for his life and losing. This was not the same man who had helped me to fight our way from the fjord and to grasp this corner of the land of the Franks. He had been taken. It would have been better if he had died in Paris as Æbbi Bonecrusher and my other heroes. Then he would be in Valhalla and when I met him again, he would be the same warrior I had fought alongside.

His eyes flickered open, "Lord Göngu-Hrólfr Rognvaldson! What brings you here to my land?"

"I came to see an old friend but found, instead, a grotesque and bloated creature who has consumed Bergil Fast Blade. What happened?"

He tried to rise and I saw that it caused him pain. "My wife left me!"

"And she took with you your strength and your honour?" I shook my head. "Your uncle was jarl. What would he say now? Rouse yourself and rise!"

He sank back into the soft bed. "I cannot. Let me die!"

I grabbed his arm and pulled him to his feet. He was overweight but I still exercised every day. I could still cleave a pig's head in two with one blow from my Long Sword. "If you are going to die then it will be on your feet with a sword in your hand. It will be as a Viking and not a pitiful excuse for a Frank!"

As he stood and looked at me, I saw him begin to gag. I moved out of the way as he vomited on the floor. I noticed specks of blood, or perhaps it was wine, in the puddle that spread across the floor.

"Come, we will get some fresh air."

He tried to resist me but I was too strong, "No Lord Göngu-Hrólfr Rognvaldson, my men cannot see me like this! Let me hide in my chamber!"

I put my face close to him. "Do you think your men do not know what you are like? This room stinks! They know already!" I opened the door and a surprised servant stood there. "Lord Bergil has been unwell. Clean his chamber and put fresh bedding upon his bed. From now on he drinks ale only! No wine!" The servant glanced at Bergil for confirmation. I roared, "I am Duke and you will obey me or die!"

"Yes, lord!"

I almost dragged my old friend out into the daylight. It was not particularly bright but he had to shade his eyes. I saw Father Geoffrey. He was smiling. He nodded, "The first steps, Duke Robert, are always the hardest!"

I headed for the ladder which led to the fighting platform over the gatehouse. I thought Bergil might vomit as we climbed the steps but he did not. When we reached the top, he began to take deep breaths. I let go of his arm and he leaned on the wooden palisades.

When I spoke, I used a quieter voice, "My friend we have both been unlucky with women. Poppa is now in a nunnery and I can take women to my bed if I need them."

"But my daughters!"

"Are gone. If you want them then stir yourself and take them back!"

He turned and looked at me, "My wife left me for a Breton!"

"And since when have Bretons worried us? We are warriors! You have forgotten that. You were Bergil Fast Blade and now you have become Bergil Big Belly!" The look he flashed me was filled with anger. I laughed, "That is better! The old Bergil hides within this bloated beast I see before me! Although if you drew your weapon now, I fear it would end badly for you!" I put my arm around his shoulder. I still towered over all of my men. I had grown old but I was not stooped as some were. "Listen, old friend. I have told the servants that you will not drink wine. You will drink small beer. You will exercise each day with your sons and hearth weru. You have two good boys there, I can see that, and you must prepare them to take over this land. When you can wear your mail once more then we will make war on the Bretons. We will seek your wife and take back your daughters! How is that?"

"Can I do it?"

I laughed, "Of course you can. Can you not hear them, Bergil Fast Blade? The Norns have been spinning; they are not yet done with us!"

"The Norns? I thought you were Christian?"

"Sprinkling a little water on my head cannot change my blood. Do you not believe that the sisters still spin?"

He nodded, "Aye, lord."

"Then, if we are fated to die, let us at least die as warriors with swords in our hands. My son can rule this land if I was to fall!"

11

He nodded and took a deep breath, "Then I will follow you once more. You are right. I need my blade in my hand!"

In the end, I stayed for three days. I impressed upon his sons and his priest the need to ensure that Bergil worked hard. It would be the only way he would defeat his demons. I also learned much of the lie of the land south of the Seine. Brittany was an obvious target. I did not think we would find Bergil's wife. She would be far away now. Brittany was just an excuse. There would be other lords like Bergil who grew fat and comfortable. I needed lean and hungry warriors. I needed Vikings. As we left to ride back to Caen I began to plan. How many other lords had become fat and complacent? I had been as negligent as Bergil. I had not become a drunk and bloated but I had lost sight of my aim and that of my grandfather. He had been told by a witch that his blood would rule a land which would be greater than the land of the Franks. I had a large land but it was nothing compared with the land of the Saxons and the Franks. I had thought the title fulfilled that prophecy. I was wrong. I would summon my lords to Rouen. It was one thing for them to pay taxes to me. They now needed to pay homage and to obey my commands.

I told Sámr of my plans when I reached Caen. The delight on his face warmed my heart. We spoke at length about the campaign to take fresh lands. His words gave flesh to the bones of the plan which was in my head. In the past, those ideas might have come from Bergil. He might become the man I once knew but Sámr Oakheart showed that I still had warriors with desire in their hearts. I relished the voyage home. I was at sea. It was a place where I was comfortable. I had fallen to the bottom of the ocean and I had lived. The sea was never an enemy to me. Watching my land slip by energised me and gave me ideas. As soon as I leapt from my ship, leaving others to see to its mooring, I raced to my hall. Before we had left for Paris, all those years ago, Padraig had shown great foresight. He had begun to train three young priests to serve as clerks for me. I also knew that he wanted me surrounded by priests so that they would act as a conscience. They were the ones who ran the business of my land. They could read and write. I could too but I did not enjoy it. They understood figures and, best of all, they were honest. Padraig had seen to that when he had chosen and trained them. Now that we were Christian, they were even happier about their job. Harold was the most senior and he was assisted by Thomas and Henry. I would meet with them once each week and they would tell me the state of my land. The price I paid was that they constantly chivvied me to build churches. I was no fool. I knew that the churches would be paid for by the Christians and the building of such churches would not only gain me favour in my own land but also at the court of King Charles. It was ironic really. When I had been a pagan, I had burned down the cathedral of Rouen. Now I had had it rebuilt. It was where I had been baptised. This had been the second baptism. The Archbishop himself had performed the act. It was symbolic for the King of the Franks wanted my people to see me baptised.

As soon as I reached my hall, I sent servants to fetch my priests. They all looked identical. Each wore a simple habit. They were clean-shaven and they had their hair so short that it was hard to see if they were bald or not! I sat at my table and waved them before me. They always brought wax tablets when they were summoned. They knew that orders would follow.

"I wish my lords summoning here to a meeting. We will have to arrange accommodation for them all. The meeting will last three days."

The other two scratched and Harold said, "When would you like this meeting to take place, lord? It will take a week for the message to reach those of your lords who live at the far end of the county."

"In one month's time."

He nodded, "That will give us time to arrange the food, the ale and the beds. Would you wish their warriors to come too?"

I shook my head, "Hearth weru only." As much as I trusted my men some were new appointments. When lords died their sons took over. Some sons I knew, others I did not.

We discussed numbers, food and the like then Harold asked, "And is there a purpose for this meeting, lord?"

I trusted my priests but they were priests and might be loose-lipped. I would give them a plausible purpose for the meeting. I leaned back, "I should have had more gatherings with my lords. I have forgotten my purpose. This will become a twice-annual event. You will need to arrange this regularly."

"Then we will need more accommodation building."

"We have the coin?"

"Not as much as we once had but enough."

"Soon we may have more. I intend war." They looked at each other. I saw the unspoken questions on their lips. I smiled, "Not the Franks. The Bretons and the Saxons have treasure. The Bretons have land. If we fight the Bretons, we gain land and coin."

There was relief on their faces. Harold, however, counselled me, "Lord you may anger the Pope by attacking Christians."

I leaned forward, "The Pope? Is he a King who commands me? Did I swear an oath to him too?"

"He is head of the Church lord. You could be excommunicated and that would negate the treaty with the King of Frankia."

I smiled, "You know that I am an ignorant barbarian so enlighten me. Did the White Christ appoint this Pope?"

"Lord, you are far from ignorant. No, Jesus, our lord, did not appoint the Pope. When the Romans adopted Christianity, they created a Pope to bring order to it."

Thomas said, "Aye, lord, Jesus said where two or three are gathered together there is my church."

"So, the Pope is a creation of the Romans?" They all nodded. "And when I ride my horse, I can choose to ride a Roman Road or not. It is my choice."

Harold knew me better than the other two. "Lord, that is a dangerous road to travel. The Pope has the ultimate power. Even King Charles and the Emperor obey him."

"What does this excommunication mean? Does it stop me from being a Christian?"

"No lord but you would not be able to receive the sacraments. You would not be able to use the church and you would not be able to confess to a priest."

They made it sound draconian but to me, it sounded perfect. "And only the Pope can do this?"

"Aye lord."

"And who is the Pope now?"

"It is a new one, lord, Pope John. Pope Lando died a couple of years since."

"And he lives in Italy?"

Thomas seemed eager to furnish me with information. "Aye lord, he is busy fighting the Saracens in Italy! He is a zealous man."

If his eyes were in the east then he might not concern himself with the west. "I will bear it in mind but we still prepare for war. Order arrows and spears. I want every drekar preparing for sea. How many do we have?"

"Your lords have twenty and there are fifteen drekar here at Rouen."

"It is not enough. How many ships are there in Rouen?"

"Including knarr and snekke there are almost a hundred."

"Good then if we have not enough drekar we commandeer those. We do not have far to sail." I waved a hand, "You have plenty to occupy you. Go."

I found my son in the warrior hall. He and Godwin were drinking with his hearth weru. Ragnar the Resolute stood as I entered. He was one of my most senior and dependable lords. William had upon his knee a young slave. He patted her bottom and whispered in her ear. She ran off giggling. "Father! You have been at sea! Were you raiding?"

I turned the frown into a smile as I looked at my son, "No, William. You are the raider!"

"It is in my blood and I have such good warriors that it would be a shame to sit here behind Rouen's walls and drink all day!"

I laughed but it was an empty laugh, "And yet that is what you are doing!"

"We are planning. Ragnar the Resolute called in to see you and we began talking about raids in the past. Godwin Red Eyes was telling him of a mighty abbey in Wessex. It is said that Alfred left all of his jewels and treasure there."

The Norns were spinning. I needed to stir my men. I had thought of Brittany. Perhaps this was a different opportunity for me. I looked at Godwin. He would not lie. "You know this how, Godwin?"

I saw him push the horn of ale away when he spoke. "The abbey is at Newminster Abbey. It is close to Wintan-Caestre. There was always a rumour that Alfred favoured this abbey at Newminster Abbey. His son Edward had it extended and it was there they reburied the King. King Edward made a visit there two years since in the dead of winter. It is said he took six wagons and the wagons were brought back to Wintan-Caestre empty."

"How did you learn of this Godwin?"

My son said, "When we…"

I held up my hand, "I asked Godwin. Let him speak, my son."

My son subsided. He was excited I could see that. He had seen more than twenty-five summers and yet sometimes he seemed like a youth who had just learned how to use his weapon.

"We captured a ship off Haestingaceaster six months since. Most of the crew perished but one was saved. We brought him back and he told us. He hoped to win his freedom by the knowledge."

"And where is he now?"

Godwin looked at William and then said, "We made him a thrall. He tried to escape and was killed." I knew from the look that my son had had him killed. It was a typically hasty action. He would have to change if he was to take over from me.

"And why have you not raided for this treasure?" I looked at my son and nodded for him to speak.

"Wintan-Caestre is close by and there is a royal burgh there. We have raided Hamwic so many times that they have now begun to build it in stone. We would need more than one ship."

"You need me, in fact."

My son grinned. He had a winning way with him. It was said that he just needed to flash a smile and women would open their legs for him. I knew he had fathered at least five children. "Aye, father, but you seemed so comfortable that we thought it a waste of time to ask you." He suddenly saw my face and realised that was no longer true. "You would raid?"

"Perhaps."

Godwin shook his head, "Lord, this is an abbey. It is one thing for pagans to raid an abbey but you are a Christian Duke. The church would frown upon such activity. We might get away with it but you are well known and we could not hide you."

"Thank you for your concern, Godwin Red Eyes. Let me worry about upsetting this Pope." I stood. "I have invited my lords to a meeting here in a month. We will be trying to take land from the Bretons. Do not raid them in the meantime. Let them think that we have turned our axes into ploughshares."

My son looked pleased. Ragnar the Resolute had remained silent. He had farmed land in the west and the Bretons had destroyed it while he had been raiding the Irish. His wife and children had been taken as slaves. He was still bitter about it and hated the Bretons more than any. He said, "Count Gourmaëlon of Brittany is a cunning man, lord. It was he who destroyed my family and many others in the borderlands. He is Count of Cornouaille and has many fortresses in the west of Brittany. It is why I came to speak with you. I live close to the land of the Bretons and I have heard rumours."

"Ragnar, is he more cunning than me?"

Ragnar allowed a smile to play upon his face, "No, lord. Only Sven Blue Cheek could match you for cunning." He nodded. "Then I look forward to the time I can stick the Breton count's skull upon a spear!"

After I had left my son I sent for Father Thomas and Egil. My priest had maps. I had him bring the maps to my chamber. I studied the maps and questioned him at length. I used Egil to sound out my ideas. A priest knew nothing of war. I learned a great deal. I learned that the son of Alan the Great now lived in England at the court of King Edward. This Count of Cornouaille was not given the title of Count of Brittany. That suggested he was not as strong as my men thought. The land of Cornouaille was, indeed, filled with narrow inlets and strongholds but Nantes was not. I sent for Erik Leifsson and he joined us. I needed a navigator and Erik was the best. After half a day I had my plan. I knew what I would do and I could prepare to meet my men and let them know my intentions.

Chapter 2

My lords were so keen to meet me that many arrived early. They were the ones who lived south of the River Seine. The last to arrive were the ones who lived further north. These were the ones I knew the least well. These were the sons of lords who had followed my banners. Erik Gillesson was my horse lord. He had more mounted warriors than any other lord. It was he who bred the larger horses such as the ones I rode. When he arrived, I took him and Sámr to one side. Before I spoke with all of my lords, I needed them to know my mind. I told them what I had planned. Sámr was already party to some of it for I had spoken with him in Caen. The voyage home and my conversation with Godwin had clarified my thoughts. I was not seeking permission. I was Lord of Normandy, I needed no man's approval. I wanted their opinion. I needed to know if they had any thoughts. Erik and his horsemen were vital to my plans. They both liked the idea in principle but also thought of ways of doing things differently.

"Lord, it seems to me that we would not need as many ships to raid this abbey. In fact, the smaller the number the greater the chance of success. We can use knarr and snekke to attack the Count of the Bretons but we cannot risk them carrying men across the open sea."

I nodded, "You may be right, Sámr. That would also allow us more time to convert the knarr to become warships. And you, Erik, you are happy with your task?"

He smiled and I saw his father in that smile, "You wish us to ride the borders and keep them safe. Riding is a joy and the chance to protect our land is a privilege. Besides, I would not wish to board my horses on ships and risk the voyage to Wessex."

"Good then I have my plan and when all are here, I will tell them."

As men arrived, I greeted them. Some of them were chosen by me for a special greeting. Bergil, Harold Mighty Fist, Haraldr, Bjorn the Brave,

Gandálfr and Leif. I spoke with each of them individually so that they knew my mind. For the rest, I gave the same greeting. I was their liege lord.

Father Harold knew how to organise and we had food and ale which was of the highest quality. We had plenty of servants and slaves. I feasted my lords before I spoke with them. Bergil now looked a lot healthier. He had lost weight and was no longer as heavy. In the time since I had last seen him, he had worked hard. I had given him a purpose. I had him at my right hand and Sámr my left. My son and Erik Gillesson were not put out. They knew the bond I had with my two oldest friends.

We had not all met together for a long time. Men who had fought and raided together were eager to catch up. Those who still remained from the Paris raid relived those days when we had humbled the Franks and won our land. The younger ones, the sons who might have been on the raid but did not lead spoke of their future glory. That was a risk for they were tempting The Norns. Skuld did not like men to plan for a future they determined. I said the least of any. I let the words flow around me. I looked at faces. I saw, in some men, the fathers I had led. Habor the Rus' son, Henry, looked exactly like his father. Yet Olaf Olafsson looked nothing like Olaf Two Teeth. Of course, he had not lost his front teeth yet but he looked more like a Frank than a Viking. He did a good job for he held Djupr for me. That had increasingly become an important port. It traded with the Frisians, the Flemish, even the Saxons of Lundenwic. He was prosperous and I saw rings upon his fingers. They looked to be made of silver. Vikings did not wear rings on their fingers. That was a Frankish affectation. If nothing else that told me that my people were changing. I saw Harold Mighty Fist's sons: Ragnar and Harold. They flanked their father. He looked old. The three looked like Vikings. Their hair was still wild and they wore battle rings about their arms. They had the weathered looks of men who spent more time outdoors than in. As I gazed around my hall, I saw that there were more men who looked like Vikings than Franks.

The ones who were missing from my feast were priests. The three I employed were nowhere to be seen. They would be in the kitchens organising the servants but they would not share my table. I knew that in the land of the Franks the Bishops and Archbishops were important men. Archbishop Franco was the Archbishop of Rouen but he had not been invited. If he took that as a slight then I would lose no sleep over the matter. I knew that in the cities of the Franks such an oversight would have brought censure. Archbishop Franco and I had an understanding and we rarely had to speak to each other. I attended his church when I could. It was not often.

When I was ready, I nodded to Mauger. He nodded back and the doors were closed. Men would guard them. When I spoke to my lords the words I used would be for their ears only. They would tell others, of that I had no doubt, but that was their choice. I was giving them the courtesy of hearing them from my own lips.

"My lords it has been many years since Paris. We have all prospered." I pointed to Haraldr Blue Eyes, "Haraldr you show your prosperity about your waist!" That made all the men laugh. He had not become bloated like Bergil but he had grown. "Perhaps we should call you Harold Beer Belly eh?" That brought more guffaws. In answer, Haraldr raised his horn and quaffed it in one.

"We have sat idle too long. There is a count of the Bretons who seeks to rule that land. There are many Viking farms that are now ruled by Bretons. Alan the Great took advantage of our distraction in Paris and stole them." I paused for effect and looked around the room. "It is time we took them back!"

That evoked the response I hoped. Men banged dagger hilts and their hands upon the table. It sounded like thunder. A cacophony of noise rose. I looked down at Sámr, he was grinning. He mouthed, "I told you!"

I held up my hands and the noise gradually subsided, "We leave at Tvímánuður. Caen and Ouistreham will be the muster points."

Gandálfr shouted, "This time we keep what we take?"

"Aye. We hold all that we can grab. We make our borders safe and we become richer."

Olaf Olafsson said, "What of the Church? Will not the Pope object to us making war on a Christian lord?"

The reaction of men like Harold Mighty Fist and his sons as well as the other Viking warriors told him what the majority of my men thought. They howled him down. I had been baptised but more than half of my men had not. Of course, some of their sons were Christian. Olaf was one but Harold's sons still followed the old ways.

I quietened down the howling. "Olaf Olafsson is right to bring up the matter and I have thought about this. I have spoken with priests, Olaf. They tell me that the risk is to me! If the Pope disapproves then I may well be excommunicated." I saw then the handful of truly Christian lords I had for their hands went to their crosses. Olaf was one of them. I smiled, "That means I will not be able to hear the services from Archbishop Franco. That saddens me!" My Vikings saw the grin on my face and they all laughed. I held up my hands for silence. "However, I do not think that will happen. King Charles will be happy that a potential enemy is destroyed. I have kept my word to the King and he is now more secure. That should keep us safe. If, Olaf Olafsson, you do not wish to risk censure from the church then speak with me before you leave."

He smiled and shook his head, "Oh no, lord, I just wondered. The Bretons are rich and I would like to take their treasure."

"Good. I have not yet fully finalised my plans and so the details will be given to you on the first day of Tvímánuður when you are gathered at Caen. For the rest enjoy the ale and then, Haraldr Blue Eyes, prepare to go to war. Either that or have a new byrnie made!"

I sat down and Sámr said, "They are keen. I am surprised none asked why we delay so long."

"As am I. We will see if they ask before they go."

William leaned over and said, as quietly as he could, "Of course if the Bretons are prepared then we know there are traitors amongst our men, father."

I smiled for the thought had already crossed my mind. "There is that, my son. However, none, not even you, know the target yet." I tapped my head, "That is still in here. Some may be unhappy that they were not included in the Wessex raid. We will see if they object when they do hear of it."

When the majority of my captains left, a couple of days later, they might have wondered why some did not. They were the ones who would raid Wessex with me. All had brought, at my request, their own drekar and they were moored in my river. My ship and my son's drekar were already prepared for sea. Erik Leifsson had spent the time since I had returned from Caen preparing for the voyage. While the crews prepared their ships and their weapons for the raid, I gathered my handful of captains in my Great Hall.

"We have created many of our own problems. We have raided Hamwic and Wintan-Ceastre so many times that they have improved their defences to the point that we would lose more than we would gain by attempting them." Godwin Red Eyes was invited to the meeting. He knew the land and I had spoken to him at length. I pointed to him, "Godwin here has given me the solution. There is a small village of a hundred or so people. It lies on the coast to the south of the abbey. They call it Hamafunta. There is also an island close by. Men use it to collect salt but none live there. We will sail to this island. When it is dark, we approach the village from two directions. We capture it. We do not burn it. We do not slaughter the inhabitants. We hold them. They guarantee that we can leave. We take their horses. It is twenty miles to the abbey. We will need to approach it from the north. Scouts can use the horses to guide us through the forests and greenways during the day."

Haraldr said, "We risk being seen, lord."

"The only place which has a number of people on our route is Drokensford. There is an abbey there but no burgh. We hold that one too. This way we have two places that are defensible when we fall back. I hope to get to the abbey with the treasure by dark. We raid at night. They will know we have raided but, by then, we will be on our way back to our ships. They will search towards Hamwic first. By the time they know we have left for the south coast, we should be at Drokensford."

Sámr nodded, "You have thought this out well, lord."

I laughed, "I may be old but my mind still functions. This is just to warm us up for the attack on Brittany. I confess that there will be little glory in this raid. We go for treasure and to see if my senior warriors still have that which they need."

Harold Mighty Fist said, indignantly, "We do, lord!"

"Do not be offended. I speak of myself. The last time I raised a weapon in anger was in the battle of Paris. When we raid the Bretons there will young warriors who are keen to show how brave they are. I need you, warriors, to be the older wiser heads."

We spent the rest of the day looking at what we knew of the coast and the tides. We identified who would watch Drokensford and who would guard Hamafunta. I gave Bergil the task of watching Hamafunta and Harold Mighty Fist, Drokensford. Now that they knew we would not face warriors it was not a problem. Father Harold had secured many arrows and, before they left, they were distributed. We would leave in two days' time. It would take all day and more to reach the island. Once we were there then time would be of the essence.

As well as my hearth weru I was taking some of the young warriors from Rouen. When they heard that I was raiding they were keen to join me. Some were the sons of warriors who had died. Others were not Vikings but the children of Franks who lived in Rouen and the lands close by. I allowed Mauger and Erik to choose them. These men were not rowers but they had good weapons and helmets. The days when Lord

Göngu-Hrólfr Rognvaldson chose his crew were long gone. Duke Robert allowed his men to pick them. Erik would choose those with broad backs while Mauger would choose those who could use a sword. They did not need mail nor even a helmet. When and if they went on the Breton raid then they would. I had a servant. Galmr had been one of Sven's warriors. He had been hamstrung at the battle of Paris. When Sven died, he begged me to take him on as a servant. I did so for he was a brave man and his lameness did not impair his ability to lift and carry. He would come with us and remain at Hamafunta with Bergil. He carried my chest aboard and laid it by the steering board. His own chest he put by the prow. We were the first aboard for I wanted to see my new crew. I wanted to gauge their potential. The way they boarded would tell me much about them. Mauger and Erik had chosen the best that there was. I needed to know how they would fare in battle.

Erik and his ship's boys were already there. "How are the winds, Leif?"

"They are from the south and west, lord." He sniffed the air, almost like a hound. Good navigators had the ability to smell the wind. "It will last a few days. See how the clouds are scudding. We will have a wet voyage but a swift one."

My hearth weru followed me and placed their chests closest to the steering board. They then went to select their oars. All were experienced rowers. They all had their own preferences. I watched the crew as they followed. I saw some with their father's old byrnie or helmet. All of them had a sword and some had a spear. This was not Norway and most men did not have the sealskin boots I wore. They had leather ones. Sealskin was better. Their chests looked lighter than mine. I had acquired things over the years. Some I might not need but I carried them anyway. I doubted that they would have sealskin capes. If Erik was right, and he was rarely wrong, then we would have wet weather. It would not hurt the younger men but they would not be as comfortable as I was. I also noticed that none had a seax. It was an old-fashioned weapon. The Saxons used them. Most had a dagger. It was a handy weapon but a seax could gut a man better than any dagger. It was a slashing, ripping weapon. A warrior did not thrust with it. I frowned when I saw most of their shields. They were the smaller type favoured by Franks. They were of more use on a horse than on foot. They were easier to make and lighter. Mine could take a blow from a Danish axe and survive. We would not be fighting housecarls but it was something I would need to bear in mind when we went to Brittany.

When the last man came aboard and Erik prepared to sail, I found myself become excited. I had been doing this for so many years that there were none who had done it longer yet I was still excited. Perhaps that kept me young. I had seen well over sixty summers but I did not feel the years. I was going to raid Wessex. I was doing that for which I had been born.

"We are ready, lord. We just await the others!"

I nodded, "Let us hurry them up. We will set sail." I roared, "To your oars!" As I had intended my voice carried and I saw my other captains beginning to hurry their crews on the other drekar. We were all having to relearn what had been second nature to us. The exception was William, my son. I saw that his crew on *'Dragon Wolf'* were already preparing to row. I stood with my hands on my hips and addressed the crew, "Today we will see your worth! I know not many of you. This voyage will show me what you are made of. I will find your flaws as we row. I will lead you in a chant! It will help you row and remind you of our heritage. We are called Normans now but never forget whence we came! We were Vikings." I stamped my foot so hard that the ship shivered, "I still am!"

Ragnvald Ragnvaldson was cursed from his birth
Through his dark life, he was a curse to the earth
A brother nearly drowned and father stabbed
The fortunes of the clan ever ebbed
The Norns they wove and Hrólfr lived
From the dark waters, he survived.
Göngu-Hrólfr Rognvaldson he became
A giant of a man with a mighty name
Göngu-Hrólfr Rognvaldson with the Longsword
Göngu-Hrólfr Rognvaldson with his Longsword
When the brothers met by Rouen's walls
Warriors emptied from warrior halls
Then Ragnvald Ragnvaldson became the snake
Letting others' shields the chances take
Arne the Breton Slayer used a knife in the back
Longsword he beat that treacherous attack
When the snake it tired and dropped its guard

Then Longsword struck swift and hard
Göngu-Hrólfr Rognvaldson with the Longsword
Göngu-Hrólfr Rognvaldson with his Longsword
And with that sword, he took the hand
That killed his father and his land
With no sword, the snake was doomed
To rot with Hel in darkness entombed
When the head was struck and the brother died
The battle ended and the clan all cried
Göngu-Hrólfr Rognvaldson with the Longsword
Göngu-Hrólfr Rognvaldson with his Longsword
Göngu-Hrólfr Rognvaldson with the Longsword
Göngu-Hrólfr Rognvaldson with his Longsword

We did not row hard but we and my son's ship soon left the others far behind. I saw that Erik was pleased. "They were trying to impress you, lord."

I laughed, "Good, that was what I intended. In oars. We will let the current take the ship until the others catch us up."

When they did catch us up, we rowed down my river. It took more than half a day to reach the sea. We did not row hard, there was no need. The current was strong. Once we reached the sea we continued to row for an hour. The hourglass we now used meant we were much more accurate. Then Erik let loose the sail and '*Fafnir*' flew! I sat on my chest and enjoyed the horn of ale from Galmr. "Bread and cheese too, Galmr. This sea air has given me an appetite."

Mauger joined me, "It will be easier sailing from Caen, lord." He was thinking of the Breton raid.

"Aye, I like my port but all those bends make for a long journey to reach the sea." I looked at the young warrior. Everyone looked young to me and Mauger was older than William. He had gone with William and Godwin on raids. That was how he had become one of my hearth weru. He had saved William when they had been ambushed by some Northumbrians. William had his own hearth weru and had known I sought younger warriors. He was a thoughtful warrior and one of the strongest men I had ever known. I was confident that he and his men could protect me from danger.

"You have fought the Saxons for many years, lord."

"Aye, I fought the Franks more but I know the Saxons. They are not as easy to defeat as they once were. They have learned to make and sail ships. They know how to fight us at sea. My friend Guthrum defeated them but, in the end, they tamed him and defeated him."

"They made him Christian." He said it quietly for he was asking me if it had tamed me.

I nodded, "I took a Christian bath. I said what I had to gain land. Look in my eyes, Mauger. What do you see?"

He did as I asked and I saw him smile, "I do not see a priest. I see a Viking."

We laboured across the sea and then when we turned north *'Fafnir'* raced. Erik Gillesson had bred some horses which were incredibly fast. They could not carry a mailed warrior but if we had to send a message across my land quickly then they were as fast as the wind. So was *'Fafnir'*. She had no weed on her hull and she was well designed. Behind us, I saw the other drekar spread out like an eagle's wing as they tried to stay with us. I had eaten fresh bread and drunk three horns of ale. I took my sleeping fur and laid it next to my chest. "Leif, I will sleep. Wake me when we sight the island."

I saw Erik and Mauger exchange a knowing look. I did not care. I now enjoyed a sleep in the afternoon. I could still stand a watch in the night but I liked a short rest. As soon as my head hit the rolling deck I was asleep and I dreamed. My dreams no longer told me of the future. They visited my past. They were, in the main, pleasurable although sometimes Poppa, my former wife, would appear and the dream would be spoiled. When I woke, the sun was setting in the west. I looked up at Leif, "Well?"

"Not yet, lord. I see a smudge which is the land of the Saxons but until we are closer, I cannot say if we are near to our landing site or not."

Some warriors were too impatient. We would get there when we got there. It was not as though there was an urgency to the task. The abbey was not going anywhere. "Aye, well I shall take a turn around the deck!"

I saw that my hearth weru were also sleeping. The younger warriors were talking or throwing bones. They would learn. I went to the prow and made water. Then I strolled back. I spoke to those who looked up at me expectantly. I saw that my other drekar had closed up. Night would be upon us and they did not wish to become separated. We had pot lanterns we could use but it was not ideal.

I had just reached the steering board when one of the ship's boys shouted, "Land ahead! It is an island."

Some of the men cheered. I shook my head. There were other islands and we had to determine which this was. It was Erik who identified it. "That is Wihtwara."

"Good, then we are close." Erik put the steerboard over to take us north and east. The wind from the south and west pushed us hard. I smiled. "And the gods wish us to get there before dark!" As soon as I had said it, I realised that I would have offended any Christians on my drekar. I could not control my mouth. I had always been outspoken. I was now too set in my ways to change.

"Galmr, come, it is time to don my mail!"

Being older meant that some things which had been easier even ten years ago now took more time. He brought my padded gambeson. It was lined with calfskin. It was still light but it afforded me a little more protection during battle. Then he slid my mail byrnie over my head. That in itself took time for I was the biggest man on the drekar. He had to stand on my chest to do so. He put my coif so that it was on my shoulders. I would not raise it until just before combat. The helmet and shield would be handed to me when I went ashore. He then strapped on my belt and hung my scabbard and Long Sword from it. Even my son, who was tall, could not have worn Long Sword from his belt. He also had a long sword but his weapon hung over his back. Finally, Galmr handed me a dagger and a seax. The seax was slipped into the top of my sealskin boot and the dagger in my belt. There was a second seax in a scabbard behind my shield. When you fought close, in a shield wall, then a long sword was not much use. You needed weapons you could insinuate into a warrior's body.

In the time it took to dress we heard the cry from the masthead. "I see a small island!"

Erik nodded, "That will be the island which lies across from Hamafunta."

I looked astern. The sun had almost dipped below the horizon. There would be just enough light for us to reach the island and take down the masts of our drekar. The mast, yard and sail would be placed on the mast fish. We would rest before we rowed around the island to land and take the Saxon settlement.

Chapter 3

We split into two groups of ships when we were ready to round the island. William led half to the west and I led the other half east. We rowed slowly around the island and saw the huts. They were lit by fires from within. The light flickered as people moved in and out of them. It was still relatively early. None would be abed yet. Our two small fleets would each land a mile to the east and west of the village and land our men. Those forty men, taken from all of the ships, would race to surround the houses. We would row slowly along the coast. There was no reason why they should keep sentries but I would send men ashore to make certain that they did not send for help. We wanted our presence a secret until we raided Newminster Abbey.

We edged toward the beach and I heard the tolling of a church bell. I saw some of the younger warriors look up anxiously, I smiled at those close to me, "They are monks at the abbey which lies close to the village. These men pray three or four times a night. It is a regular peel of bells. If it was an urgent sound then we would have been spotted."

All of them were now armed. Some wore their helmets. The men from our boat slipped over the side. They were led by Halfdan. He was one of my hearth weru. As soon as they reached the beach, we backed water and then rowed down the coast. With neither mast nor sail, we were invisible. The mast and sail would remain on the mast fish until it was time to leave.

We had the harder row for my son and his ships had the wind with them. There were fishing boats drawn up on the beach. I pointed to an empty patch of sand close to the boat which lay the furthest east. Erik began to head for it. I heard a shout from ahead. My son and his ships had landed. Erik put the steering board over and shouted, "In oars!" The wind, tide and our momentum slid us onto the beach. As ship's boys jumped ashore to tie us up the younger warriors leapt into the water.

Gone were the days when I would be the first ashore. As I waded through the sea, surrounded by my hearth weru, I heard the clash of steel and the cries of men dying. It would not be a bloodbath. Once resistance ended then we would cease killing. These were hostages we took. Bergil Fast Blade and his men would already be racing to the church. That was a prize and would be the place we held the hostages securely until we needed them. As I walked through the huts, I saw that the resistance had not tested my men. Four Saxons lay dead and five others were nursing wounds. I nodded to my men.

"Godwin!"

Godwin Red Eyes ran towards me, "Aye, lord."

"You know the way." My son walked up to me. He was sheathing his sword behind his back. "William, take Godwin and your crew. Head to Drokensford. Keep us hidden and if you deviate from the path leave a man to guard it for us. Find horses for your scouts."

I heard neighing and saw his men leading six small horses. My son grinned, "Aye, lord. We have already found some. Come, Godwin."

I turned to Sámr, "Organise the men and follow my son. We can leave the village to Bergil Fast Blade. He has more than enough men. I will go and speak to him. Do not wait for me. I will catch you up."

With my men behind me, I soon reached the church. I saw that Bergil had the priests all kneeling on the ground before him. He would be using terror to impose his will. They would expect to die. They did not know that they were safe; for the time being, at least. "I am searching the church for treasure before my men bring the villagers here. There are just two doors to this church. Once we have taken that which we need then we will bar the doors."

"Good. You have to keep this beach safe for us Bergil. When we come back, we may well find ourselves pursued. Have your men ready with bows. Load the drekar as soon as the treasure is taken and the captives safe."

He smiled, "You need not fear for me, my friend. I am not the whale you discovered wallowing in self-pity. Your words shook me from the dark place in which I was hiding. I have already forgotten my wife. It is best if I assume my daughters died. That way I can mourn them. I am on the road to recovery. By the time we leave for the next raid, I will be back to my normal self."

I clapped him about the shoulders. "I never doubted it for a moment."

I headed after my men feeling much more confident. We marched up the road through the dark. It took all night to reach Drokensford. My son and his men had captured it. It was the same size as Hamafunta and there was a monastery there. King Alfred had been very pious. There seemed to be as many monasteries, priories and abbeys as there were burghs! By the time I reached the town the five men who had died defending it were being piled on a pyre. The monks glared angrily at us. The Prior pointed an accusing finger at me, "And you call yourself a Christian. May you burn in hell!"

I walked close to him. I spoke Saxon well. "Have you a death wish, old man? At the moment you live for I am in a generous mood. Annoy me and that state will end!" I turned to Harold Mighty Fist, "Find their treasure and send it back to Hamafunta then put all of the monks and villagers in the church."

"Aye, lord!" He turned to his sons and said, "You heard the Duke, obey him." They hurried off and Harold grinned. This was the life he was born for.

"We will eat and rest. We do not have far to go. Once it is dark leave sentries armed with bows."

"The plan is a good one, lord! You have no need to fear."

I shook my head, "Harold, the Norns!"

"Sorry, lord!" He clutched his horse amulet. All of my older lords had them hung around their necks.

I did not sit and rest as I had ordered my men. I sent scouts out along the road, "If any come down the roads then stop them. Take them prisoner if you can, but if not then just stop them." I then walked the line of sentries to make sure they were all alert. Harold's men would have no further walking. They could endure a longer watch.

I sat with, Sámr, Ragnar the Resolute, Gandálfr and Harold Mighty Fist. My son and Godwin sat with their men for they would leave as soon as they had eaten. The monks had a good table and we had slow cooked fowl with local mead. I still had a good appetite and I retained most of my teeth. Others, I knew, were not as lucky. Sámr smiled, "Back in Wessex, lord. It is strange but this feels right. Why we waited years to raid again I know not."

Ragnar nodded, "Aye lord, life has been dull."

I shook my head, "If I did not know better, I would assume that the pair of you were criticising me!"

Sámr smiled, "Perhaps we are."

"And you would be right to do so. At least Bergil had the excuse of a lost wife to make him indolent. I had no such excuse. That changes now."

We had just finished the food when William walked up to our camp. "We have eaten. I have sent Godwin and the scouts ahead."

I waved, "Go and we will follow. We are old men, William. We need to make water before we march!"

With Godwin and the scouts leading we headed the last few miles to the Abbey. The Abbey was close to the walls of the burgh. My plan was bold. The position of the Abbey, north of the walls, meant that a normal attack by Vikings would come from the south. That would give the Benedictine monks the opportunity to take their valuables into Wintan-Caestre. Of course, they could not take Alfred's body with them. I was not a fool. We would not touch the body. It had no value to me. By attacking from the other side and surrounding the Abbey then none would escape and there would be no one to warn the burgh. It would not take many men to strip the Abbey of its treasures and make the monks captive. The majority of my crews would be ready to repel the defenders. The Saxons relied on their Bondi warriors, the so-called hundreds. This was the local levy and they would be led by a thegn. There were a number of thegns around Wintan-Caestre and when the bell sounded the alarm, they would make their way to the town. By the time they reached us, we would be gone.

We could smell Newminster Abbey before we saw it. The monks had candles and used incense. Even without our scouts, we could have found it. The monks rose early. They would soon rise but, when we arrived, they were all still abed. The discipline of my most experienced men came to the fore. There was no talking for there was no need. Gandálfr and his men silently surrounded the Abbey. He would take the abbey and he would be responsible for taking the treasure and the captives. The scouts secured the abbey's stables and the rest of us closed to within a hundred paces of the walls. There was a watch but we were cloaked and we were silent. We arrayed in three ranks. The third rank was made up of the warriors without mail. They held bows and arrows were already nocked. I stood in the front rank with my hearth weru, William and his bodyguards, Ragnar the Resolute and Sámr. The rest lined up behind us. William and I drew our swords. The rest of the front rank used spears. We waited.

31

Inevitably there was a cry. It came from the abbey. I would have been surprised if there had not been one. What there was not was the sound of the abbey's bell. Gandálfr was too seasoned a warrior to have overlooked that. The bell, when it came a short while later, sounded from Wintan-Caestre. We had learned, from a thrall at Drokensford that King Edward was in the north with his army. His family were in Lundenwic. Despite that, there would be guards in the burgh. It was an important town. They would be the town watch and the fyrd. The shouts from inside the burgh were accompanied by the thunder of feet running along the fighting platform. I glanced to the east. Dawn was still some time away. I smiled when torches were brought to the walls. They helped us and not the Saxons. Their night vision would be destroyed and they illuminated the wall. That would allow my archers to see their targets. By their light, I saw men peering over the walls as they sought to see the size of the problem. Our cloaks and shields would just be a dark shadow.

"Archers! Draw!" My voice pierced the darkness. I saw a spear pointed in my direction as the defenders identified me. "Release!" It sounded like a flock of disturbed birds as the forty arrows soared over our heads. I heard cries as the watch perished. They had not taken the precaution of having shields ready.

William laughed, "You know, father, we could take this burgh!"

"And what would we gain? The treasure is in the church. We let Gandálfr set off down the road and when it is daylight, we follow him and his men."

My son sounded disappointed, "I had hoped to hew some heads."

Sámr sounded the voice of reason, "We will have to draw our swords before we reach our ships, William Longsword. This is the tomb of their great king. We have offended them and honour will be at stake."

"Aye, son, Sámr is right. Use your head. Save your passion for the Bretons!" I allowed five flights of arrows and then shouted, "Hold!" I had heard arrows striking the wood of shields. There was little purpose in wasting arrows.

I heard, from the south, the sound of hooves. As I had expected, they had sent for help. Dawn was breaking when Sven, one of Gandálfr's men, found me, "We have the treasure, lord, and we found a wagon. There are thirty monks. Five died resisting us. Lord Gandálfr had no choice."

"I know. Head for Drokensford. When you reach it leave the monks there and carry on to Hamafunta."

"Aye lord. It is a mighty treasure. We have six chests not to mention the candlesticks and church ornaments. The Abbot had fingers adorned with gold and silver rings."

"You have done well. We will follow."

William asked, a short while later, "And how long do we wait?"

"It will take our men some hours to reach Harold Mighty Fist. Let us wait until the Saxons try to shift us."

We had no hourglass and we had to rely upon the sun to gauge the passage of time. I guessed that three hours had passed since Gandálfr had left us when the gates opened and men began to spill out. As the gates began to swing open, I shouted, "Archers!"

A thegn wearing a full-face helmet and a long byrnie led men out. I saw ten housecarls. They also had good helmets, mail byrnies and axes. The rest had a variety of helmets and shields. These were the burghers of the town. I would not underestimate them. King Alfred had trained them well enough to defeat my friend Guthrum.

"Release!"

My archers sent their arrows as the Saxons formed up. We had archers and the Saxons did not. Their slingers were scurrying before their shields when the arrows struck. Some slingers fell as did some of the men who were slow to raise their shields. Once the shields formed a wall I shouted, "Hold!" Turning to Sámr I said, "Let us see if we can make them charge us, eh?"

He chuckled, "Aye lord!"

"Men of Rouen, fall back fifty paces! Keep facing the foe." I paused, "Now!" We walked backwards slowly. As I had expected, it made the Saxons, who now outnumbered us, think we were retreating. The thegn held up his sword but the burghers saw us backing towards their precious abbey. They thought we were fleeing and they charged. As soon as they charged, I shouted, "Shield wall!" I slipped my shield around my back and held Long Sword in two hands. William did the same with his own long sword. The rest of our men swung their shields to lock them with their neighbours and then poked their spears over them. Spears appeared over the shoulders of our front rank. In the case of William and I, they came through the gap. None were tall enough to rest their spears on our shoulders. It was not bravado from my son and me. Our swords were so long that they would strike the enemy when our spears did. We were also helped by the fact that the Saxons ran at us wildly with no order. The thegn and the housecarls had only managed to form a hundred or so of their men into a shield wall.

My archers thinned out the numbers. Even so, there were so many that some reached us. The first to try to kill us were burghers with helmet, shield and spear. I brought my sword from over my head. The Saxon who thrust at me with his spear thought he had me and jabbed his long spear at my chest. The tip had just touched my mail and his face had lit up with the joy of killing a giant when my sword came down and split helmet, skull and the upper body of the man. Even as he was falling William's scything, sideways strike had taken the head of the man next to my victim. I saw, behind these Saxons, the rest of the line of charging men slow a little. They chose not to run at William and me. Instead, they ran into a wall of spears held by hearth weru; the best we had. The Saxons thought they had avoided the long swords of William and myself but they were wrong. We swept them into the sides of the Saxons fighting the warriors to our side. A Saxon horn sounded and the chastened survivors ran back to the safety of the shield wall. Their retreat cost them another fifteen warriors as arrows struck them.

I said, "Now is the time! Charge!"

We ran. We did not run fast. We advanced at the speed of men who had rowed with the warriors next to them and had their rhythm. We ran as one for that was what we were. We were the Clan of the Horse. We had yet to taste defeat. The Saxons would be soiling their breeks and wondering if they could make the safety of their own walls before our blades hacked, sliced and butchered them. We ran knowing that the Saxons would be disordered when the fleeing men tried to get behind the housecarls. And we ran knowing that we would be victorious. William and I, with our best warriors, ran at the thegn and the housecarls. They had axes held in two hands and that meant they had no shields. I heard them keening a song. They knew they would die. Had they been in a shield wall with thirty or more of their fellow then they would have believed they could stop us. They had done so before. When King Alfred had led them then they had been the equal of Vikings. Now a thegn led them. He was their lord but I doubted that he was Alfred. He was a thegn who watched the King's town. They would be hoping, as they swung their axes in a figure of eight, that they might get lucky and take me with them. They would know who I was. The giant Viking was a legend. The housecarls would not be cowards. They would be brave and they would want to save the people of Wintan-Caestre. Then they would have died

34

with honour. We had to ensure that it was they who died and we who lived.

I was not as fast as I once had been. It was Godwin and William who reached the line first. Godwin's spear and the spears of my son's men ripped into the housecarls as William's sword hacked flesh. A couple of spears had their heads splintered. But a splintered spear shaft can still be rammed into the eye socket of a warrior. William's sword hacked across the neck of one housecarl who did not wear a coif. I saw Godwin's spear ram into the screaming mouth of his companion. He had been unlucky with his axe. It had missed Godwin's spear by a handspan. His open helmet had no protection. I heard the spearhead grate through the back of his skull. The thegn was facing me and he held his shield before him. A lord, he used a sword. He thrust rather than slashed with his sword at my neck as I brought my sword from on high. He held up his shield and, while his sword pricked my coif, his shield was shattered by my blow. When I wielded Long Sword, I used two hands. It meant I had no shield but the power and weight of the sword could hack through mail! Splinters of wood flew into his face. I suspect I broke his arm too. He staggered a little and I swung again. This time it was a diagonal blow from the opposite side. It came down on his sword side. His own sword came up and the two blades cracked together. Sparks flew but he had merely reacted. There was no strength to the blow and the sword was knocked aside. I hit his coif halfway along the length of my sword. I ripped it downwards. It severed links as though they were made of cord. There was nothing beneath the coif and Long Sword sliced and sawed through flesh, muscle and bone. I took his head. His body stood for a moment and then crumpled as though it had been emptied of life in an instant. As Sámr slew the last housecarl the survivors ran back to the safety of Wintan-Caestre's walls.

"Hold!"

My men were perfectly trained. They heeded my roared command and they halted. They presented their shields and they looked for more opposition to fight. When they saw none, they looked down at the men they had killed, assessing the treasure that might be carried. Each of the dead housecarls would be rich. They had mail and they had a position. They were Christians but they were also warriors. They had battle bands. Some would be silver. They might have a silver cross. They would wear rings on their fingers. Housecarls were vain. They liked others to know how good they were and that was displayed on their fingers and around their necks. Some would even have purses. They might be concealed beneath their mail but they would be there.

I looked at the town walls. William was right. We could have taken the town but what would have been the point? They had summoned help. We would soon have to fight many more men and the town held nothing we wanted. We had gold and silver. We had the ornaments from the abbey. In the town, we would have had to fight men for pathetically small pots of coins. It was not worth it. We had time. Gandálfr was still heading towards Hamafunta. I could allow my men the opportunity to plunder the dead.

"Fetch our wounded. We are done here. The Clan of the Horse has won! You can take from the Saxons but be hasty. We leave in five hundred heartbeats!"

Some of those who had crewed *'Fafnir'* ran forward, "Lord, the mail?"

I looked at William. He shrugged, "My men do not need it." Already the ones who had fought in the front rank were taking from the housecarls. They would not bother with the mail for they already had a byrnie.

"Take it but do not tarry. If you are caught it will go ill with you."

I saw that we had lost men but they would not lie here. Oar brothers picked up the bodies of their dead comrades. Before men fought, they made promises. The families of their dead friends would be given a share of whatever we took. The swords of the dead would be killed if there was no son to give the blade to. The dead were cared for before the rest of their oar brothers took the treasure. That was why we fought as we did. We would bury them at sea. We would not allow the Saxons to display their heads! As we headed back, I positioned good men to the side and the rear as well as the front. It was a foolish leader who assumed that he had destroyed all of his enemies. I thought we had but why take chances? We had a day to reach our ships and then we could relax. Once we were at sea, we were safe. This time we used the road for we wanted to move quickly and we wanted to draw any attackers to us and not my men who hurried ahead of us. We did not need to move silently. The whole of the land would know we were here. Even as we headed south, we heard the distant tolling of bells. The Saxons had learned that when Vikings attacked you gathered your men and you met them with large numbers. Unless Saxons outnumbered Vikings then they had no chance of defeating them. We were not true Vikings any longer. We were better for we were Normans and we were even stronger than our forebears had been. We had honed our skills. We had fought more enemies than they had. We understood how to fight against horsemen and we knew how the Saxons organised. They would already be raising the levy, their fyrd. Each one hundred would be taking their weapons from the sacks in which they were kept. They would be donning helmets that they had not used in five years or more. They would be taking a tearful farewell from their wives and families and they would march together towards a muster point. It would all take time and we would be heading south while they did so.

I was confident. As we moved south, I looked at the new, younger warriors. Some had taken the mail from the dead housecarls. They had taken weapons too. They had had little to do in their first battle. They had had to stand in the face of greater numbers and they had done so. Some would have weapons that had not been used. That did not matter. The experience of standing there and seeing an enemy flee would give them confidence the next time we fought. Watching my best men hew the enemy without suffering losses would have been a lesson in fighting. They would be blooded one day. Now they tramped along burdened by the booty they had taken. Now, as they laboured along the road it would be a test of their strength. None of us had rested much on the journey to the Abbey. Food had been in short supply. Their stomachs would crave food. Their mouths would be dry. They would be desperate for ale. These were also lessons in war. Many of the young men had never been on a raid. Once we reached the ship, they would go over every detail. They would relive every blow and arrow. What happened to these men would be magnified when we attacked the Bretons. It had been years since I had led men into battle and I had to know their strengths and their weaknesses.

Sámr marched next to me. I was aware that my long legs ate up the ground. I was setting a hard pace. Sámr Oakheart had fought with me so many times that he was used to my pace. He could not only keep up with me, but he also seemed to be able to read my mind, "They did well, lord." I grunted in reply. "They obeyed orders. I remember some of Guthrum's men. They were brave enough but, it is said, they lost the battle to Alfred when they did not heed Guthrum's commands."

"If we had fought a stronger foe then I might agree with you. A handful of mailed warriors do not make a good test. Many of them have weapons with sharp edges still. We do not."

Sámr was not afraid to argue with me. We had shared much in the past and he was bold in his words. "You wish we had had a harder test? You would we had lost some of them?"

"Losing one or two would have made some of them more thoughtful. Listen to them!" There was laughter and even songs. Had the younger ones fought I would have understood it but they had just had to watch. That was my fault. I had not trusted them and I had used my best warriors.

"You are wrong, lord. I agree that not all had to fight but some did and some died." I heard an intake of breath from Mauger and my hearth weru. "More mailed warriors would have given us a harder test but the Saxons fled twice. We beat them twice. We defeated the best that they had with consummate ease. Their town was ripe for the taking and we had lost few men. All of those facts show that even the new warriors know how to obey you. I think this was a good test."

I strode more steps and reflected. He was right. Some had fought. Some had wounds. I was wanting perfection in the battle. That never happened. "You are right, Sámr! I am getting old and, perhaps, a little foolish."

"No, lord, we both know that is not true."

We moved along in silence. I was deep in thought. Sámr was right. I had been guilty of seeing the horn of ale as half empty. I fingered the horse amulet which hung from my neck. If I was wrong about that then what of the raid on the Bretons? I had thought to send a fleet to attack Nantes and the Count's capital. I did not have enough ships and I now wondered if that was the right strategy. The days when we had sailed to fight was in the past. We could still raid using drekar but even Bjorn the Brave lived three days from the sea. As we moved through the heartland of Wessex, I changed my plans. I needed men like Sámr and Bergil with me. Sven Blue Cheek was sorely missed. He would have given me sage advice when I had first suggested the attack.

We reached Drokensford without incident. Harold Mighty Fist awaited us there. "Gandálfr left with the captives a couple of hours since."

"Good. We rest for a short time and eat. Choose five priests to accompany us. When we leave, we bar the rest in their church."

Harold laughed, "They will think we mean to burn them."

I shook my head, "I will leave a message with those in the church. If we are attacked then the priests who are hostages will die. We need to move quickly. I would not stop save that the younger warriors need rest and food." I pointed. Those who had taken from the dead Saxons now looked weary and we still had many miles to go. "They will reach us before we have embarked. I want the Saxons wary and cautious. Perhaps I am becoming cautious too. I would lose as few men as possible."

"That is not a bad thing, lord. The younger ones still have much to learn. Aye lord. I have hot food ready. The monks know how to cook. The ones we take with us will be leaner by the time we reach Hamafunta."

It was the early afternoon when we left. Our dead were placed on a wagon and we used some of the captured horses to draw it. After I had spoken to those left in the church, we hammered wood across the doors of the stone church. They would be found for I knew there would be pursuit. A chase did not worry us. We could move faster than those who chased us. Hamwic was my worry. That was a strong burgh. Word must have reached it and they would send men to slow us. They would need to muster and therein lay hope. That would take time. As we had left, I waved William and Godwin forward. "I want your men in the fore as a screen. Those who took treasure can stay with me. Kill any scouts you find but if you see a large force then return to me without alerting them."

"Aye, father."

I was proud of my son. He reminded me of me when I had been a young warrior. He was bold and fearless. He did not panic and he knew how to command men. Godwin Red Eyes did for him what Sven Blue Cheek had done for me. He was a voice of reason. William still had much to learn. His fearlessness on the battlefield became recklessness in his dealing with women. I had never been one to hop from bed to bed. William was.

We were five miles from Hamafunta when my son came back. Godwin was not with him. "The Saxons are waiting for us. They have blocked the road at a small hamlet. They have put barriers across the road."

"Any sign that Gandálfr and his captives were stopped?"

"No, father. There were no bodies. They were still building barriers. Had you not ordered otherwise we would have attacked them."

I almost ignored his words. He had obeyed my orders and that was what I had wanted. He was right. Gandálfr must have escaped. "Then they do not know how close we are?"

He shook his head, "I do not think so."

"And how many are there?"

"They look to have the hundred from Hamwic and another one. The men were sprinkled with those who wore mail."

I turned, "Harold Mighty Fist." He stepped forward. "Take your warband and all of the men without armour. Head to the west. There are Saxons ahead in a hamlet. I want you to attack them from both sides. Wait until you hear our horns before you begin."

"Aye, lord. My lads are keen to gain some honour this day."

Harold nodded and he headed off to gather his men. I turned and waved forward the young men from my crew who had taken the mail. "Alan son of Erik, you and the others who carry the mail. Don it and guard the captives. Take the wagons with our dead. When we attack move them down the road after us. Your task is to get them to the ships."

"Aye lord." I watched Alan son of Erik head back to his oar brothers. I walked to my hearth weru and William.

I had chosen the young warriors because they looked weary. They could be exhausted and they would still be able to cope with a handful of priests. I drew Long Sword, "The rest of you, we have some Saxons to shift. We move silently until we find Godwin Red Eyes. Mauger, when I say, have the horn sounded. We hit them hard. This is the levy. They are farmers with bill hooks and ancient helmets. They will be thinking of their farms and their wives. They will run if they are given the chance."

"Aye, lord."

This was still the land that the kings of Wessex had used for hunting. The forest had only been thinned a little. The farms and houses were clustered in the open areas and we found Godwin Red Eyes and William's men some twenty paces from the hamlets. I could see that the Saxons were still building a barrier. I turned, "We make a wedge and I will lead." I said it forcefully. None argued with me. They might disapprove of the idea but they would not speak out. I smiled, "I think if we move at the pace of an old man, we might be able to stay together, eh!" They smiled back. "We will start to form here. My slow pace will help us to make a mighty wedge." Without further ado, I marched towards the road. William and Sámr took their places behind me. The others formed up in organized lines. Mauger was behind William and he had Odo with the horn next to him.

As soon as we cleared the woods, I heard a shout from ahead. All work ceased and I saw the crude barricade bristle with spears. It was not solidly made. They had used hastily cut saplings, carts and willow hedging. It gave an illusion of protection. The hamlet lay about half a mile down the road. I kept the same pace. I did not look behind me. I knew that my men would be forming up. We would have ten ranks deep by the time we hit the barrier. Marching towards it I saw that it was not as high as they might have liked. It was not as tall as me. Men in mail stood atop it. They must have dragged a couple of carts and wagons behind it. I smiled. They were in for a shock when my Long Sword and that of my son struck them. When we were just two hundred paces from them and stones began to fall, I shouted, "Mauger, have the horn sounded now!" The horn sounded. We kept moving and then I heard our flank attacks. Harold Mighty Fist was keen to bring his men into action and I heard the rustle of arrows as they flew from the Saxon flanks and into their unprotected backs and sides. Men cried as they fell. The arrows did not strike mail. They struck men who had, at best, leather jerkins. They were no match for our war arrows. The stones no longer flew at us.

I started to chant. It helped us stay together and to move faster whilst unnerving the Saxons who had seen their plans thrown into disarray by my men's flank attack.

Clan of the Horseman
Warriors strong
Clan of the Horseman
Our reach is long
Clan of the Horseman
Fight as one
Clan of the Horseman
Death will come

I lowered my head as we advanced. The stones and spears would not hurt me. I wore a good helmet with padding beneath as well as my byrnie. The helmet had a conical, angled crown. Stones and arrows would slide along it. If they had had axes, I might have been in danger but the men standing on the barricade, although mailed, held spears. As we neared the barricade, we, inevitably, moved faster. It could not be helped. The ones at the rear of the wedge were anxious to get to grips with the enemy. They pushed into our backs. As I swung my sword at the legs of the Saxons whose spears cracked and rattled off my mail and helmet, I felt myself pushed along as though by a fast tide. My sword hacked through first one leg and then a second of the Saxon above me. Even as he fell, dying, my blade hacked into the leg of the next Saxon and grated off the bone of his knee. Sámr's spear went up under the byrnie of a third and William took the legs of a fourth. Above us, the centre of the barricade was clear and then my body was rammed against the barricade. It had been hurriedly erected. The weight of my men was behind me. I struggled to keep my feet but managed it until the barricade disintegrated before me. It was as though a dam had been burst and I tumbled forward and landed, somewhat awkwardly, across the wrecked barricade. If I had not been followed by my son and hearth weru I would have been trampled to death but they formed a wall around me. The wedge was broken but the barricade was no more. The whole structure crumbled and the men at the rear, having seen me fall, were eager to get at the Saxons. It was like a mailed tide flowing over the shattered Saxons. From the side, Harold's men fell upon the Saxons who were attacked from all sides but one. Mauger and Erik held their hands out for me and I pulled myself up.

Mauger shook his head, "That was foolish, lord! Next time one of us leads!"

"We are all warriors, Mauger!"

"No, lord, you are our leader and without you, we lose our heart!"

My battle was over. I watched as my men tore through the Saxons. They had gambled upon stopping us at a barricade and they had failed. The only way left for the Saxons was south and they fled. They would keep running until they could see no more Vikings. Then they would crawl home grateful that their God had saved their lives. They would talk of us as though we had many more men than we had. It would justify their flight. King Edward would hear of the skirmish and it would become a battle. He would fear an invasion and he would strengthen his burghs. He would not know this was a raid to give us funds and to blood young men. While my men took all that there was to be taken from the field my son and my hearth weru insisted that I get to Hamafunta. I reluctantly agreed. The fall had hurt me. I had landed badly. I was sure I had broken a rib or two. We walked with the wagon and the captives.

Bergil Fast Blade and Gandálfr had already loaded the ships. The monks had their hands bound and were kneeling with the villagers from Hamafunta, on the beach. "The rest of the men will be here shortly." I pointed at the wagon. "First, we load our dead and then, when they arrive, our men. Are the houses of the villagers empty?"

"Aye, lord. They have been stripped of all that is valuable."

"Then fire them!"

42

Even as my men lit fires to make torches, my men began to arrive. The dead and the wounded were loaded first and then I saw black smoke begin to rise from the houses. It was at that moment that the rest of the Saxons, sent no doubt from the land around Wintan-Caestre, arrived. There were over two hundred of them and some were mounted. Sámr said, "We should leave now!"

I shook my head, "Have men stand behind the priests. Put a sword at their throats. Let the villagers go!"

"They will try to put out the fires."

I smiled, "I know and the Saxons will see their priests more clearly."

As the villagers raced to their homes, thirty riders detached themselves and galloped towards us. The rest of the Saxons formed three lines. I took out Long Sword. "Come, William, let us go and speak with these Saxons and test their resolve."

We walked towards the galloping horsemen. Saxons did not use stiraps. They had spears but they could not thrust. They rode ponies. They were not a threat. I held up my left hand when they were thirty paces from us. I knew that Sámr had archers ready to unleash arrows if we were in danger. The three lines of Saxons moved steadily across the sands towards us. They began to spread out.

"Halt or your priests die!"

Their leader, who had a shield with a white horse painted upon it, pointed his spear at me, "You will all die! I am Eorledman Edgar and I swear, Viking, that I will have your head."

"The first to die will be your priests. When I drop my hand then arrows will fly and you will die. Are you so keen to meet your god?" He looked beyond me at the fifty archers with arrows nocked. "Tell your men to halt. Pull back to the ridge and we will let the priests go!"

"I thought you were a Christian, Robert of Rouen!"

"And do not Christians make war on Christians? I do not bandy words with Saxons. I have spoken enough. Give the command for my arm tires."

He turned in his saddle, "Halt!" His men stopped. He turned to his men, "Ride back and tell my thegns to pull back to the ridge." As his men rode off, he said, "This is not over. I swear that I will have vengeance on you Norman scum!"

I sheathed my sword. If words and oaths could kill me then I would have died many times over. "Let the priests go. Board the ships! We return home!" I turned my back deliberately and walked towards my drekar. I was confident that I was safe. If nothing else the shield across my back protected me.

Chapter 4

It took three days to reach home. Our river had too many twists and turns to manage the voyage upstream any quicker. It became obvious that I had broken ribs. We strapped them up but they still hurt when I moved. They made me bad-tempered. I knew there was little I could do to make them heal faster and they were a reminder that I was getting no younger. A warrior endured such things. The lack of sleep helped me to focus my mind on the war I would begin at Tvímánuður. The Bretons would know we were going to attack. I could not rely on all of my lord's discretion. The hard core of men who had followed me for a long time I could trust. But there were sons who now led warbands. They were often an unknown quantity. Some would enjoy boasting of what we were going to do while others might have more sinister motives. I was not naïve. I was getting old and some of my lords were half Breton or half Frank. They had uncles who were our enemies. It did not matter as the plans for the attack were still in my head. I had months to plan. Brittany had a coastline and a long land border. There were no standing armies. My men were farmers or fishermen until I called them to arms. It was the same with the Bretons. They would be stiffer opposition than the men of Wessex but they would not be professional warriors. Only the warriors of my hearth weru were that. The bare bones of my plan were formulated as we headed across the sea to my river. They gained flesh as we wound around the loops in the river that was now the Norman River, the Seine. By the time I stepped ashore I knew what we would do. I just needed to speak with Sámr, Bergil and my son. All would be visiting with me as I had the treasure on my ship. It would need to be divided. My men carried it to my Great Hall. My three priests would divide it for me. They would roll their eyes and tut at the religious artefacts but they would be fair. They would remind me that what I had done was not a Christian act. I would smile. Words could not hurt. They would warn me that my soul was in danger and I would nod. Half of the treasure would go to my coffers. Once I would have had half of the weapons and mail but I no longer needed them. I had a room which was an armoury. I could fully equip another twenty hearth weru if they were needed. The other half of the treasure would be divided equally between my lords. Any family who had lost their provider would be given extra. I did not think that would be many. The ones who had died had been the younger warriors who wore little mail. Half of them had been warriors who had come to my land seeking adventure. They had been buried at sea. Their oar brothers would remember them.

My injuries meant I could not travel my land for a while and so I made sure that the lords who visited with me stayed long enough for me to pick through their ideas for the coming war. The simple logistics of horses, arrows, spears and food, could be left to my priests. Erik Gillesson would advise them on the feed for the horses. We had more horses and horsemen now than we once had. All were trained by Erik, his sons and his men. Every lord knew how to ride. Some were better than others. William had inherited his great grandfather's skill. Bergil and Sámr were not as good as the younger lords. They had been men grown when they were introduced to horses. Our riders used smaller shields. They used a couched lance and Erik had taught them all how to attack in tight lines. Every lord had at least four or five horsemen. Not all were mailed and most wore just a simple leather burnie studded with metal. They were used as scouts and bodyguards. The Franks liked their horses. We were becoming as proficient as they were.

Our better warriors still fought on foot. Protected by long mail byrnies, they were made of mail, scale or leather. Some were a combination of two. Warriors had their own preferences. I did not like the scale ones but they were cheaper and easier to make. The wisdom of mail had been shown when we had attacked the barricade. My helmet had suffered dents but not a ring had been broken. Our archers were becoming almost as valuable as our shield wall. They, along with our slingers, were more than a match for Franks although the Bretons used crossbows and they could hurt us. My archers could loose four or five arrows in the time it took a crossbow to send one bolt towards us. Of course, the bolts, if they were released accurately, could be deadly.

We had been home for three weeks and I was about to summon my leaders to a council of war when the Archbishop of Rouen asked for a meeting. I acceded to his request. I liked him. He was a pragmatic man. Normandy was safer because of my presence and if I did not always attend church, he could turn a blind eye to that. Father Harold had told me that he had been less than pleased with my raid on the three churches. I expected censure for the act. I could live with censure so long as it was not public. No man criticised me!

"Yes, Archbishop, how can I be of service?"

He smiled and spread his hands, "It is not me who wishes to speak with you. It is the King."

"And what does the King wish?"

"He would have you meet with him. His daughter, your wife, has not seen you for some time and he thought you might meet with him at his hunting lodge. It is close to the priory of St. Julian. It is in the forest to the west of Paris." He leaned forward. "It is a discreet hall. There the King can be relaxed and away from prying eyes. He asks that you take just a few men."

I immediately became suspicious. Was this a trap? Would I be lured there to be murdered? Even as I thought it, I knew that my death would not harm Normandy. My son would rule after me and he had advisers like Sámr and Bergil. In fact, killing me might be the worst decision the Frank would make. I had kept my word. If I died then there was no pact with the Normans! "Of course. I shall just take my hearth weru. Will you be coming with me, Archbishop?"

He shook his head, "No, Count Robert, I do not enjoy hunting and I think the King would like as few other people there as possible." He could not call me Duke for the King had not accorded me that title. As I said, he was a pragmatic man. We might discuss things that might not be in the interests of the church. The Archbishop could honestly say he knew nothing about what was said.

After he had gone, I summoned William and spoke with him. I explained where I was going and what I thought it might be about. "I think I am going to have my hands slapped for the raid on Wessex. King Charles is no fool. If he did it publicly then he might risk my anger. He does not want the treaty broken."

He was concerned for my safety. "You are riding deep in the heart of West Frankia, father. This is too great an opportunity for our enemies. What if another, not the King, has you ambushed?"

I shook my head. "My son, soon I will have seen seventy summers. I should have died many years ago. Who knows there may be a wild boar in the King's forests and the Norns may have spun my death on his tusks? I might be hurt whilst hunting. I have clawed a land for you and the clan. It is called Normandy. It is not as large as I would have liked it to be and if this is not a trap and I return then we will, together, make it larger! If I am taken as a hostage then let me die! If I am murdered then with it dies my oath not to fight the French King. That oath is what keeps me alive. If I die or the King dies then it is null and void. You can attack the Franks as well as the Bretons. So, you see, there is no danger for me. I will, however, take care."

I left the next day. I rode my mighty horse, Blue, and my ten hearth weru rode as well. They wore the same cloaks, helmets and carried the same shields which had been made by Alain of Auxerre. The dark blue hue and the sign of the sword had been created by Alain. On the battlefield, they looked effective. The only difference was that the sword on the breast was longer than Alain's had been. It made us look less like Vikings and more like Franks. That was no bad thing riding through Frankia. I also wore an open helmet with a nasal. I did not think we would be fighting and it was more comfortable than my masked helm.

We stayed at the stronghold of Bjorn the Brave at Évreux. He was one of my lords who had left the sea. He and his son farmed and they did so successfully. This was not the hard land of Norway. This was fertile land. It was said if you threw a seed into the ground you could almost watch it grow before your eyes! He raised cattle, sheep and pigs. His vineyards produced wine. Bjorn still preferred ale but wine sold! When we fought the Bretons, he would not have his own ship. As we ate, I told him the purpose of my journey to visit the King. Like my son he was suspicious, "Lord, let me come with you. You need to be protected."

I laughed, "If the Norns have spun and it is my turn to die then so be it. If the Franks are foolish enough to murder the Duke who has kept the peace then they deserve the tidal wave which would engulf them." He nodded. "I need you to prepare for war. You have good horsemen here as well as shield brothers. I will be counting on you and your men."

He nodded, "Like you, lord, I am getting old but my son, William, is a good warrior. I will ride at his side and give him my guidance."

"You are right Bjorn, the future is with our sons but we are not relics yet. There is still work for our swords."

After leaving Bjorn my men and I headed for the lodge. We would be met at a small village on the Paris road for the ways to the lodge and hall were secret. That alone gave me comfort. I did not worry about assassination from Charles the Simple but his lords were a different matter. It was one of his bodyguards who met us. I recognised the small stars he wore on his tunic. I gathered, from his curt manner, that he did not approve of us. That was no surprise. We had killed many of his fellows in battle.

"Follow me, Count Robert." To the Franks, I was still just a count. He led us down a narrow track. It was not big enough for a wagon. This truly was a retreat. As we rode, I noticed men in the eaves of the forest. I turned to Frank, "Are they a threat to us?"

He smiled, "No, Count. They are here to protect the King."

The hall was made of wood and looked like the halls I had seen in Wessex. Next to it were two smaller halls and I guessed that one was the stables while the other would house servants. Men were gutting a pair of deer and a wild boar. The King had been hunting already. When we dismounted the bodyguard pointed to the smaller hall. "Your men will be housed there. Next to it are the stables. If you would follow me, Count."

I saw the worry on Mauger's face. I smiled, "If I need your help, I will shout but I have seen nothing here to make me fear for my life!"

I was reassured when I entered the hall. It looked like my grandfather's hall in the Haugr. King Charles was a much younger man than I was but he looked to have the cares of the world upon his shoulders. His eyes showed that he did not sleep well. "Count Robert, it is good to see you. You are ageing well."

I laughed, "I live the way I always did. And you, King Charles, what of you?"

"I am beset with enemies."

I looked around, "Gisela?" I did not necessarily need to see my wife for she had barely attained double figures but I had been told that she would be here and I was being polite.

"She is a little unwell. She is in Paris with her mother and sisters. It will be men only. There will be good hunting. This forest is renowned for its wild boar and deer."

I nodded as one of the King's servants handed me a goblet of wine. I was right. Gisela had been the smokescreen for the Archbishop and others who might have heard of my clandestine visit into the Kingdom of the Franks. "I think, King Charles, that you have asked me here for a different purpose."

"Your mind is as sharp as ever. We will leave such talk until the morrow. For tonight we eat and we drink. We talk like civilised men for, despite the act you put on, I believe you are one of the cleverest men I have ever met." He did not deserve the title Charles the Simple. I think he earned the name because he was not a complicated man. Others used it to mock him.

In truth, I enjoyed my first meal with the King. It was not a feast but it was the kind of food I liked. We ate wild boar. This was not the one we had seen being taken to the kitchens. This had been slow-roasted. The crackling was well salted and to my taste. The juices ran from the flesh. It was served with honeyed apples and bread made from wheat! He had ale for me and it was good. We talked, not of politics but of hunting and of our families. Having only daughters, he was envious of my son.

"Aye King Charles but he is my only child. If anything happened to me then I would have none. A man worries about his inheritance but William is in good health and one day will marry."

He shook his head, "You may be right, Count Robert. I know that you are a man as I am. You have needs that must be filled. You have spilt your seed. There are young warriors and maidens who have your blood. I know I have bastards. They cannot have the crown but they are of my blood."

Of course, he was right. I had lain with women other than Poppa. While I had been married to her, she had been the only woman in my life but before and after was another matter. I had no idea how many there were and it did not matter. William was my heir.

"Then that is the difference between us, King Charles. I have someone to inherit Normandy."

"And if we both live long enough, I may have one. When Gisela is of an age then you and she could produce a son." He smiled. "I can hope. Without that hope then my future is bleak."

"Bleak?"

We were alone but he looked around, "There are men who seek my crown. Count Arnulf and Count Robert of Poitiers both plot and conspire. Count Robert's father ruled Frankia briefly. His son seeks the crown. Arnulf wishes a larger Flanders." He leaned back. "I know, Count, that you may have been apprehensive about coming here today. We will touch on Wessex tomorrow but your survival and presence in Normandy is the only thing preventing my enemies from taking my crown." He looked at his goblet and pushed it away. "I have said too much. It is the drink. We will talk in the morning when I have a clearer head." He stood, "You are a clever man and belie your reputation. Would that I had spoken to you before you burned my bridges, eh?" He left me alone in his feasting hall.

I finished the jug of ale and watched the fire. I had much to occupy my mind. I had more power and influence than I knew. It explained much. Now I understood why the Archbishop was slow to censure my lack of enthusiasm for Christianity. The King needed me. The Church in Frankia needed me. I went to bed when the jug was finished but my mind was a maelstrom.

The King, despite his libations the previous night, was bright-eyed when I saw him the next morning. There was a table laden with food. "Having you at my table, Count, seems to do me good. I slept well last night. I have invited your men and mine to join us. We will be hunting this morning and after we can talk." He gave me a wry smile. "It might put their minds at rest for they fear I have had you murdered in your sleep! My captain tells me that they are loyal men!"

I saw the relief on the face of Mauger and the others as they saw me when they arrived. The hunting hall was filled with all manner of hunting gear. There were even clothes. I guessed that some of those who came here were ill-equipped for hunting in these woods. Nothing would have fitted me but the leather byrnie I had brought was perfect. I would have brought my Saami bow had I known what we would be hunting. I took one of the Frankish ones. I now saw why the Franks were such poor archers. They had inferior bows. The boar spears and javelins were more to my taste. We would be riding to the hunt and dismounting to actually kill. I preferred that. My horse, Blue, was a good one but he was neither fast nor nimble. You needed both to be able to hunt from the back of a horse.

His woodsmen led us down a trail. They walked and it soon became clear that they knew their business. My grandfather had been a good tracker. He had been trained by Ulf Big Nose. Those skills had been passed down to me but I was not as good as my grandfather had been. The three men who took us deep into the forest were as good as the legendary Hrólfr the Horseman. We said nothing as we headed into the heart of the hunting grounds. The straining leashes of the men with the dogs told us when we were getting close to the animals. The leading tracker held up his hand and then waved at the King. The King dismounted and we followed.

I knew there was an etiquette to hunting with a king. He would have the first strike and only then would the rest of us be allowed to make a kill. The leading woodsman spoke with the King and then he led the hounds and their handlers to head further into the forest. I saw that they headed south. We were facing west and the wind came from the northwest.

The King smiled, "We now wait for the animals to come to us." He waved over a servant. We were each given a horn of ale. The King and I were served first. The King raised his horn, "To a successful hunt and a good outcome to this day!" We toasted and then handed back our emptied horns.

The King took a bow. I chose a pair of javelins and a boar spear. The huntsmen had told us that we sought deer but there were wild boars in this forest. We moved, when the King commanded, further into the forest. Servants watched our horses. The King and I were surrounded by our bodyguards. When we heard the horns and then the barking of dogs we stopped. The King nocked an arrow. I rammed the spear and one of the javelins into the soft earth. Being the tallest I had the best view. I was the one who saw the deer hurtling towards us. I grabbed a javelin. This was a large herd. The dogs had terrified them. A huge stag led them and it was coming for us. The King loosed his arrow. It was a well-aimed arrow. It went into the shoulder of the stag but both the arrow and bow were inferior to those used by my best archers. It merely angered the beast and it turned to come at us. We were all free to release our arrows and javelins. I pulled back and hurled my javelin. It hit the stag close to where the arrow of the King had struck but it was not a mortal blow. I picked up the boar spear as one of my hearth weru stepped towards the stag with his javelin held before him. It was brave but foolish. Even as I braced myself and my spear Siggi Svensson stabbed the stag in the chest and was then struck by its antlers. Blood sprayed over us as the antlers gored him. He was mortally wounded. I lunged with my boar spear. I hit the stag beneath its skull and the iron spearhead drove up into its brain. My strike saved my life for the antlers just missed my head as its head was lifted up and life went from the stag's eyes.

I let go of the spear and ran to Siggi. Even as I reached him, I saw that he was dying but he had managed to grasp the hilt of his sword. He opened his mouth to speak but all that came out was his death sigh. "Farewell, Siggi. You kept your oath to the end."

The hunt had disappeared behind us. I felt a hand on my shoulder and I looked up at the King. "I am sorry Count. This man's death can be laid at my door. I am not as good an archer as I thought. I should have gone for a doe."

I stood. "Do not blame yourself, King Charles. This was meant to be. Siggi was a warrior and he died a warrior."

The King looked down and saw the sword in Siggi's hands, "Scratch a Norman and you see a pagan."

I shrugged, "We would bury him here if that is permitted."

The King nodded, "Not in a churchyard. I understand. We will be with the horses."

I stood, "Mauger, fetch the heart of the stag. These two warriors will be laid together."

We used Siggi's sword and the boar spears to dig the grave. When it was deep enough my men found stones in the forest and made the shape of a boat. We curled Siggi into the position of a babe in his mother's womb and placed his sword in his hands. Then we put the deer's heart in the grave with him and covered the body. Standing in a circle we were alone in the forest. "Allfather, take this warrior. He deserves the honour of sitting with you and those around your table. He kept his oath and died well. We will see you soon enough, Siggi Svensson."

We washed and cleansed ourselves in the hall. The mood was more sombre than it might have been. As well as the stag we had taken more than eight deer. It was a good hunt but Siggi had died. I sat with the King and we spoke.

"The death of your man told me all that I need to know about you, Count Robert. You are still a pagan at heart." He held up a hand to stop any argument. "You are a pragmatic man. I am too. However, you raided Wessex and I cannot allow you to do so again."

My eyes flashed angrily at the King. I was not a man who was told what he could and could not do. "King Charles, I have not broken my oath. I did not attack Franks!"

He shook his head, "I care not if you attack Franks so long as they are not Western Franks!" He sighed, "Let me explain. King Edward is an ally. In a sea of enemies, he is one who would watch my back and he is no threat to my land. Had I had a son then he would be betrothed to King Edward's daughter, Eadgifu. Wessex now controls the island that was Britannia. I beg you, for my sake, do not lose me an ally."

Had he said this before I had attacked it would not have prevented the raid but the raid had served its purpose. We had coin and new men had been blooded. I had no intention of raiding again for we had taken all that they had. The treasure we had taken was almost the same as the payment King Charles had made after the battle of Paris. I could be magnanimous, "For our friendship, King Charles, I will accede to your request."

The relief on the King's face made me smile. He then went on to tell me about his enemies. They were all counts and they ringed him. The Count of Poitiers, Count of Paris and Marquis of Neustria and Orléans, Robert of Neustria was the most dangerous of them. The fact that he had three such titles told me how powerful he was. Each of his lands was bigger than Normandy. He was the son of Robert the Strong who had been, briefly, King of the West Franks. This Count also hated me for I had helped to defeat his father. Count Arnulf of Flanders was the most treacherous. He appeared to support King Charles but he sided with the Count of Poitiers. The last enemy he named was known to me. Count Gourmaëlon of Cornouaille sought to become Duke of Brittany. The King could not allow that.

"And have you no allies, King Charles?"

"Two who have power, you and King Edward of England. So, you can see the dilemma you placed me in when you raided Wessex."

"Aye, I can see that."

"Hagano of Lothringia, my wife's cousin, is an ally but he is not popular in my court. You can see, Count Robert, that I tread a fine line. It is like a line of stepping stones across a raging river. One slip means my doom." We were both silent as we considered the situation. When he spoke, his words made me jump for I was thinking about how I could use this knowledge. "I would ask a favour of you. You can refuse although I suspect that you will agree."

My eyes narrowed, "Is this the price for my raid? I aid you and I am forgiven?"

He smiled, "No, Count, you are forgiven so long as the act of raiding Wessex is not repeated. My request is this, I would have you deal with the Count of Cornouaille. Unlike the other two his lands are close to yours and my spies tell me that he has plans to take back the land of the Bretons from the Normans!"

I nodded, "Did your spies also tell you that I was considering attacking him?" The answer he gave would determine our future relationship.

He looked me in the eyes and answered honestly. He passed the test. "Your men were not close-mouthed. Yes, Count Robert."

"And you know that if I take Brittany then the land I will control will be enormous, a Dukedom, in fact?"

He laughed. "I have heard that you title yourself, Duke of Normandy, anyway. Does it really matter?"

It was my turn to laugh, "My lords seem to think I deserve it."

"You probably do but that is a step too far. It would give my enemies more fuel to use against me. I do not mind what your men call you in your own land. I will continue to call you Count." I nodded. He was admitting that I was Duke. "And I take it you will attack the Bretons?"

"I will but I will do so without informing you of the time or the manner. That is for your protection. You have enemies and they might well use that against you. This suits me anyway. I have told my men to keep word of our attack secret and some did not. This will allow me to discover whom I can trust."

"Good. I am pleased that I invited you. My lords may not understand it but I trust you more than any of my lords. You are still a barbarian and, at heart, a pagan but I believe you have honour and that is rare in leaders."

I gave a mock bow, "That does not sound like praise but I will take it for I have always been a man of my word."

He stood, as did I, and we clasped arms. It was a bond between a duke and a king. Neither of us broke that bond. We were both faithful until, well that is the future, and it does not do to upset Skuld. In all, I spent three days with the King and we learned much about each other. That would be the only time we met. We needed no further meetings for we knew each other's minds. I would not raid Wessex and he would support me if the Pope demanded action. I could go to war and know that Frankia would not intervene. Brittany was alone and was isolated. It was a plum ripe for the picking.

Chapter 5

When I returned to Rouen I spoke at length with William. He was my
heir and he deserved to know all that had been said. He was as happy as I
was that our war had been sanctioned but, like me, he was concerned
about the fact that the attack was common knowledge. I summoned Egil.
He had a clever mind and the three of us, along with Godwin Red Eyes,
spoke of how we could smoke out our enemies. We came up with a
cunning plan. We had just two months before the raid. William and I
divided my land into two halves. We would ride my land and speak to
my lords face to face. We would look into their eyes and we would see if
we could start our prey. This would be the first real test for my son as a
leader. We would tell each of the lords something slightly different in the
hope that when we heard rumours, we could identify whence they
emanated. I took north of the river and William the south. The real
reason for that was that I was more confident about the lords who lived
south of the river. From things the King had said I was more suspicious
of the ones whose lands bordered Flanders.

I headed north with my nine hearth weru. We had not replaced Siggi.
In truth, I would not select one. One would be selected for me in battle.
Nine would do when we fought the Bretons. We headed first for Djupr. I
could speak with my lords who lived between Rouen and Djupr. It would
allow me to gauge the mettle of the men I would lead in battle. Olaf
Olafsson held the most important town north of me. As his port was on
the coast it handled more trade than Rouen. What concerned me, as I
headed north, was the accounts Father Harold had shown me before I had
left. Djupr appeared to pay fewer taxes than any other of my towns and
that included Caen. I wondered if it was an oversight or something more
sinister. I had no evidence that there was any wrongdoing. Once I had
met with Olaf, I would travel the borderlands and then head back to
Rouen. There were just five lords north of the river. Olaf was the most

important and, after visiting Leif Galmrsson and seeing no deception in his eyes, I headed to Djupr. We met four lords on our way north. I saw nothing but honesty in their eyes. My hearth weru concurred. While I spoke with the lords, they spoke with the hearth weru of each lord. I felt more at ease as we headed to the coast.

The loss of Siggi had affected my men. They rode closer to me and viewed all we met with suspicion. Their attitude towards others bordered on rudeness. When we reached Djupr they looked at the sentries as though they were enemies and not friends. My hearth weru were powerful warriors. They dressed for war and their weapons showed them to be men to fear. Olaf's sentries recoiled when we entered their gates.

Djupr was a bustling port. It looked and felt prosperous. As I had expected we were treated as though I was a king. Olaf fawned. His father would not have done so. He would treat me with respect. I had never fought with Olaf, his son. I did not know him. This would be my first opportunity to get to know him. I was given fine quarters. I was accorded a thrall to look after me. I had never needed such things. All that Olaf did, made me suspicious and I should not have been.

He had laid on a great feast. I had not warned him of my arrival but he was rich and accommodation was not a problem. The lords north of my river all deferred to Olaf. He wielded great power. He taxed, for me, all that came and went from Djupr. That was the main reason for Father Harold's surprise. The taxes he collected should have rivalled Caen or Rouen. They did not. Something did not add up. I wondered if he was being robbed by his own clerks. I did not drink as much as Olaf wished. I wanted answers.

First, I spoke to him of the gathering of ships at Caen. He nodded. He had already been warned of the muster when he had visited me in Rouen. I told him that we would be attacking by sea only and that we would need his ships. With that out of the way, I sought other answers. "You have done well here, Olaf. Your father would be proud."

"I hope so but he set his standards too low. The lord of Djupr is a powerful man and should be treated accordingly. He was content with a small hall. He allowed all to speak to him as though they were his equals."

I put down my goblet, "As do I. You are saying I am wrong?"

He knew he had said what he should not and he backtracked, "No, lord. It does you great credit but you deserve honour for what you have done. It is just that I am half Frank. Perhaps that half of me makes me different from my father and from you."

"My mother was a Frank."

I could see in his eyes that he had wished he had drunk less and been more guarded in his words. "Perhaps you are right. I will try to change."

I nodded and ran my finger around the edge of the goblet. It was made of silver. I did not have silver goblets. I used horns or wooden beakers. "Tell me, Olaf, have you and your port had a bad year this year?"

He grinned and waved an expansive hand, "No, Duke, we have done well! The crops were good and we have many ships which use the port. I have added two quays and three warehouses."

"Then why do you pay fewer taxes than Caen, Bayeux and my other towns?"

He almost choked on the wine he was drinking. "I am certain that there has been a mistake, lord. Are you sure?" He recoiled when my eyes bored into him. He was treating me like a fool.

"There may have but it was not mine. It was yours. If it was a clerk with sticky fingers then the fault is still yours. If you want a fine hall and silver goblets then the price you pay is vigilance and, most importantly, honesty! After we have chastised our foes I will return with my clerks. We will look at your accounts. If you have been cheated by your men, we will discover it and we will punish them."

He looked relieved, "Good. I confess that I am not as knowledgeable about such matters. I will make amends. I will go over every figure myself. I will find who has been cheating us!" I saw his eyes. He was shifty. "And how do we attack the Bretons?"

"You have the greatest fleet of ships. We rely on you. Bring your fleet and all of your men to Caen at the start of Tvímánuður."

"Surely I should leave men to watch my borders?"

"No, Olaf, there are other lords who do not have ships. They can watch your borders. I need you. I need the ships and sailors of Djupr!"

"Then I am honoured that you think so highly of me."

That night I did not sleep well. Perhaps it was the food. Olaf had served us dishes I did not recognise. Whatever the reason my sleep was disrupted by disquieting dreams and voices. When my brother's face loomed up out of the dark with a dagger in his hand I woke. I was sweating. What did the dreams mean? Were these voices from the dead warning me and what was their warning?

Olaf insisted on giving us a fine breakfast before we left. The result was that we did not leave until a couple of hours before noon. As we headed, with full bellies, north and east, I spoke to my bodyguards. They had spent the night with Olaf's men. Often, they heard more than I did. "What did you learn?"

"You were right, lord. Lord Olaf has been denying you the coin you are due. It is common knowledge." Mauger hesitated.

"Speak! I will not be offended."

"His men think you are old, lord, and cannot discover the fraud. They were boasting of how clever Olaf Olafsson is. We pretended that we could not hold our ale. They were deceived."

I laughed, "Then he is in for a rude shock."

Before we had left Olaf had shown concern for me. He had asked if he should send men to accompany me. When I told him where I was going, he said that bandits often raided that part of my land. I was surprised. Lord Henry, who had been Harold Sorenson, was a dependable lord and he held that rich piece of farmland for me. He was the next lord I would visit. His words acted as a warning and we rode as though in enemy territory. We were less than four miles from Lord Henry's home when Snorri Larsson, who was riding as a scout, suddenly stopped and dismounted. He went to his horse's hind quarter and pretended to examine its fetlock. It was the signal that there was danger. My men did not react overtly but we all became wary. I pulled up my mail hood and leaned forward to stroke my horse's ears. I saw my men slip their shields onto their arms. To a watcher, it would appear as though we had not reacted but we were ready. Snorri had told us that there was an ambush ahead.

My horse, Blue, afforded me a good view of the land and I could not see where the ambush lay. There was a farm ahead but as there was no smoke coming from its roof, I assumed it was abandoned. There were no fowl clucking in the yard and the place had an abandoned feel about it. We reined in next to Snorri as he mounted his horse.

He pulled himself up into his saddle and as he did so he spoke to me, "Lord there are men hiding up ahead. Men who hide do not mean well. They have unsheathed weapons and they are trying to hide. While I have been stopped, I have seen other men on the opposite side of this road."

We walked slowly down the road. I looked ahead. The farm was to the south of the road and to the north was what had once been an orchard. The trees were overgrown. I began to become angry for this was

Normandy. This was my land. We were mailed and we were armed.
These were bandits. When we were less than two hundred paces from the
farm, I turned in my saddle, "Draw your weapons." As they did, I stood
in my stirrups, "I am Robert, Duke of Normandy. Show yourselves or
die!" The response was a flurry of arrows. I wore leather gauntlets and as
a pair of arrows came at me, I flicked up my hand. It was just a reaction.
Although I managed to hit both arrows one was deflected and I felt it
strike my cheek. Blood dripped down.

My men needed no orders. Their horses were smaller and nimbler than
Blue. They dug in their heels and galloped towards the archers. I did the
same with Blue. He lumbered down the road. Once he got up to speed, he
was unstoppable but we would not reach his full speed by the time we
reached the farm. I drew Long Sword. I now saw the ambushers. There
were more than fourteen of them. They had been forced to stand to send
their arrows at us. They were Vikings. They knew how to use a bow.
That was shown when one of my oathsworn, Stephen son of Sven was
thrown from his saddle having been hit by three arrows. Mauger and
Snorri avenged their shield brother and their swords hacked into the
necks of two of the bowmen.

My helmet hung from my saddle but my coif protected my head. It
saved my life for the arrow which came at my head hit the coif and just
made my head ring as the missile was deflected. I galloped down the
road towards two bowmen who stood drawing back their arms. Blue was
much faster now. He had been bred not only to carry my body but also to
fight. His mouth opened and revealed his teeth. I do not think the two
men had faced a charging horse. They had certainly never seen such a
huge horse. As I closed, I saw fear in their faces. It made them panic.
Men who panic do not fight well. They fumbled with their arrows. They
wore no helmets and had no mail. Instead of concentrating on killing me,
they were worried about their survival. It cost them their lives. The two
arrows they sent at me missed me by a sword's length. They had loosed
too quickly. As Blue's hooves smashed into the legs of one, Long Sword
swung from on high and sliced into the skull and then the chest of the
other. It laid him open to his ribs. I wheeled Blue around and used Long
Sword to split open the head of the man with the crushed and shattered
legs. I saw Mauger slay the last one. We had won but I had lost another
oathsworn.

"Are any left alive?"

Mauger shook his head, "I am sorry, lord. When young Stephen died then the blood rushed to our heads."

It was regrettable but understandable. I nodded, "Put Stephen on his horse. We will bury him later. Then search the bodies. Take everything you can find. There may be clues as to their paymaster."

Beorn Yellow Hair asked, "Are these not bandits, lord?"

"Bandits, who risk death by attacking the Duke of Normandy?" I shook my head. "These were sent here. They were killers."

Mauger dismounted and began to take the purse from the man he had just killed, "Olaf Olafsson?"

"Perhaps, although it is a little obvious if that is true. He warned us of bandits and offered to send men with us. His name, however, is now in my mind."

The weapons were not worth anything and after killing their swords we headed towards the hall of Harold Sorenson. The evidence we had discovered was inconclusive. There seemed to be more coins from Flanders than from Normandy. That, in itself, was not a surprise. Flanders lay just ten miles or so to the north of us. What was suspicious was that they each had silver coins amongst the copper and one, obviously the leader, had a gold piece from the land of the Franks. They were not bandits. They were mercenaries and they had been sent to kill me.

Harold Sorenson lived on the borderlands. He had a hall which was like the Haugr. He had dug a ditch and used the spoil to build a rampart with a wooden palisade. His hall was large enough to accommodate him, his family, his hearth weru and his animals. He had taken the name Henry when he had married the daughter of the lord whose land we had taken. His wife was Christian and had insisted upon Harold taking a Christian name if they were to be married. Harold had not killed her father. He had been killed by another in a battle far to the south. The people of this land were both practical and pragmatic. They were far from Paris and had learned to adapt to new masters. Flanders had fought Frankia for this land. We were just a new combatant. Lord Henry, as he was now titled, and his wife appeared to be happy enough. Certainly, the smile she gave me appeared genuine. His son, Robert, looked a fine young man. Not yet with a beard, his body showed that his father had begun to train him for war.

"You should have warned us, my lord."

I dismounted, "Your husband will tell you, my lady, that I am a rough and ready lord. I need nothing special. Whatever food you were going to eat this night will suffice and we only stay one night."

"Then I will go and prepare your accommodation."

I smiled. Accommodation would be another mattress placed close to the fire. Turning to my lord I said, simply, "We were attacked four miles down the road at the deserted farmhouse."

He nodded although his face showed both shock and concern. He was surprised. He had had nothing to do with the attack, "Arne's place. He and his family were killed by bandits four years since. None will live there for they fear it is haunted. I am sorry you lost a man."

"And we should bury him. You have a cemetery?"

"In the village, there is a church. We can bury him there. I will see that his grave is honoured."

It was dark by the time we had laid Stephen to rest and I was weary as I entered the hall. The delay had enabled Lady Popa to have more food prepared. The ale helped to revive me and as we ate, I was able to speak to Lord Henry. His young son, Robert, who looked to be ten or eleven summers old listened with rapt attention. I smiled for he was the future of this land. He would grow up as a Norman. His father was a Viking and his mother a Frank but he would be Norman.

"They could have come from Flanders. Count Arnulf gathers mercenaries like farmers gather apples in autumn. These walls, lord, are not here for show. They serve a purpose. We bar our gate at night and I have two men on watch. We fear those from across the border. This is rich farmland and the Flemish want it."

I was here to see into the hearts of my men and I saw no deception in Lord Henry's eyes. I told him of my plans for the attack. I explained his part. He nodded, "I can bring twenty men and still leave my walls guarded but I have no drekar."

"Then you and your men will come to Rouen. I have men who will march to war."

He looked surprised, "I thought we were attacking by sea?"

I smiled, "You and your son can keep this secret safe. Our enemies still expect a fleet to appear off their coast. I want their eyes there. When you reach Rouen then all will be revealed." He nodded. "Will your son be coming with you?"

"His mother does not wish it for the sons of Frankish lords wait until they have a beard before they fight. My son is the son of a Viking. He can use a sling. He has shown that he can use a practice sword too. He works with Ivar, the leader of my hearth weru. I learned the same way. The sooner a boy learns to fight the sooner he becomes a man. You wish to come, do you not, Robert?"

"Aye, father. I would like to say that I fought in a battle with this great lord."

When we left, the next morning, I was happier than I had been when I had left Djupr. Lord Henry paid his taxes and there was no hint of deception in his words. I would have spent the rest of my wanderings well if it was not for the disquiet amongst some of my lords. The lords close to Flanders spoke of unrest amongst their people. The Franks objected to the taxes which were levied. The taxes were exactly the same as the ones they had paid to King Charles. The reasons were vague. Some of my lords thought it was because we were Vikings and they thought us barbarians. Others thought that it was the church while a number believed that Count Arnulf was behind it. I could do little about Count Arnulf and I could not change their perception of Vikings but I could do something about the Church. The day after my return I had Father Harold summon the Archbishop. The Archbishop came with other priests. I had William with me. Although I was keen to know what had happened in the south I had other matters, more pressing, to deal with. There was rebellion afoot.

I had thought we had an understanding and so I began the discussion. "Archbishop, I am disappointed."

"Disappointed, lord?"

"You have a fine cathedral have you not? I have given the coin to improve it."

"Yes, lord, and we thank you." He looked at me as though I spoke a foreign language.

"Your priests and your churches are treated well? My lords look out for them?"

I could see him looking from me to Father Harold and back. He was confused. Father Harold was too for I had deliberately not spoken to him. "Yes, lord. Do you seek thanks? We pray for you and your son each day."

"And I thank you in return but what of the priests who live close to Flanders? Why are they fermenting rebellion?"

"Are they, lord?" He seemed both relieved that he had discovered the cause of my concern and confused because he did not think it was true.

"Some of my lords seem to think so. I have important matters to deal with but come Ýlir, the month you call December, I intend to visit the priests along the border and if they are found to be inciting rebellion then I will deal with them."

"Lord, they are priests and subject only to God's law!"

"If they live in my land then they are subject to my law! Deal with it, Archbishop, or I shall!"

He nodded, "I am certain that they only do God's work and have nothing to do with fermenting rebellion but I will speak with them." He and his priests scurried out.

I turned to William, "What do you think?"

"That you dealt with him a little more harshly than I expected but I think he was genuinely unaware of any rebellion."

I nodded, "My choice of words and tone were as a result of my words with the King. He needs us more than we need him. He is beset by enemies. When we fight the Bretons, we fight his war. I will not break my oath but I am less worried about our position. A greater worry is this talk of insurrection."

"You saw no evidence of it did you?"

"No, but as I was returning home, I realised that our raid on Wessex only benefitted the lords south of the River Seine. That means all of their people gained. Perhaps those lords north of the river see the riches of the south and are resentful."

"They could have raided. They are Vikings at heart. I raided. I filled my own coffers. That is why my men all wear mail, have the best of helmets and the finest of swords. My men pay well for their food and ale. My people are satisfied. The ones in Rouen and Caen are satisfied." He looked at the table and then back up at me. "I am surprised at Olaf Olafsson. His father was a rock. He would have snuffed out talk of rebellion when he first heard of it. Perhaps he is at the heart of this unrest. We found no sign of it south of the river. The lords there were eager to fight and spoke from their hearts."

"And that is why I want you to command the fleet when it sails for Nantes. Olaf has more ships than we do but you will command. You will watch him. I am getting old and it will be you who leads the lords like Olaf, Henry and the others. The days of Sámr, Bjorn the Brave and Bergil Fast Blade are numbered."

"You are still a mighty warrior. Mauger told me how you almost split one of those who attacked you in two. That is not the act of a warrior who should hang up his sword. When you were taken to the bottom of the ocean and then freed the gods chose you. They chose the Dragonheart when they touched his sword. You died and were reborn. There is still magic about you."

I laughed, "Do not mention that to the Archbishop, eh?"

We were both thrown into preparations for the war. My ships would be coming to Caen and William took his drekar and his men there. I sent Erik Leifsson with the young crew of *'Fafnir'*. I would not be travelling with the fleet. Instead, I would be leading those who headed across my land. To that end, I invited Bergil Fast Blade, Erik Gillesson, Gandálfr, Harold Mighty Fist and my other lords to muster at Bjorn the Brave's hall at Évreux. Although closer to the land of the Bretons than Rouen it was still far enough away so that the muster would go unnoticed. Before he left, William and I pored over the maps and my plans. William and the fleet would be the bait who would draw the eyes of the Bretons to Nantes and Vannes. Our fleet would be seen as a threat. In their eyes, we were still Vikings and Vikings raided using the river! I would lead my horsemen and the rest of the army overland. Our first target was Alençon. It was ostensibly still a Frankish town but the Bretons had insinuated themselves there. It was a Breton lord who ruled. We would have to reduce it first before we moved on to Rennes. Nantes and Vannes were seaports. Our fleet could blockade them. Rennes was a rat hole to which they could flee. I intended to take it and deny the Count of Cornouaille a place he could spend the winter. There were other strongholds to which he could flee but if I held his three most powerful then I had won.

Bjorn the Brave sent me word when my men were mustered. The ones I trusted I had ordered to meet at Bjorn's. The ones I did not trust would be sent for when I left Rouen. They might be late to the muster but it meant I would lead men in whom I had complete faith. My presence in Rouen was important. It would lull my enemies into a false sense of security. While I was in Rouen there would be no attack. When I slipped out it was with my eight oathsworn and twenty riders. They were the sons of the rich men of Rouen. I had enough warriors for my shield wall and what I needed was horsemen. These young men had good horses. Their fathers could afford fine mail and swords. Each had sworn an oath to me. They were Christians and so I had a Bible as well as their swords. We were changing. They had all spent time with Erik at his training camp. He vouched for their skills and honesty. They would be an extra layer of protection for me when we went to war. I would use Blue to travel wherever the battle was at its fiercest. My twenty-eight men would be able to protect me. We left before dawn. Egil and the men who remained were more than enough to protect my town from an attack. To add to the illusion Egil dressed Sven Long Legs, the tallest man in the garrison, in my clothes. It would only fool an observer from a distance but that was all we needed. We rode south and east while darkness and early mist hid us from observers and spies.

Although they were well-armed, trained and mailed, the young men of my town were untried. As we rode, I saw Mauger and the rest of my hearth weru viewing them with suspicion. Until they had been tested in battle then my eight bodyguards would not trust them. I confess that I was curious. If the experiment was successful then it could be repeated throughout my land. Each of my towns had men whose fathers were rich. They were the merchants. They were the men who produced pots, goblets and platters used throughout the land. They were the owners of merchant ships. If I could harness their potential and their coin then we would be more powerful than any Viking army had ever been for we would have mailed horsemen who could fight from the back of a horse. Such a thing had been the dream of my grandfather. I hoped that I would see that dream fulfilled.

There was now a mighty camp at Évreux. After the news of unrest, he and my other lords had each road leading into the camp well-guarded. Word of our presence would not get out. We would not spend long at Évreux and once we left it would not matter if word spread of the Norman army heading for Brittany. My plans meant I would try to sow confusion. I held a council of war and appointed six men to lead my six warbands. Erik Gillesson would lead the largest warband. They were the horsemen. Each lord had brought some men on horses and they joined Erik. Each of my six warbands would travel separately. The warbands would take a different road but our destination was the same. Once we neared Valframbert then we would be using just three roads. Warbands would combine. Six would become three. One would be from the north and west. One from the north and east and one from the south. We would keep the three warbands separate. I would lead the one from the north and east and we would approach Alençon. In a perfect world, the burghers would welcome us as allies but I doubted that outcome. It was more likely that they would bar their gates and try to hold us off. The town had a wall but it was wooden and the stronghold was not a daunting one.

We carried enough food to reach Alençon. After that, in the land of our foes, we would live off the land. It was almost harvest time and I hoped that the Bretons would be busy in their fields. Even as we headed towards Valframbert and Alençon my son would be leading more than two hundred ships to blockade Nantes. He would land men to the north and south of the port and begin to besiege it. I did not care if the Count of Cornouaille laughed off what he would see as paltry numbers so long as his eye was fixed on the sea. Once we reached Valframbert then he would know he had an even bigger army heading from the east. The lord of Valframbert was one of my men. Sámr had spoken with him and Tostig Sharp Tongue had not joined the muster. He was at the border town ensuring that no word of our arrival reached Alençon. Erik Gillesson would lead his mounted column to head to the far side of Alençon where they would hide. Bergil Fast Blade, now more like the warrior I had known for more than half of my life, would lead five hundred men to the south and east of Alençon. My band of one thousand men would march down the road.

We camped by the River Londeau but I was accommodated in Tostig's stronghold. Gandálfr was with me and we dined with Tostig. "So, Tostig, what can you tell me of Alençon?"

"It is not a large town and the men there are practical. They dare not offend the Bretons for they are too far from Rouen. I am the nearest Norman lord. I command forty men. I can keep an enemy at bay but I cannot protect their burghers."

"And who is the lord there?"

"There is none. The Frank who ruled the town, Gilles d'Alençon, died of the pox. No other lord replaced him. There is a council of merchants and farmers. They have a Breton merchant, Stephen of the Seed. He controls the town council."

I stared at Tostig, "I should have been told of this. I could have appointed a lord."

"I know, lord but…"

"Speak."

"I have two sons. I hoped that when Richard, my eldest, was of an age, he might be a lord."

That reason I could understand and my anger began to subside, "And how old is your son?"

"He has seen eighteen summers."

"A man then; and has he been blooded?"

"He was my shield-bearer at Paris."

"Then I will attach him to my hearth weru. Let us see how he shapes up when he has to endure the enemy trying to kill me."

I thought Tostig might refuse but, instead, he smiled and nodded, "That is the best answer I could have had." He waved over a youth who had broad shoulders and the dark hair of a Frank. He got his looks from his mother. "This is Richard Tostigsson. Richard, the Duke would have you attached to his bodyguard."

"It is an honour, lord."

I shook my head. "It is a poisoned chalice, Richard, for every Breton will try to kill me. This will make or break you. Do not answer yet. Sleep on it. Give me your answer in the morning. If you accept my offer then, should you survive, there may well be land for you to rule. I make no promises."

"I have a chance, lord, and that is all I need." I liked his earnest face and honest answer.

When we left, the next day, I allowed the young warriors of Rouen to ride ahead of me. They were honoured but I had another motive. All of them had burnished helms and shiny mail which had yet to be tarnished by battle. Their horses were all groomed so that they shone and each of the young warriors had a banner flying from his spear. My seasoned warriors had mocked them. Secretly so had I for they were an unnecessary encumbrance but they looked effective and the colourful host of warriors heralded the rest of our more mundane army. I wanted to impress those within the walls. We halted before the gates of the town. If we had to assault them then they would not hinder us. My young horsemen pranced their horses before the walls. I heard the snorts of derision from Haraldr's men. I hid my smile as I edged to within bowshot of the walls. I was showing the men of the town that I was not afraid of them.

I waited until faces appeared on the gatehouse. "I am Duke Robert of Normandy! I have been given this land by King Charles. I am here to claim Alençon. Hitherto you have enjoyed the freedom of no taxes and no lord. That changes this day."

I watched the faces on the gate as they looked at each other. Eventually, a grey beard took off his helmet. "I am Fulk of Alençon. I own half of the houses in the town and I am mayor."

"What happened to this Stephen of the Seed? I thought he was mayor?"

He shook his head, "He was but when we heard you were heading here, he left in the night with his chests of gold and silver. He has gone to Nantes." I nodded. That was an honest answer. They were doing what we would do. They were being defiant even though the odds were in our favour. "We could fight you, Duke Robert."

I nodded. I had to be brutal and make a threat that would stop them from fighting us. "Aye you could and you might kill some of my men. If you killed just one then I would throw down your walls. Then I would blind every man who resisted us and take his arms and feet. I would give the women to my men to be used then sell what was left in the slave markets of Bruggas." I shrugged, "It is your choice. Resist and you know your fate. Open your gates and you are my friend. I will afford you protection and when the Bretons are defeated you will enjoy the riches of that land too. That is a generous offer. Fight and die or live without the threat of Brittany." I smiled and waited. "The sun is hot and I am no longer as patient as I once was. Make a decision now!"

"Open the gates! Let us welcome the Duke of Normandy!"

Chapter 6

We stayed but one night. There was no need to stay longer. The Breton merchant had not had the courage of his convictions and the merchant had fled. We learned from Fulk that Stephen of the Seed took twenty mailed men with him. Had they remained then we might have had to fight. When the burghers saw the size of my army their faces filled with the relief of knowing they had taken the correct decision. I learned a lesson that day. The Franks were still terrified of us for they thought we were still Vikings. We needed to have our army led by men who dressed like my horsemen of Rouen. The likes of Bjorn the Brave, Gandálfr and Harold Mighty Fist would make them fight for they feared for their women. I told Fulk that he could continue to lead the town until I had appointed a successor. As I left, I reminded him that I expected the taxes that they had not yet paid.

I allowed the young men of Rouen to lead our victorious column. My son would have to change. He was still the wild warrior. He dressed like Godwin and the other men he led. I dressed like my horsemen. I wore the blue cloak with the white sword. As I fingered my moustache and beard, I realised that they would have to be trimmed too. In truth, the only reasons Vikings did not trim them were of a practical nature; at sea, it was hard and unnecessary to do so and when we raided, we needed terror. We had taken our last raid. Now we would be conquering other lands. We might still need terror but the last thing we needed was for men to fight to the death because they thought we would just kill them and take their families.

The next town, Rennes, would not be so easy. This was also Breton. Stephen the Seed would have warned them of our approach. Perhaps the word was already racing to Nantes and to Vannes too. Riding ahead of us like a screen, Erik had sent scouts to discover the state of the walls and to see if the town was alerted to danger from the east. It took two days for the three columns to close with the walls of Rennes. We were given constant reports from Erik's scouts. Rennes was ready. They had, as I had expected, been warned of our approach. It had been anticipated. It would not change my plans for the battle and I was not put out. Erik cut off the road to Nantes. The assault this time would be more difficult for there were walls of stone and they were topped by a wooden palisade. I rode, with my hearth weru and the horsemen of Rouen, around the walls. It took half a morning to do so for I wanted to look for weaknesses. The river protected half of the circumference. That left a smaller area for us to attack and for them to defend. When I returned to the camp, I summoned my lords and held a council of war.

"Erik, take every rider and put the land around the town to the torch. Every animal you can find must be captured and brought here. Empty their granaries. I want all of their food. Kill the men and drive the women hence." He nodded.

Gandálfr asked, "There is a good reason not to kill them, lord?"

"Aye, old friend. I want word of what we do to spread. We do not need Breton slaves and we would rule this land in the future. When we win and win we shall, then we can give some of their farms back to them. The other reason is that they will flee to neighbouring towns, perhaps even Nantes, and they will have to be fed. War is fought with food as well as the sword."

Bjorn said, "And do we build siege engines?"

I shook my head, "There is no need. They will not have laid in supplies for they can only have had one or two day's notice. When they see the smoke rising from the Norman fires surrounding them and when they smell Breton cattle being cooked, then I will speak with them."

"That seems a risk, lord."

I smiled, "Why? My son has Nantes and Vannes blockaded. This is harvest time. If their men are in their three large towns and we are burning their farms then they have only one choice. They will have to fight for the alternative is surrender. I would rather have one battle which we win than a lengthy siege which would not guarantee victory. I will send two of my men to the fleet and they can advise my son of our position. He can safely land his men now and they can feed from the Bretons. Surely you do not mind sitting in the sun and eating beef, do you?"

Bergil Fast Blade laughed, "It seems perfect to me, lord. I had forgotten what a clever mind you have!" Bergil was back to the man I had known. His wife and her infidelity were forgotten.

We had taken over a farmhouse and that became my home while we lined the outside of Rennes with fires. The paucity of their defences was shown by the fact that our men could close to within two hundred paces and they were not subjected to either bolts or arrows. They had laid in too few to waste. They would save them for our attack. When Erik's men drove their captured cattle to our fires then the air was filled with the smell of roasting beef. After five days word reached us that my son had landed his men and burned the ships in Vannes and Nantes harbours. Brittany was a mercantile land. We had destroyed that livelihood. King Charles had wished me to destroy any opposition in Brittany. We were well on the way to accomplishing that but we had still to fight a battle. I was a warrior and I knew that it would come down to a battle. We had to destroy the Bretons so that I could put my own lords in the place of the Bretons we would kill.

Each night I rode to the gates with my hearth weru, the young horsemen from Rouen and Richard Tostigsson. I learned much about the young men when I did so. Many older warriors resented young warriors. I was not one of those. I had been a young warrior who had led men from an early age. I knew how to look for that within young warriors which would make them great warriors. Richard impressed me as did Guy the cloth merchant's son. While the other young warriors boasted of what they would do to the Bretons those two studied the walls and the men who topped them.

Richard asked me, as we returned to the farmhouse, three nights after news of my son's success reached us, "Duke, how will we assault the walls?"

"We make pavise. We advance our archers behind them and we clear their walls. They should have had stone throwers or bolt throwers on their walls but they do not. There is no ditch. They rely upon the river and that only protects one side. When the walls are cleared then we move closer to the walls and let our axemen hack at the gate. The only thing they can do is to use fire or oil. Thus far I have not seen them preparing either. If we see smoke on their walls then that means they intend to give us a hot welcome. When you have wooden walls then fire is dangerous. We build ladders and, when the gate is about to fall, we use ladders to assault the walls along its entire length. We have more warriors than they do and the town will fall."

Guy said, "But you do not believe it will come to that do you, Duke?"

"You are both clever young men. No, I believe that the Count of Cornouaille will bring his army from Nantes to relieve the siege. My men's blockade will force him to do so. He cannot use his ports and Rennes is the most important town in Brittany. My son and our men can retreat to their ships if he attacks them. He will still be blockaded. He needs to relieve Rennes and then rid the land of us so that his people can harvest what is left of their crops."

Richard asked, "Then, Duke Robert, why do you ride around each night?"

I smiled, "To frighten them. I am the Viking who defeated King Charles, who defeated Alan the Great. I am the giant. I am the barbarian. I am not the warrior I once was but they do not know that and the sight of me riding around their walls on the largest horse they have ever seen will give them nightmares. I still hope that they will surrender before the Count of Cornouaille arrives but it matters not for their spirit will be broken. They will have tightened belts and we are eating their beef. My men are drinking their cider, wine and ale. Our men are using the river to empty their bowels and bladders. The people of Rennes are drinking that water. Their spirits will be sinking. There will be farmers on the walls looking out and seeing their farms being burned and their animals slaughtered. There will be worrying thoughts in their heads. When this is over what will they have to return to?"

It was four days later when Erik's scouts galloped in with the news that an enormous army was heading from the south. I would have the battle I wanted. I convened a council of war. When my captains knew what I wanted I immediately ordered two of my men to ride to my son. I needed the crews of our drekar now. The Count had sixty miles to travel. He would move more slowly than my son with his men. My men would just run up the road. They would not travel with carts and wagons. They would use the byways and live off the land. They would travel as boat's crews. Leaving some men to watch the main gate, I took the rest of my army south of the river. With Erik Gillesson and his men guarding my left flank and the river guarding my right, we waited for the Bretons to lumber up the road towards us.

It took two days for them to reach us. In that time, we had dug a ditch before us. I had archers and slingers camped just behind it. My warbands were in three lines although, until the enemy arrayed, they lounged before fires which cooked more of the Breton beef. The Bretons outnumbered us. Many of the farmers had fled to Vannes and Nantes. The Count had gathered every man he could. The majority of his men were not warriors. They were farmers who would fight. I did not doubt that they would fight hard but they were fighting my men. More than half of my army was made up of men who had recently raided Wessex. We were a honed sword. The Bretons were a sharpened bill hook. His most dangerous men were his horsemen. His crossbows were good but my archers were better. The aim of the Bretons was to break the siege and to do that they had to attack us. I think they thought we would just be waiting for them at Rennes. When their scouts saw us, they galloped back to tell their leader that they had found us.

When they arrived, they built a camp. They were taking no chances and they dug a ditch and lined it with wooden stakes they had brought. I let them. All the time they were preparing my son was bringing more of my men from the south. The next day the Bretons arrayed. A large body of horsemen went to their right to fight the threat that was Erik Gillesson. The rest of his horsemen formed a thin line across the front of their foot. Before them were their crossbows. When I saw his formation, I knew what he intended. He would neutralize my horsemen and then weaken our centre before launching an attack by his horsemen. It would be a test of wills between his best and mine. I was confident. Only Erik and I truly knew the worth of my horsemen. It had been my grandfather and Erik's father who had begun to build the horsemen Erik led. We had not used them in Paris. They were seen as scouts who wore armour. They did not know that they had been as well trained as any shield wall. I knew that in the battle between horsemen there would be one victor; Lord Erik of Montfort!

I had dismounted the young men of Rouen and they were before me. They would be used as bodyguards now. My hearth weru stood at my side. We had spears and we had darts. Our men had good shields. The Breton line knelt. The warriors were blessed by priests and then horns sounded. The crossbowmen advanced and the horses on their right flank charged. Erik sounded his own horns and then countercharged. I could leave that battle to Erik. The crossbows moved towards us. A crossbow has a flat trajectory. Arrows can be launched into the air. The pavise we had prepared for an attack on the walls now gave my archers protection. The crossbowmen came within range and knelt. A crossbow is incredibly inaccurate when used from a standing position. Even before they had taken aim the crossbows suffered casualties. If the crossbows were in range of us then it followed that my archers had their range too. Arrows fell as men knelt. A quarter did not even get to launch a bolt. Then a duel began. Some of my archers were hit. A crossbow is a powerful weapon and some of them penetrated the pavise. My archers slew more of their men. The more crossbowmen who fell then the slower was their rate of release. More men died. They were losing the duel. While the cavalry battle raged my archers and slingers gradually overcame the crossbows. The survivors, less than half of the ones who had advanced, fell back.

I had Egil Flame Bearer's son, Leif, with me and he held his father's horn. As the crossbowmen fled, I saw the enemy horsemen preparing to charge. "When I give the command then sound the horn twice. It will order the archers and slingers to retire."

"Aye, lord."

I could tell he was nervous, "Leif, do not fear. You are your father's son. Do not panic and sound it twice, then twice more and twice more after that. All will be well. When that is done then wave my standard. I would have the enemy drawn on to me!"

The horsemen came with couched lances. Some were mailed, most were not. My archers and slingers sent a storm of arrows and stones. Horses and men fell. When they were less than forty paces from our archers I said, "Now!"

The horn sounded clearly. The archers and slingers ran. We opened our lines to let them through and then locked shields. I had no shield but Mauger and Arne locked theirs before me. I held Long Sword above my head. Our men had known there was a ditch. The Bretons did not. Most cleared it but some did not and both horses and riders fell. It broke the cohesion of a line that was already thinned by arrows and stones. My men had spears. From behind us came the spears of our second rank. They were charging into a hedgehog of steel.

Mauger said, as the horsemen neared us, "Lord Erik has driven the other horsemen from the field."

I just nodded. Leif Egilsson held my banner and he waved it high above my head. I twirled my sword above too. I was a head taller than any other warrior and I saw an arrow of riders coming directly for me. The young men of Rouen were brave. They held their spears and braced themselves. The leading Bretons were not stopped. Four of my young warriors in the centre died in the initial attack. They managed to unhorse two riders but five more came towards us. I swung my sword, not at the warrior who rode the leading horse, but his mount. My sword hacked through the chestnut's head. The animal had tried to swerve away from the long sword and, when it was hit, its dying carcass fell against the next horse. Both riders were unhorsed. Mauger and Arne stepped forward to spear the two riders. I brought my sword down on the Breton lord who tried to wriggle free from under the dead horse. We now had a barrier of horses and men before our centre. These were the best horsemen the Bretons had and two of them made their horses rear. Fearlessly Richard Tostigsson held his shield before him and rammed his sword into the chest of one of the horses. It tumbled and knocked over the other rearing horse. Robert and Guy of Rouen ran forward to slay the horsemen. The men on the two sides of their arrowhead were outnumbered and when half had fallen the rest retreated.

Guy looked at me. His mail was covered in blood. It looked like he had been working in an abattoir. I could not tell if any of the blood was his. He asked, "Is it over, lord?"

Bergil Fast Blade laughed, "No, young warrior. We have beaten off the attack they thought would win the day quickly. Now they use the sheer weight of numbers. They will bring men on foot to fight us."

I shouted, "Move the wounded! Leave the dead. Our warriors can still fight for us even though they are in the Otherworld!"

I saw the young warriors from Rouen clutch their crosses as they heard what they thought was blasphemy! They had lost a fifth of their number already and three others were wounded. Was their leader still a pagan? If they stood it would be a real test of their courage and their loyalty.

The Count had gambled on his best warriors, his horsemen and crossbowmen, breaking our line. That had not worked. Now he would have to resort to the levy. I saw men in mail with helmets. There were others with improvised weapons and quickly made wooden shields. The one advantage the Bretons had was that they outnumbered us. Erik and his horsemen were still chasing the Breton horsemen from the field. Until my son arrived with the rest of my men, we would have to hold the line. I glanced down the spears of my warriors. My lords were still dotted along it. Their hearth weru were around them. The second rank had our mailed veterans and it was only the third rank and the archers behind who were vulnerable. The young men of Rouen had shown me enough of their courage to give me hope for our third rank. This would be bloody and I did not want them wasted.

"Guy, take the young horsemen and guard Leif and my standard. Leif, stand behind the archers and wave my banner."

"Aye lord."

We opened our ranks to allow the men to slip through. They had impressed me. The three who had been wounded had stayed at the fore. They did not lack courage. When this was over, they would just need to be trained properly. As the Bretons steeled themselves for their attack, I saw Gandálfr step forward. One of the Breton horses still lived. I heard him say, "Go to the Allfather, warrior! You have earned your place in the Otherworld!" He mercifully ended its life and stepped back. My men were not cruel.

I saw the Count of Cornouaille. He rode a good horse and he had an entourage of eight men with him. They wore red cloaks. A priest rode a horse next to him. His rich robes told me that he was a bishop. They rode down the Breton line. The Count was speaking and, as he passed each group of men they cheered. At one point he turned and gestured towards me. Men shook their fists and weapons. Then he returned to the centre of the line. The Bishop dismounted. The whole Breton army knelt and the Bishop blessed them. If he had been a good leader then the Count of Cornouaille would have dismounted and joined his men in the next attack. He did not. The horsemen rode through their men and took their place at the rear. One of the red-cloaked horsemen dismounted and stood in the centre. It was obvious that he would lead. His position in the centre meant that he would come for me. The front rank shuffled around so that he was surrounded by mailed men.

"They will come for us."

Bergil Fast Blade said, "And that is how it should be for we are the best."

Gandálfr chuckled, "And these have fine mail and weapons. They oblige us by bringing their riches to it. I am gambling that the ones with the fine cloaks are wealthy. Let us hope they bring their coin to pay the ferryman!"

My men laughed. I studied the red-cloaked warrior. His helmet was unusual. It was high domed. I could see little of his face. The range was three hundred paces, and his mail coif covered all but his eyes. As he raised his spear to begin the attack, I saw that he had mailed gloves on his hands. This was a well-protected warrior. Then a horn sounded and, with banners fluttering in the breeze the line lurched forward. Our ditch was no longer an obstacle for it was filled with dead and dying men. The obstacles would be the bodies of the Breton dead.

I began chanting. It was soon taken up. My men banged their spears and swords against their shields. The cracks echoed across the battlefield like Thor's thunder. The chant put steel in our hearts and, for the levy, made them fear the foe they faced.

> *Clan of the Horseman*
> *Warriors strong*
> *Clan of the Horseman*
> *Our reach is long*
> *Clan of the Horseman*
> *Fight as one*
> *Clan of the Horseman*
> *Death will come*

The Bretons should have chanted. It would have kept the rhythm for them. Some of their men stumbled for they were not in step. Some fell behind and some, especially those on the flanks who were unencumbered by mail and bodies hurried forward. The secret of a successful attack is to hit as one. In the first fifty paces, their line became ragged and had gaps in it. I was hopeful that this attack would be doomed to failure. Still, they came on. I saw the leader use his spear to try to control the advance of the Bretons. Some of the younger ones were eager to close with us. Some would have filled their breeks. The shame would make them want to fight and cover the breeks with Norman blood. Those within thirty men of the red-cloaked leader obeyed and that alone told me that they were the best of his warriors. They would be worthy opponents. I held my sword above my head and Arne and Mauger locked their shields. Galmr Leifsson and Leif Siggison, on the other side of those two, did the same. I heard laughter and looked down to see Bergil Fast Blade laughing with his men. He had recovered from his pit of despair. He did not fear the enemy who came on. Like me, he fought with a sword. His hands were still fast despite his age.

When I glanced to the fore once more, I saw that the enemy was less than a hundred paces from us. "Archers! Now!" It sounded like a flock of birds had taken flight as arrows soared over our heads. They were loosing blindly but the Bretons filled the ground. Some would look up and they would die. Even those with shields might die for they did not have shields that were as good as ours and arrows could shatter a poorly made one. Shields came up. Some were slow and men were struck. Holes appeared in their lines but not in the centre. The solid phalanx came on. Their raised shields actually helped them for they could pick their way over the bodies littering the battlefield. Men fell. They were the ones who were poorly armed and protected. That would have an effect on their fellows who survived. It would sap their will to fight.

The red-cloaked leader waited until they were twenty paces from us and then, raising his spear shouted, "Charge!" They broke into a run. He and those around him all set off on the same leg. There were three dead horses before us and the red-cloaked Breton and his men clambered up to use the height they provided. I swung my sword as their spears were thrust down. The uneven nature of the horses' carcasses meant that the red-cloaked Breton did not manage to thrust his spear at me but at Leif Siggison. My sword swung in an arc as a Breton spear was rammed at my helmet. Two things happened at once. The spearhead came from on high and it caught my eyepiece. My helmet was pushed down and I was temporarily blinded. My sword struck flesh, then mail and finally more flesh. I heard a scream and the falling spear released my helmet. I saw the Breton had had his right arm severed. My sword was stuck in his side. He fell backwards and his fall released it.

Next, to me, Arne snarled, "Bastard!"

I looked and saw that the red-cloaked Breton had taken Leif Siggison's head and was holding it aloft. Another of my oathsworn had died. Mauger and Arne had slain the men before them and I pointed my sword at Leif's killer, "He dies!" I turned and my men followed me. It was calculated. All along the line were combats between my lords, backed by their hearth weru, and knots of Bretons. We fought better this way. I swung my sword two-handed into the side of the warrior protecting Red Cloak's side. Even had my blade not severed the links then the sword would have broken bones. As it was his scale armour was not good enough and my blade tore through to reveal his organs. He fell backwards. Red Cloak had lost his spear and he wielded a sword. He turned to swing at me. His sword was not a long one and although he hit my mail the links held. He had taken his strike. I raised my sword and brought it down. He lifted his shield to protect himself. The sword split the shield and I heard a grunt as his arm was broken. He was forced back and he slipped on a dead horse. As he fell backwards his arms instinctively spread open. He looked like the White Christ in Rouen Cathedral. I brought Long Sword down to split him in twain.

The better Bretons in the front ranks had perished but there were still many men who were fighting. Suddenly, I heard a wail from ahead. I stepped onto the dead horse which had been the Breton's bane and I saw, at the rear of the enemy line, Bretons fleeing. Their Count was leaving. His banner marked his departure. Then I saw my son's banner and, from the east, heard the thunder of hooves as Erik Gillesson and his men returned to the battlefield. The Bretons before us would not know that they had lost and they fought on but I knew and I roared, "William Longsword comes! We have victory! Let us end this!"

That and the death of Leif put heart into my men and we began to scythe our way through Bretons. None could stand before Long Sword. The blade was now blunted and dull but it was a long bar of steel and it broke bones as we advanced towards William. It was almost dusk when we met in the middle of a sea of bloody battered bodies.

I clasped my son's arm, "Well met, William! Did you catch the Count?"

He shook his head, "He is as slippery as an eel. He took off with his horsemen. We could not stop him." He waved his own long sword, "We have victory! Brittany is ours!"

We camped at the battlefield. The enemy wounded were despatched. My warriors passed over the battlefield and took from the enemy dead. We would have better-armed warriors now. Our men would all have Breton coins in their purses. Some would wear expensive boots and fine leather belts and baldrics. I saw Sven Ship Sealer sporting a red cloak. Our healers tended to our men. We buried our dead. There were many good warriors who had died. None of my lords had perished but all had lost, as I had, oathsworn. We had paid a high price for this land. Erik and his horsemen gathered the loose horses. We had roasted horse for food. As the bodies of the Breton dead were burned the wind took the smell and the smoke south. It would pass across Brittany and tell the people that their Count had lost.

I sat with my son and my closest lords around a fire and William told me of his battle. "They were expecting our fleet, father. Their ships were safe inside their harbours. They lined their walls. You were right to change your plans. Our men are loose-lipped or worse."

I looked at the men who had come with my son. He had brought half of the lords he had led. Sámr was there and his bloody mail showed that he had fought. Olaf Olafsson was still with the fleet. My son had left him to command. He had known we would need our best warriors! "And how did you destroy their ships if they were in the harbour?"

He grinned, "We had knarr with us for treasure. Erik Leifsson suggested we fill them with kindling and use them as fire ships. The Bretons had made it easy for us. Their ships in the harbour were like a longphort. They could not be moved. The fire spread to the houses close by the strongholds. When their armies had left, they took their best men. We took Nantes straightaway. I brought half the army here and sent Olaf to take Vannes. I did right did I not?"

I waved an arm at the battlefield. "This is evidence that you did. You are ready to lead the clan!"

We had much treasure from the battlefield. Gandálfr was quite right. The Breton lords came with no thought of defeat. Their purses were full. I sent Erik and his horsemen home. We would not be needing them and I was aware that we had taken most of our men from the heartland of Normandy. Count Arnulf might seek to take advantage of our war. We marched to Nantes. The Count had fled. From some survivors, we discovered that he had ridden to Count Robert of Neustria in his Poitevin home. King Charles' enemies were gathering. I realised that they were now my enemies too. While we awaited news from Olaf Olafsson, I began to examine Nantes. It had potential. It was closer to the sea than Rouen and there was land to the south which could be raided. If we raided Robert of Neustria, I would be doing that which King Charles wished. When news came, two days later, that Vannes had surrendered to Olaf Olafsson then I knew that Brittany was ours.

I had decisions to make. I needed three counts: one for each of Rennes, Vannes and Nantes. They had to be strong men for if we held these three towns then the rest of the land would have to obey us. I wondered about taking one for myself and, as soon as the thought entered my head, I dismissed it. I liked Rouen and I was getting too old and set in my ways to move. I decided to wait until Olaf Olafsson returned. We had enough to occupy us. We had the treasure to divide and we had a town to loot. We had killed many lords. Their wives and families had fled to Poitiers, following the Count. By the time Olaf arrived, we had chests for all of my lords. They would divide it amongst their own men. For my part, I did not intend to keep any. I had enough and the men who had followed me deserved it. Erik Leifsson had been the one who had the idea of fireships and he would be rewarded as though he was a lord.

We held a feast to celebrate and I had made the decision who would be my counts. I decided to wait until after the meal to declare them. During the feast, men drank too much. That was normal. My son, Sámr, Bergil and my other senior lords did not. I watched men as they drank. The young horsemen of Rouen drank heavily but I noticed that they were more reflective than they had been when we had left Rouen. Richard Tostigsson was another who was reflective. He had shown me that he too had learned from the battle. He had impressed me. His father had said he would. I would give him a lordship. He would rule Alençon for me. I had spoken to some of my men before the meal. Sámr, and Ragnar, not to mention Bergil, deserved the first refusal of the three towns. Sámr and Ragnar chose not to accept my offer. I was not insulted. I had offered them to myself first and I had refused. I understood their reasons. Bergil had accepted. He would have Rennes.

I had decided on two others when Olaf Olafsson began to raise his voice. He was drunk and he boasted of his success. Taking Vannes had all been down to him. I heard his voice telling all of his prowess. No one else had taken such credit. I had spoken to Erik Leifsson. My captain had watched the attack and he knew the truth. I knew that others deserved as much credit for the victory. Not least my captain himself. I dismissed his words as the results of too much to drink until he began to tell those around him that he would be the new Count of Vannes. I had not spoken to him although I had a title planned for him. The more he went on the angrier I became. I did not like boastful men. I did not like warriors who took me for granted. I was Duke and the decision would be mine. By the time I was ready to make my announcement I had changed my mind. He would not have the title and the land I had previously planned.

I stood and banged on the table for silence. All faces looked at me. The only one who looked in expectation was Olaf Olafsson. He was in for a shock. "My friends, we have had a great victory. We have taken Brittany. We have doubled the size of the land we rule and all of you will benefit. There are chests of treasure for you to take home. All will be rewarded. I have four prizes to give. Rennes, I give to Bergil Fast Blade. He will be the new Count of Rouen." It was a popular choice and men banged the table to show their approval. I will leave Nantes for the moment. Gandálfr would you exchange Lisieux for Vannes?"

I had not spoken to Gandálfr but the joy on his face was clear, "Aye lord and gladly. I am both honoured and humbled."

A flicker of doubt crossed Olaf Olafsson's face and then disappeared for he now expected the prize that was Nantes. "Good. Richard Tostigsson you performed heroically in the battle and your reward is Alençon."

Like Gandálfr he had not expected it and he stammered his thanks, "I, I, thank you, lord. I do not deserve it."

"But you do! You and Guy of Rouen saved your lord from the two Breton horsemen. It is right and fitting." He nodded. "Guy of Rouen I give to you Lisieux." He sat open-mouthed and nodded. I smiled. "And that leaves Nantes. I give Nantes to my son William Longsword and with it the title of Count of Brittany."

That was a popular choice for all of them liked my son. He was a man's man and a fearless warrior. The only dark face belonged to Olaf Olafsson. I smiled, "And, of course, Olaf Olafsson contributed to our victory as did Sámr Oakheart. They are both accorded the title of Count! Count of Caen and Count of Djupr." Sámr was overjoyed but Olaf had a sour face as though he had just eaten a lemon! He stood and left. It was rude and would be punished. I saw that he took with him half a dozen lords from the land north of the Seine.

William said, angrily, "That is lacking honour and disrespectful! Do not give him the title! He does not deserve it."

I spoke quietly. William was still learning. "My son, I had already planned on giving him the title of Count of Vannes but he told all that it was his already. I will speak with him but first, we have much to do here. Tomorrow we send the fleet home and our men. I will stay with you, Gandálfr and Bergil until the land is secure."

I did not get to speak with Olaf for he left before the rest of the fleet. I would have to travel to Djupr and chastise the new Count of Djupr personally.

Chapter 7

In the end, it took a month or more to make the three towns secure. I had men to hang. I had to make an example of them. These were men who thought I was a barbarian and did not understand figures and coin. They tried to cheat us. They learned that the Normans did not suffer fools. The lesson was quickly learned and no others tried to emulate the men. I spared the warriors who had fought against us but we let them know that they would now fight for us. If they did not then they were free to leave my land. My three new counts had families to bring from their homes and I felt duty-bound to stay and see them settled in. The result was that I did not head for Rouen until the start of Gormánuður. I had been away far longer than I had intended. The journey back was not quick either. I visited with many of my lords. It was not just Rennes, Vannes, Nantes and Alençon which had new lords. I had rewarded all those warriors who had shown heroism and courage during the battle. I was weary when I reached Rouen. However, my weariness left me when I saw that my town had prospered in my absence. The Archbishop came to see me almost as soon as I reached my hall. He seemed agitated.

"Is there a problem, Archbishop?"

He nodded, "Before you left for Brittany you spoke of unrest in your northern marches. I was mindful of your words and I took it upon myself to travel my parishes. It is not the priests who ferment discord, lord. It is Count Arnulf and, I fear, some of your lords."

He spoke so earnestly that I knew he was speaking the truth. The Archbishop was King Charles' man and he knew that he had to be honest with me or risk being responsible for the breaking of the treaty.

"Names?" He hesitated, "Come, you cannot fear them."

He nodded, "I can for one is close to you, Olaf Olafsson, the Count of Djupr."

I folded my hands together. "Thank you, Archbishop. I have a chest of treasure for the cathedral. I am sure you can put it to good use."

"Thank you, lord. I have not angered you?"

"The truth might be unpalatable but it cannot anger me." I had been suspicious of Olaf but I had put it down to ambition. I thought that he saw me as something from a past age and he wanted our land to move in a different direction. Now I saw the plan clearly. He and Arnulf planned to usurp me. The attack by the bandits had been planned by Olaf. He had delayed our start that day so that his men could be in place. I discovered that the Archbishop had discovered the plot by speaking with loyal priests. The confessional had not been violated but priests were almost invisible and they had heard pieces of conversations. It had taken the Archbishop to put all of the pieces together.

When he had gone, I sent to Caen for Sámr and to Montfort for Erik. Sámr would take a few days to reach me as would Erik. With my son and Bergil in the south, I now needed men I could trust. Harold Mighty Fist and Ragnar the Resolute had shown me that they were ready for the life of a grandfather. If war came, I would use them but now I needed men who could act and act quickly. I did not act as I might have done twenty years earlier and that cost both me and my people. It was at such times I missed my right hand. I missed Sven Blue Cheek. And of course, I missed Hrólfr the Horseman. My grandfather would not have done as I did. He would not have dallied and delayed. He would have ridden north and dealt with Olaf Olafsson. I waited for my two lords. In the time it took for Erik and Sámr to arrive, the north of the Seine erupted in rebellion and disorder. I was in my Great Hall speaking with the two of them when Robert, son of Henry Sorenson rode into my stronghold. I heard the noise from my sentries and I went to the fighting platform. I saw Mauger speaking with the young son of Lord Henry. He looked both distraught and dishevelled. His horse had been ridden almost to death.

I returned to my hall. I waved over Father Harold and asked him to bring his wax tablet, "I fear there is mischief afoot." He hurried out and Erik, Sámr and I waited for the boy to be brought to us. None of us spoke for we were busy trying to guess what news he brought.

Mauger and Arne brought the young man into my hall. I saw that his clothes were covered in blood. He could barely get his breath and his eyes were wild. Arne went to my table and poured a horn of ale for the boy. Mauger shook his head, "What he spoke was garbled, lord, but from his words, his mother and father have been slain. He said rebellion over and over."

Father Thomas had been summoned by Father Harold and when he entered he looked at Robert. Concern was written all over his face. "Father, tend to this boy. I need to speak with him and for him to be calm."

"Aye lord. Come, boy, let me look at you. Fetch water and a cloth." Servants hurried to do his bidding.

While the priest took the shaking boy away, I said to Mauger, "What exactly did he say?"

"Just what I reported, lord. His horse is broken. We may have to put it down. He has ridden here from his home in the north. That is a long ride. Can it be that there is rebellion?"

Erik Gillesson said, "There is one way to find out. With your permission, lord, I will send ten of my men north. They can discover the truth of the matter and I will send to Montfort for the rest of my horsemen. If this is rebellion then you will need horsemen to deal with it."

"Let us not get over-excited about the words of one young man. He has not seen enough summers to take his words without confirmation."

Sámr shook his head, "Lord, in your heart you know. This is Olaf Olafsson. The Archbishop spoke of unrest and conspiracy. This boy now repeats rebellion."

"That is a sudden decision from so little evidence, my friend. Gossip from priests and a wild-eyed boy does not mean that Olaf Olafsson is trying to take my land." Sámr was right of course and I was just trying to rid myself of the image of the son of one of my most loyal men not only rebelling but trying to take my land.

"It is measured, lord. When we blockaded Nantes and Vannes he wanted to command. He questioned every decision your son made. He tried to undermine him. I had to have words. After that, he kept apart from your son and me. I thought nothing of it at the time but I can see now that I should have spoken to you. When he was not accorded the title he desired, he was angry. It is gossip but some of those who were seated near him heard him curse you. I put it down to drink and thought that going back to Djupr would bring him back to his senses but now that I think back, I believe he had bad thoughts in his head. I am sorry for I have failed you."

"No, Sámr, I have failed my grandfather and Normandy!"

Mauger nodded, "Remember, lord, the accounts? I think that Count Sámr has the right of it. I too heard Count Olaf's words and he sounded bitter." He shook his head. "Had I not dwelt on our dead comrades I might have acted. I was not vigilant."

"Do not blame yourselves. I am as guilty as any. I had misgivings and voices in my head warned me but I ignored them. We ignore such thoughts at our peril."

Father Thomas returned. The boy was still upset but he was no longer shaking. Father Thomas said, "I would speak quietly and calmly, lord. I have given him a draught to slow him down. His heart was beating too quickly."

"Thank you. Fetch my other clerks. I have orders to give." He left and I smiled, "Speak, Robert, Henry's son, and tell me all."

He nodded and I saw the enormity of telling the story to me sinking in. His voice wavered as he spoke. I kept my face as expressionless as I could. He was like a frightened and fey animal. I saw that he had grown since the last time I had spoken to him. There were wisps of hair on his top lip. He was no longer a boy. "My father returned from the war and he brought great treasure. His men returned to their farms. All was well for our men had prospered. The border seemed quiet and he had the weaponsmith begin to make my first helmet. It was a happy time." I heard his voice begin to break and he coughed to steady himself. "And then, three days ago, the men of the village suddenly rose. These were not the warriors who had followed my father. These were the Franks and Flemish who lived close by our stronghold. We heard the sound of fighting. My father and I went into the square and saw the Franks butchering our handful of warriors. One threw a spear at my father. He was badly wounded and I went to him. He drew his sword and told me to ride to you and tell you of the attack. I obeyed." He looked at me, "Should I have stayed?".

"What happened to your father and mother?"

"When I mounted my horse and came from the stables, I saw that my father had had his head removed. My mother had come out to tend to him and she lay... lord two men were upon her.

"Then you have your answer. That would have been your fate. You obeyed your father and your parents will be avenged. That I swear. What happened next?"

I had to wheel my horse away for the men who were attacking my mother saw me and came at me with spears. I used my dagger to mark the face of one. I will know him again. The villagers were too busy ransacking my father's hall and I was able to ride from the stables. I was seen and they chased me but I was mounted."

I pointed to the blood on his tunic, "The blood?"

"My father's."

"You did well to ride here in three days."

"I had no choice, lord. Each village I passed seemed to have the same chaos. I saw halls burning. I passed dead warriors on the road. I recognised some as the men who had fought alongside my father. It was only when I reached the land just north of the river that I found friendly folk." His voice was now much calmer. I think the telling of the tale had helped him. His face looked determined.

I turned to Mauger, "Take Robert to the warrior hall. Find clothes for him. Have the men prepare to ride."

"We only have the boy's word, lord."

"I know Sámr but look in your heart. What do you think?"

He nodded, "There is rebellion."

Erik returned, "I have sent forth my men. Is it true?"

"It is, Erik. With half of our men in the south occupying Brittany, we now have a rebellion in the north and few men to deal with it. Sámr, send for your men and then send for Ragnar, Haraldr and the others. They will go with you, Sámr. I could do with my son, Gandálfr and Bergil but I cannot take them from their new homes." I shook my head. This may be a Christian land but the Norns still spin!"

Sámr nodded, "And what then, lord?"

"We have no evidence yet that Olaf Olafsson is at the heart of this. I would have you march to Djupr and ask the son of our old shipmate if he knows anything about the revolt. Tell him that I am still with my son. It is a small deception but it might help you to discover the truth of the matter." I looked hard at him. "Take no risks. If you suspect treachery then wait for me. I will march to the border with Erik and his men. I intend to recapture these fiefs before Count Arnulf can take them. We will all be mounted. I hope that speed and our horses will be enough to snuff out this rebellion."

We left the next morning. I led barely two hundred men. They were, however, battle-hardened, mounted and well-armed. More they were all eager for vengeance! Erik's riders had returned to confirm that some of the fiefs had revolted and their lords had been slain. The horsemen had had to flee for their lives from at least two places. All was not lost for there were still places where strong lords had resisted the attacks. We headed for the first such village. Saint-Saëns had had an abbey which we had destroyed before we made peace with the Franks. The stone from the abbey had been reused by Sven Mighty Arm. One of my older warriors, he had not fought with us in Brittany and that may have been the reason why he had not succumbed. His warriors lived in his warrior hall and they had fought back. We reached his stone walls and the old warhorse emerged.

"You are all well, old friend?"

"Aye. Although it was touch and go. I lost some fine warriors."

I nodded, "Erik, round up every man who is older than ten summers and bring them here."

"Aye, lord."

"Sven, have your weaponsmith light his fire. We have need of heat!"

The fifty males were brought, some of them screaming, to the outer bailey of the stronghold. One shouted, "I am innocent, lord! I did nothing!"

I looked at Sven, "Is he innocent?"

In answer, he walked up to the man and struck him so hard with the back of his hand that he was knocked to the ground. "This bastard killed Arne Three Fingers."

I nodded, "Mauger have him held and then blind him!" We went down the line and in all twenty-five men were blinded. Their womenfolk led them away. I shouted, "These men are banished from Normandy! Take what you can carry and leave. This is the punishment for rebellion in my land!"

That first day we visited five fiefs. Four had held out against the rebels and their men were blinded. At the next village, we saw the burned-out remains of the hall and found the bodies of Benni Silver Helm and his family. The village was empty and the men and their families had fled. Word was spreading of my punishment. The hearths were still warm. The people had run away at our approach. We camped in the village and I reflected upon the scale of the revolt. This had been planned for some time. Olaf was not just reacting to his perceived slight and that meant the Flemish were involved. I had another enemy and, once again, I would be doing the bidding of Charles of Frankia. *Wyrd*!

"Erik, tomorrow we use your horsemen. I will keep my oathsworn and the young men of Rouen." The survivors of the battle of Rennes were now led by Roger of Rouen. They had proved themselves and I could trust them. "We are now in the land of rebels. Your men will ride around each village which we approach. We will stop them from leaving."

Erik nodded, "And you blind them all?"

"The next village will see the men lose their hands."

"That will make this land a wasteland, lord."

"Then so be it. I will not brook rebellion. Our men can spread their seed and in the fullness of time, the fiefs will be occupied once more. I am getting old, Erik. I have my son to consider. He is yet to be married and I must think of the future. I will be as harsh as I must to leave the land for my heirs. Hrólfr the Horseman had a dream. A Norn prophesied. I have to keep that dream and prophesy alive."

My protective ring of horsemen was alert, the next day, as we headed north. We were approaching the home of Lord Henry. There were two fiefs before we reached it. I knew that there were no lords left this close to the border. My men had all been slaughtered. That they had died as warriors was small compensation. As we neared the next village, we heard shouts and screams. Swords clashed and I urged Blue on. We found Erik and his men fighting with the men of the village. The blackened shell of the hall of Einar Alfsson told me that another of my lords had perished. I drew my sword and galloped, recklessly, into the heart of the fighting. My first blow split a man from his rump to his neck. None surrendered. When the men were all dead, I glowered at the survivors. They were women and children but they had condoned what their men had done. As the women cowered, I pointed Longsword at them. "Erik Gillesson, have your men bind their feet and hands. Take them back to Rouen. They are now thralls."

One woman, a grey-haired mother dropped to her knees, "Mercy, Duke Robert!"

I laughed, "This is mercy and more mercy than was shown to Anya wife of Einar and their three children! Your men did not even bother to bury their bodies. Your priest is slain too! Not another word or I will punish you!"

I guess someone must have escaped for the next four villages, including that of Lord Henry, were abandoned. We did as we had all the way north. We buried the lords and their families in the churchyards. My heart was hardening even more. Many of these people had been with me since Norway! I had let them down. Some of the wives of my men had been abused before they had been killed. This would be a long, hard winter for northern Normandy. It took another week to reach Djupr as we continued with the purging of the north. We had found no lords left alive. It was now obvious that Olaf Olafsson and Count Arnulf had colluded. Why else was Olaf still alive? Why had he not sent me a message to warn me of the rebellion? We reached Sámr Oakheart's camp at dusk. He had the town ringed on the landward side.

"Well?"

"We found villages close to the river which still had a lord but the closer we came to Djupr the fewer we found."

"What did you do to the men in the villages?"

"Disarmed them."

I shook my head, "That is not enough. Ragnar the Resolute, take your warband. I would have you chop off the right hand and right leg of every man who rebelled against us. Banish them and their families from my land. Leave on the morrow."

He nodded. Ragnar was a man who lived up to his name, "Aye, lord."

"And Olaf?"

"He invited me alone into his walls. I was suspicious and did not go. His men loosed arrows and bolts at us. I lost four men. Three of them were oathsworn. This is now a blood feud. I will have blood for the blood I have lost. Weregeld will not be enough!"

"That is true, old friend, for all of us. Tomorrow I will go and speak with him."

"Speak?"

"The words are intended for the ears of those within his walls. I want them to be in no doubt as to their fate if they resist me. The perimeter is secure?"

"It is but he can still escape by sea."

I turned to Haraldr, "Tomorrow take our horses and return to Rouen. Bring *'Fafnir'* and any other ships in port. Blockade Djupr."

That night I told Sámr what we had discovered. His face hardened, "All the time we were in the south fighting the Bretons, the Count of Flanders and his man were plotting. I cannot believe it of Olaf's son."

I turned to him. "I should have known it better than any. My brother slew our father and tried to kill me. Just because it is family does not make a difference to some men."

"You may be right and we saw little of Olaf in the last years and nothing of his son."

"Neither was with us at Paris. Suddenly many things are clearer. What I do know is that I will have to choose my next Count of Djupr more carefully."

The next morning, I mounted Blue and, with my men around me, I rode to within three hundred paces of the walls. I held my shield in my left hand. It hung loosely. I was still in arrow range but at that distance, the arrow would not penetrate my mail and leather. I shouted, "I would speak with Olaf Olafsson."

I was made to wait an inordinately long time and I wondered if he had fled. Eventually, he came and stood on his gatehouse. It was a wooden one. Djupr had been a dependable port in the past and had suffered no attacks. If we had to assault it then it would not be as hard as some of my men's strongholds.

"Why, Olaf? Why have you betrayed me? Did I not reward you? Why did you join with Count Arnulf?" My words were carefully chosen for I was trying to discover the size of the problem.

"Why choose the Count of Flanders rather than a barbarian like you? That is easy! When you are dead, I will be Count of Normandy."

"That will not happen. I am still alive and sitting astride my horse. You are the one cowering behind your walls. You are the one who is afraid to meet us beard to beard."

His voice sounded contemptuous but I knew he feared me. "What is it that you want, old man?"

I felt my bodyguards begin to murmur at his insults. I held up my hand and said, quietly, "Peace!" Then I raised my voice. "I cannot believe that all of your warriors rebelled against me. I fought alongside many of them. Let them come to me and ask for my forgiveness! If they do then they shall live."

He laughed, "You want those who oppose me?"

His words should have warned me but I could not see his purpose, "Aye, I would have them!"

He turned, "Let the barbarian have his men."

His warriors must have been waiting behind the wooden palisade for suddenly twenty naked and mutilated bodies were thrown into the ditch and beyond. I recognised some despite the mutilations. They were the older warriors who had fought alongside Old Olaf. My voice was like ice, "I will leave you with one message. We are coming for you. If you surrender now, we will give you a warrior's death and we will spare your womenfolk. If we attack and we lose one warrior then I will give the blood eagle to the survivors and the women will be given to my men. Your children will be sold into slavery!"

He laughed, "You have not enough men and Count Arnulf will come to my aid! Your words are empty. You had power but no longer." He dropped his arm and a flurry of crossbow bolts came at me and my men. My hand came up. Four bolts hit my shield. One struck Blue in the shoulder but it barely penetrated. Another one hit Geoffrey d'Honfleur, one of my young horsemen, but his mail was good. I shook my head, "Treachery seems to come as second nature to you, Olaf. This will not end well for you." I wheeled my horse around and led my men back to our lines.

When I reached my men I waved over Erik, "Have your men ride to the border. If the men of Flanders come let me know. I would meet them north of here. Do not engage them, just watch."

"Aye, lord."

"Sámr, follow Haraldr. I need you with the ships which blockade the port. You have watched him when he commanded ships. Use that knowledge."

"Aye, lord, I will ride until my horse drops!"

I did not have enough men with me to fight an invading army of Flemish warriors. Olaf had sounded confident. I calculated that it would take two or three days, at least, for Sámr to blockade the port. I had enough warriors to contain Olaf and, possibly, to assault his walls but if Count Arnulf came then I would be in trouble. Was this a bluff from the traitor?

We found out the next day. A column of men was heading from the north. They were the men of Flanders and there were four hundred of them. That was more than I had. Leaving my men surrounding the port I rode north with Erik, his horsemen and my horsemen. We had just over a hundred and twenty men. It would not be enough to fight a battle. Thanks to our mounted scouts we knew where the Flemish army was. The Flemish army did not know where we were. They knew they were being shadowed but could do nothing about horsemen. We met them twenty miles northeast of Djupr.

Erik had a good eye for a battlefield and he had found a good place to greet them. The land was flat but he had found a mall rise and we waited behind it. He and his men were hidden to the north and south of us. The Flemish warriors saw first my banner and then me as we crested the rise. Immediately they went into a defensive formation. Shields and spears were presented. I was flanked by Erik, Mauger and Arne. Leif Egilsson was behind me with my banner and a horn. The men of Flanders had some nobles with them. They were mailed and armed as we were but there were just thirty of them. I guessed the Count was with them for I recognised his banner. We waited.

Roger of Rouen asked, nervously, "They outnumber us, lord. Should we not retreat?"

"You, Roger of Rouen, are a Frank who, one day, will become a Norman. We are Vikings. We do not worry about large numbers facing us. For my men, that is the challenge. How many can we kill before we are slain? Never worry about losing. Let the enemy do that! It is a state of mind."

I took off my helmet and said, "Erik, Mauger, Leif, with me. The rest, wait here."

When a man has died and been brought back to life then little frightens him. I had been to the bottom of the ocean. My brother had tried to kill me. I knew that I had been chosen by the gods. That gave me belief in myself. If there was treachery then I would be the one they would target and I had lived long enough. I smiled as I rode towards the Flemish. I halted forty paces from them and waited. Their spears did not intimidate me. It would take a brave man to advance towards the Duke of Normandy on his giant horse.

Eventually, a priest, four nobles and a man I took to be the Count of Flanders nudged their horses towards me. I waited until they were just ten paces from me and I spoke, "I am guessing you must be the Count of Flanders."

"I am Count Arnulf."

"It is good that you visit with us but I am a little concerned that you feel you need to bring an army. Unless, of course, this is an invasion."

I could see that my easy manner had disconcerted him. He looked at the priest, who, from his robes, I took to be a bishop and then back to me, "The Count of Djupr has invited me here. He says this land is no longer Norman." He looked around. "We outnumber you, Count Robert. Do not make this harder than it should be. You have lost."

I nodded and smiled, "The number of times I have been told that you think it would be true but it is not. We have not lost. By this time tomorrow, the Count of Djupr will be enduring what we call the blood eagle and you will be back in Flanders."

He looked at the small number of men facing him and laughed, "You are old Count Robert. Leave now and I will spare your life."

I turned and said, quietly, "Erik."

My master of horse raised his spear and then lowered it. Suddenly horsemen appeared along the flanks of the Flemish army. They were fifty paces from them and they had spears levelled. Horsemen always appear to be greater in number and I saw the fear on the faces of the men on foot. They were not prepared. They were in a column and if my men charged then they would die.

"You were saying?"

"A few horsemen cannot make a difference."

"How about a few horsemen and Viking warriors?" I dug my heels into Blue and edge him towards the Count. I leaned down. I saw his nobles fingering their weapons but they would do nothing. I said, quietly, "I am willing to overlook this incursion into my land if you leave now. If you do not then there will be war. Brittany is no more. It is now part of Normandy. Perhaps I should add Flanders. It is your choice. Who do you believe, me, the lord who took Paris, or a foresworn traitor?" I saw his face as he sought a solution with honour. There was none. "I am an old man and I need to make water. Decide now. I have my Long Sword and it can be out of its scabbard in a heartbeat. I am happy to settle the matter, are you?"

He shook his head, "We have been misled. We return home!" He turned his horse and rode back through his men. They were happy to follow.

We waited until they had quit the field. "Thank you, Erik. Now let us go and deal with a traitor!"

As we rode back Roger asked, "Why did they back off, lord?"

"He looked in my eyes and saw a man who was not afraid to die. He looked into the eyes of a Viking. I am the last of a dying breed, Roger. I have fought for over fifty years and I am still a powerful warrior. My son is a new warrior. He is a Norman!"

The next morning, I rode to the gatehouse and shouted, "I have met with Count Arnulf. He has returned home. We come for you tomorrow, Olaf Olafsson!"

I returned to our camp and joined my men. We had enough men to assault but I was waiting for our drekar to arrive. Mauger woke me in the middle of the night, "Lord, we have heard noises from the port. Our sentries report ships leaving."

I stood and smacked one fist into the palm of the other, "Then he has fled! The snake has escaped us."

"Do we attack, lord?"

"No, we wait for Sámr and our ships. I know now that they will be here tomorrow but that is a day too late." I shook my head, "The White Christ does not know all. The sisters are spinning!"

I went back to bed but I did not sleep. I was planning my revenge. It would not be swift. We had to consolidate Brittany. I needed to appoint new lords for the towns and fiefs north of the Seine and I needed to reduce Djupr and make it mine once more. That it would be bloody I knew already.

My men were arrayed by the third hour of the day. This was not a task for the horsemen. This would take the men who fought with a spear and a shield. It would take axemen to hew down the door. It would take the Duke of Normandy to lead the men. I led a huge wedge towards the gate. We were within arrow range when I heard a shout, "Drekar!"

It was Sámr. The effect was dramatic. The men who had been on the walls suddenly disappeared. We marched to the gates and my oathsworn took axes and began to hew the wood. It did not take long. Within were traitors and my men wanted to get at them. Once we were inside the walls, I saw the chaos and panic. There were other gates. They were smaller ones and the people of Djupr raced for them. It was futile. Sámr and his men landed and we began to kill every man we found. The women and children were taken. Some were destined to be our thralls while others would be sold in the slave markets of Dyflin. I slew no one. None dared face me. I went with Mauger and my men to the Great Hall. As I had expected, all the treasure had been taken. Olaf had fled with the treasure I had given him in Nantes. It fuelled my anger. I turned, "Mauger, I no longer need you as captain of my oathsworn!" I saw his face fall, "I need you to be Count of Djupr and rule this port with a fist of iron! We have been weak for too long!"

Chapter 8

It was Mörsugur before I was able to return to Rouen. I had selected some of the young warriors of Rouen to become my lords. It was calculated. They looked and dressed less like Vikings and might appear more acceptable to the Franks who remained. They were the concession I made to the rebels. I had had a valuable lesson. I would have to rule in a more aggressive way. I would have to become the barbarian they all thought me to make the land safe for my son. And I needed to get him wed.

It was a wet journey back to Rouen. There were flecks of snow mixed in with the sleet and the rain. It did little to improve my mood. Olaf Olafsson had escaped me. I had another enemy in Count Arnulf. I had thought, with the greater part of Brittany under my control, that I had a secure land. I had been wrong. I also learned a little more about myself. The wetting of my head had not changed me. The old ways were still the best. If a man believed in the Norns then all would be well. They gave an explanation to life that was lacking in the Christian world. That religion promised hope and resolution. The real world was nothing like that. I would continue to pay lip service to the White Christ but I would also seek to respect the sisters.

I had not only given Mauger a fief, but I had also done the same with all of my oathsworn. Arne was given the fief which had belonged to Lord Henry. There were still people living in those places. I had only slain those in the villages. I had just punished the wrongdoers. My men would have to begin again. They would have to encourage farmers to come to their fiefs. I told them all that they need not pay taxes for a year. We still had the coin from the Bretons. I rode back with the young horsemen of Rouen. I would need to find oathsworn.

When we reached my stronghold, I began to organize my land. I sat with my three priest clerks and had them draw up titles for the new lords.

We lived in a world of writing and documents. It was not the Viking way but we now lived in a Frankish world. I had to adapt. The papers appeared to me to be the same as the stone for the Franks. They were reassuring foundations upon which their world was built.

My son could write. That was thanks to Padraig and he sent me letters which told me of his life in Brittany. He was changing. Each letter showed me a more mature warrior. He was adapting and becoming more like a Frank. Inside he was still a Viking. He would fight like a Viking but he thought a little more like a Frank. Outside of the three major towns, life went on as it had before. The difference was that their lord was now a man appointed by me or my son. There was neither rebellion nor even the embers of one. The people there lived as they had under Alan the Great. They were used to paying taxes and my son showed great wisdom by neither increasing them nor by adding to the tax burden. So long as there was no war then the ordinary people were happy enough. The letters I sent him urged him to take a wife and sire children. I knew not if he would heed my words. There would be women who would wish to be married to such a powerful lord. It all depended upon him. Did he have more of Poppa in him than of me? I prayed to any god who would hear me that my son should marry and sire a son.

Someone must have heard my prayers. As summer drew closer and we entered Sólmánuður I received the letter which gave me hope for the future. My son had taken the daughter of one of the Breton lords we had slain. Her name was Sprota, the same name as the servant of my former wife. That was not a surprise. Poppa and Sprota were popular Breton names. They were not married in a church. He took her as I had taken his mother. It was our way. The next letter, in high summer, told me that his wife was with child. The old Göngu-Hrólfr Rognvaldson would have made a blót but Duke Robert just went with his young horsemen to the forests, hunted and left the heart of the stag in the river. The young men of Rouen did not understand why I did what I did and I offered no explanation but my mood improved from that moment on.

Rouen was a busy port. We were a prosperous people and had much to trade. We had many ships arriving from the Saxon kingdoms. It meant we now knew more about the island to the north of us. They were talking about it as England now. King Alfred, the father of King Edward, had united some of the smaller Kingdoms. Cent and Essex, Mercia and Northumbria were now part of Wessex. Jorvik was not under the control of King Edward of Wessex, neither were the lands of Wales and

Scotland. King Edward was a powerful man. I made certain that my men spoke with their captains. Wessex, Northumbria and Mercia were all neighbours. We could trade and we could raid. They were rich kingdoms and the more I knew the better it would be for my land.

Queen Frederuna, the wife of King Charles, died. I was invited to the funeral. I would not have gone save that I was aware of my position. I owed my land to the King of Frankia. He would be insulted if I did not attend. The real reason was that I knew the other lords would attend. I would get to meet men like Count Arnulf, Robert of Neustria, King Edward and King Henry the Fowler of East Frankia. I had learned long ago that looking into a man's eyes when there was peace helped you to defeat them when there was war. I knew there would be war in the future and I would be ready.

My young horsemen were not only from Rouen but also from the fiefs of my lords. Sámr's son, Richard, and Erik's son, Gilles, were amongst them. Bjorn the Brave's second son, Berenger, was a third. These warriors looked different from the sons of the Rouen merchants. They were broader and more muscled. Bjorn, Sámr and Erik had made their sons work. They had taught them how to use a bow. Of course, all of my men dressed in the same uniform. I spent little money on me but I spent a great deal upon my men. All wore the same helmet. They each had a blue cloak with my Long Sword on the left breast. They all wore the short, split byrnie which made riding easier. Their shields were identical and they all rode a black horse like mine. I knew that it made a statement. When we rode abroad men knew who was approaching. My twenty riders were well drilled and presented.

I also had Leif Egilsson and Robert son of Henry. The orphan had no other family and I took him under my wing. Until my son sired me a grandson, I would be a foster father to Robert. I would mould him into a warrior. Both he and Leif were of an age and got on well. They also wore the same as my bodyguards. The difference was that they did not carry spears. They acted more like servants than warriors. If we fought then the two of them would defend my banner. I left Rouen in the hands of Leif's father, Egil. The rebellion in the north had been a warning. I needed a strong hand on Rouen and all of my lords were vigilant.

We were able to stay in the halls of my lords until we reached Évreux. Bjorn the Brave had the last stronghold before Frankia. I would not risk staying with any lord I did not know and we rode from Évreux to Paris in one long and hard day. King Charles had sent me a piece of parchment which acted as a surety to enter Paris. The last time I had been there had been many years earlier and we had had a fleet of ships. As we crossed one of the newly built bridges into the city I saw how much had been rebuilt. The buildings there put Rouen to shame. King Charles used diplomacy and not war. That was why he needed me. I had an army. The piece of parchment afforded me entry to the island in the centre of Paris. Here the buildings were even grander. My men had to camp by the river but my two young companions and I were given a chamber in the King's hall. King Charles still held me in high regard.

We did not arrive until after dark. The King and those guests who had arrived early were eating already. I was taken to a table which was far from the King. He nodded as I sat. I recognised some of the men at his table. I saw Count Arnulf. There was one there I took to be King Edward. He had some young men with him who looked like they could be two of his sons. I guessed I would know the names of the others. I had not fought them yet and so I did not know their faces. I did not mind eating with the lesser lords of Frankia. It gave me the opportunity to listen to their words while studying the faces of men who, one day, I might have to fight. I smiled as I sat for every face turned to me. I was used to that. I was well aware that old age had not diminished my size. All had heard of me. I had fought King Alfred. I had fought alongside Guthrum. Both of those legends were dead but I still remained and every eye looked at me to try to discover how. The followers of the White Christ believed I had a pact with the devil or I was the devil himself.

Servants brought me a platter and ale. I took out my seax and carved a large slice from the wild boar we were eating. The men alongside whom I was seated moved slightly further away. It may have been out of politeness but I suspected it was fear. I learned that I was seated at the table with the men of Neustria. They did not like me. Until we had begun our attacks Neustria had encompassed not only what was now Normandy but the land around Orleans, Flanders and Provence! They were guarded in their words but they thought me an illiterate barbarian who would not understand them. I did. Their leader was Robert of Neustria. His father had been Robert the Strong and had tried to take the Frankish crown. I knew that King Charles feared him. I suddenly knew why I had been invited. It was to keep his rivals in check. My treatment of my rebels had sent shockwaves through my neighbours. The Archbishop of Rouen had told me that. I had not acted in that manner to achieve the effect but I would use it.

The exception was Edgar. He was a warrior and a Saxon from Wessex. "I fought you, once, Count."

I turned to look at him. He looked to have seen fifty summers and so it could be true. I smiled, "I have fought many men but as you still live, I suspect you did not come within the compass of Long Sword."

He laughed, "No, Count. You hewed the heads of many of my friends. They were warriors." He shrugged. "It is the end most of us expect. My name is Edgar of Haestingas."

"You are from Wessex?"

"I am. I now serve Prince Athelstan, the King's eldest."

"He will be King when King Edward dies?"

"That depends. We are like the Frankish kingdom. The Eorledmen will elect the King."

I laughed, "When I die, and I do not think that death is long overdue, then my son William will rule."

"Do you not rule by the will of King Charles?"

"You have fought me, Edgar of Haestingas. What do you think?"

"I think that you are your own man and will do that which pleases you."

We both decided that politics was not a suitable subject and so we spoke of battles and weapons. For two old warriors, it was safer ground.

As I finished a servant came to me, "The King would see you, lord, privately. When you are done, I will take you hither."

I stood, "Take me now. It was good to speak with you, Eorledman Edgar. Perhaps we can talk again, in the future?" He nodded. I smiled at those who had been at my table, "I will leave you now. Perhaps you will be able to talk more freely eh? Now that the barbarian has gone!"

The servant took me up a stone staircase to a small chamber on the second floor. It looked like it would accommodate just four people. There were two goblets and a jug of wine. "The King asks if you would wait for him, lord. He will not be long."

I poured some wine. These days the closer it came to the time for sleeping the less ale I drank. I did not wish to spend all night making water. I drank more wine. It helped me to sleep. The King entered and I stood. I owed him respect. He waved me to my seat and then closed the door. "I have one of my trusted men watching the door. We can speak freely." I nodded. The King had asked for this meeting. "Thank you for dealing with the Breton problem although I think you benefitted more than I did."

"The problem is not over, lord. I have heard, from my sea captains, that Alan, son of Alan the Great is abroad seeking support." I hesitated, "From King Edward, I believe."

"You are well informed."

I shrugged, "What happens to the east of my land is a mystery to me but I keep my ear to the ground when it comes to the Saxon kingdoms and the threats to my borders."

"There are many who said you dealt harshly with your rebels."

I nodded, "And now we have peace and the rebels are gone. Count Arnulf will be dealt with when Brittany is firmly in our hands."

"And you made your son the Count of Brittany."

"I should have asked?"

"Perhaps it would have been polite to inform me. After all, Brittany is part of Frankia."

"Does it really matter what we call ourselves so long as we are your allies and we protect your land from Danes and Norse who would raid you? Have I not done that which I promised when last I came to Paris? Have there been any raids on your people?"

"I am grateful and I do not mean to censure you but there is a faction in my land which is trying to oust me. Duke Gilbert of Lothringia and King Henry both seek to unseat me. They are using Hagano, my wife's cousin, as an excuse but that is all it is, an excuse."

"You need a son."

He nodded in agreement. "I need a son." He drank some wine. He studied my face. He was building up to asking me a question. I did not make it easy. I let him struggle to broach the subject. "You know that Count Arnulf's mother was one of Alfred's daughters? He is a cousin to the King."

"I had heard that."

"King Alfred had daughters and sons in equal measure."

"I have heard that too."

"King Edward has a daughter, Eadgifu."

I laughed, "And people call us barbarians. At least we wait until our wives are in the ground before we seek another."

He had the grace to smile. "My wife was unwell for some time. I grew accustomed to the fact that she would die. She understood. I think that giving birth to six was too much for her. We kept trying for a son but..."

"I do not criticise, King Charles."

"You can see that it is even more important that you do not raid Wessex." I nodded, "And, for the time being, at least, you refrain from war with Flanders."

"That is too much to ask, King Charles. The man tried to take half of my land."

"I know but you are no longer the chief of a clan. You are a senior noble of Frankia. You must behave differently."

"I am an old man, King Charles. It is hard to learn new ways. You hurt a Viking and you had better make sure he is dead for he will have his vengeance."

"And that I understand. I just ask that you wait until my new wife has given me a son. They say that revenge is a dish best served cold."

"And I am old. I would like to enjoy my vengeance."

"Then let me sweeten the taste for you. I will confirm your son's title and make a gift of one thousand pounds of silver to ensure that you have no need to go to war with Flanders. You could use the silver to build strongholds which would make it hard for the Count to repeat his attack."

That was a tempting offer. The new lords in the north would struggle without men to farm their land. I could use the money to build halls that could be better defended and to encourage men to settle in the deserted farms and villages. I nodded, "Very well, Highness but you need to watch out for your enemies. I have also heard that Robert of Neustria is building an army."

"And I have heard the same. If he attacked me would you come to my aid?"

Robert of Neustria was every bit as much my enemy as the King's. In addition, the land to the east of Normandy and Brittany was now the only land into which we could expand. "Of course. It would be an honour."

I saw the relief on his face. He would just need to mention that and it would prevent Robert of Neustria from attacking. We were a force to be reckoned with.

"While you are here it would be good for you to speak with the other princes, dukes and kings. They are all fascinated by you and your reputation."

"They want to know if I am the barbarian they all think I am. I understand."

"You are clever, Robert. I have seen that. Your physical appearance belies the leader within."

Robert and Leif had been given food to eat with the servants and they had gone to the chamber to make it more comfortable. When I entered, I saw that they were both alert and the hands were on their daggers. I smiled, "Trouble?"

Leif shook his head, "Nothing that we cannot deal with, lord." I saw that his knuckles were bloody. He saw my look and smiled, "One of the pages of the Count of Flanders made a disparaging comment. He will not smile for a while. He lost two teeth." Egil had taught his son well.

"Keep your eyes and ears open tomorrow. We wear our byrnies beneath our tunics. We have enemies here and it may come to more than knuckles and teeth. While my horsemen are away then you two will watch my back. I do not fear any man but assassination is something they all use. I need to know where Olaf Olafsson is hiding. If you hear his name then let me know."

"Aye, lord."

"And Robert? You have seen to Blue?"

"He is content. The other horses give him space. He is like their king."

"Aye, Erik has bred a fine animal."

I had not known the Queen. I had never met her and I was detached when she was laid in the tomb in the cathedral. Instead, I watched faces. I looked at alliances. King Edward and his sons stood with Count Arnulf while Robert of Neustria huddled with Duke Gilbert and King Henry the Fowler. Eorledman Edgar stood close to the Prince of Wessex. None stood near me. Robert, Leif and myself were shunned. I saw the hated Lord Hagano. The Frankish nobles did not disguise their feelings for him. It seemed to me that he was even more unpopular than I was with them. The exception was Count Arnulf. He seemed just to glower and glare at me through the whole ceremony.

There was a feast afterwards. We did not sit. Trestle tables were laid in the cathedral and we ate standing up. I had promised the King that I would behave but I did not say I would not speak. I boldly walked up to Count Arnulf of Flanders. He was standing with King Edward. I towered over both of them. Even my two companions were as tall as the two leaders. I smiled, "Count Arnulf, tell me, does the traitor, Olaf Olafsson, still cower in your land?"

"The Count of Djupr is still my guest."

"He is no longer Count of Djupr. There is another. Count Mauger is a fierce warrior and, unlike Olaf Olafsson, is not foresworn. I can trust him."

King Edward said, "You have had great success, Count Robert, but it cannot last. We have curbed the Vikings of Northumbria. They are a relic. I accept that they once had power but my father ended that reign of terror. He humbled Guthrum."

"I would not know, King Edward, no King has ever humbled me."

Count Arnulf said, "There is time."

I turned to face him, "Count Arnulf, I have promised my friend, King Charles, that I will not attack Flanders. I keep my word, you will be pleased to hear. A word of warning, however. If any Flemish warrior crosses my border then I will regard that as an attack on me and I will respond. My response will be both swift and terrible. Before you unleash my anger think carefully and tell Olaf Olafsson that my reach is long."

"And what of my land, Count Robert? Is that safe from your privations?" King Edward's voice was curious rather than threatening.

I smiled, "Of course! There is nothing left to take!"

We left two days later. My horsemen had much to tell me. They knew where Olaf Olafsson was to be found. Richard son of Sámr Oakheart told me, "There is a fishing village to the north of Bruggas. It is surrounded by marshes and silted rivers. The Romans called it Caletum. Olaf is to be found there. It is believed he is safe. The Count of Flanders has built him a hall." I raised my eyebrows. "It is said he will become Count of Normandy when you die and your son is defeated. He has been promised as much by Count Arnulf and the King of the East Franks. The other lords who fled you when you came north live there too. They wait for the day they will be given Normandy!"

"You have done well. Do you think we will be hindered on our way home?"

Gilles, son of Erik snorted, "The ones we spoke to, lord, were not real warriors. They told a good tale but they were not warriors. They are the popinjays who dress well and never have to fight. They thought because we dressed as we do that we were the same. We let them believe that. I looked at their horses in the stable. They do not even use stiraps. They have the saddles like the Romans used. It is as though they are babies learning to ride."

Gilles knew horses. His father had had him on the back of a horse as soon as he could walk.

"Good. We will let them think we ride home but I intend to visit with my son. There is much that he needs to know."

We told no one of our destination. My men thought that there was little chance of ambush. I would take no chances. If we just disappeared when we left Paris then their chances of causing mischief would be limited. The journey to Nantes was arduous but, ultimately, proved free from danger.

My son had worked hard. He had built a good wall and there were two towers close to the waterfront. He could defend his ships. The Great Hall was like a palace anyway. He had improved it and he and his wife were comfortable. Sprota was a pretty young thing. If she resented being the wife of a Norman, she did not show it. She looked like she would be able to bear children well. I knew that Poppa, my wife, had not had an easy time. Gefn had said it was because she was not broad in the hips. Sprota had no such problem. She appeared to be in awe of me. William, for his part, looked to be genuinely fond of her. The fact that she was a Breton noble's daughter could not hurt. We went to one of his rooms and I told him all that had transpired since I had left him. As I had expected, he was angry about Olaf.

"We will make him pay!"

"I will make him pay. You need to make this land secure. Robert of Neustria is casting covetous glances here. The former Count lives in his palace at Poitiers. He is not yet done with us. There is another who seeks to be Duke of Brittany and that is Alan who lives in Wessex. He calls himself Duke of Brittany and he has the support of King Edward."

William smiled, "You have done so much for this land, father. When do you rest?"

"When I am in Valhalla!"

He laughed, "Do not let the priests hear you say that!"

"I worry not about priests. They worry about me. And I am pleased that you have settled down. Sprota looks to be a good wife."

He hung his head a little, "I know not about settled, father."

"You still lie with other women?"

He nodded, "It is in my nature."

"You have that from your mother! Have you fathered any bastards then?"

"I may have. I know not."

"You will need a son from Sprota, perhaps two or three!"

"Why? You had a brother and that did not work out so well."

Only my son, Sámr or Bergil could speak to me like that. I nodded. "Perhaps you are right. I will leave for home on the morrow. Let us not be distant. Write to me or send a trusted messenger. I need to know when you have a son! Until you do then all that we have done is at risk."

We rode home via Rennes for I wished to see if Bergil Fast Blade had fully recovered. I was delighted to see that he was looking much healthier. He had had an easier task than my son. Nantes had been the home of the Breton dukes and loyalty there ran deep. Rennes was closer to Normandy. We had never raided it and Bergil was a good ruler. He had been accepted. He had even taken another wife. She was Breton. She looked a little old for childbearing but Bergil had been hurt badly when his wife had left him. I think he needed the reassurance that it had been his wife's flaw and not his.

It was not planned but I headed to Sámr's stronghold at Caen. His son, who rode with me, was pleased. I had not told my men but I had plans to deal with Olaf Olafsson. To complete them I needed Sámr. Caen was a solid stronghold. It rivalled Rouen. The river was not as protective but if Rouen was ever lost then I would live in Caen. I told Sámr what I had learned and then explained what I had planned.

"Olaf thinks he is safe. He is on what he believes to be an island. He is well protected by Count Arnulf's men and he is counting down the days to my death for he plans on becoming Count."

"Men would not accept him, lord. There is your son."

"My son is well respected but he is not me. Besides, there were lords who rebelled against me. They reside with Olaf. There might be others. I am no fool, Sámr Oakheart. I am too honest. If a lord offends me then I tell him. I do not hold his offence against him but we both know that there are men who brood about such matters. I would sail there at Gormánuður. It is the time of the annual autumn storms and they will least expect an attack."

"Is that not a dangerous time?"

I laughed, "Sámr Oakheart, remember our voyage here? We sailed from Norway. This is a little voyage up the coast. It will take less than half a day to reach it. Olaf would not do it but we can. I need your drekar and your men. I will not be taking my horsemen. I will take *'Fafnir'*. Your son heard that the snake's lair is a well-apportioned hall. There may be treasure. King Charles did not wish me to raid the men of Flanders. He said nothing about former Normans and rebels!"

By the time I left Sámr's suggestions had improved my plan considerably. I rode back to Rouen and this time I took in the beauty of the land. My father had never seen the dream of our family come to fruition. My grandfather had but neither could have imagined what we would have achieved in my lifetime. The thought that flickered through my mind, as we approached the Seine, was, '*would I live to see a grandson?*' I looked at my two standard-bearers. If the Norns had spun and that was not to be so then I would have to make do with Robert and Leif. If nothing else I could train them to be warriors, lords even. The lands of Normandy and Brittany would need them when I was in the Otherworld. The cough I had developed, on the ride north, was a warning. I was a man and not a god. I could still suffer illnesses and I was now of an age where such things could be fatal. I was being neither maudlin nor melancholic, I was being practical.

Chapter 9

Summer came and passed. Whichever god watched over Normandy, he looked after us. Our crops were good. My son's wife gave birth to a daughter. He named her Mathilde. When I thought of King Charles and his six daughters I began to worry. My son was also getting older. Daughters and bastards were not enough. He needed a legitimate son. There were too many who would refuse to recognise a bastard. William would try again. We also heard that the date for the marriage of King Charles to Eadgifu had been set for the following year. It was my Archbishop who brought me the news. He also brought me a private message. I would not be invited to the wedding. His lords were becoming increasingly restless and my appearance at the funeral of his wife had done nothing to ease their concern. I did not mind.

In the time leading up to our raid, I threw myself into improvements on my stronghold and port. I built towers to watch the ships in the river. I had raided and knew how vulnerable ports were to Viking raids. I had enough of a reputation to stop most Vikings from attacking me but there were other raiders who did not know me and they might just be desperate enough to risk my wrath. The lower tower would be permanently manned and the other three manned during a time of danger. We improved my gatehouse and we added cauldrons that could be tipped so that we could pour boiling fat or oil upon an attacker. I had seen stone-throwers and I set Egil and my men to make a pair. To keep the church on my side I added to the cathedral and ordered a new bell to be cast. The majority of those in my town were Christians and it would do no harm to be seen to be rewarding the church. The fact that the bell could summon men to our aid was a bonus. Many of my men had done as I had done and taken the dousing for a quiet life. There were some, however, who had embraced the new religion. Thus far they had shown no sign of the weakness I saw in other Christians. Even my converted warriors still fought as hard as any.

The promised silver arrived from Paris. I sent some of it to my new lords in the northern marches. Then I took a large chest of silver and I rode to Montfort and Erik's mighty stronghold. He had built four towers and their bases were made of stone. As we neared his land, I saw that the fields were filled with horses. Erik was now one of the richest men in my land. When we raided his men had more opportunity for treasure. However, he made as much coin from breeding and then selling horses as he did from raiding. King Charles' Franks recognised quality. As well as telling Erik of my plans I intended to buy more horses from him. I had seen the efficacy of horsemen. The days of the seaborne raider were numbered. Ports like Caen, Rouen, Nantes and Vannes now had defences that could destroy an attacker who came by sea. Horsemen riding from a centrally positioned and well-defended stronghold could control vast areas and, when we attacked, could cut a town off before they had the chance to send for help. I had men in Rouen who would be trained to be riders.

Erik was pleased to see his son and, like Sámr, interested in my news. Like Bjorn the Brave, Erik lived close to the border with Frankia. If there was a change in leadership then he would be the first to be in danger. Erik was already a grandfather. His daughter had given birth to another grandson. I envied Erik for I would never see a grandchild grow to be a man. Erik would. Erik had a comfortable stronghold. It was made of stone. Part of the defences were ancient ditches and he had improved what had been there before. His feasting hall was enormous. It rivalled Rouen and Caen. I knew that some leaders and princes resented those beneath them having more than they did. I did not. I applauded Erik and his home.

As we ate and drank, he told me of his horses. "Blue is the first of the mighty horses. He is the biggest. Perhaps he is a freak of nature. I would borrow him, lord, to breed even better horses."

I nodded, "I can let you have him whenever you wish."

"I have a couple of mares in season now but if you let me have him for the winter, then he can cover more of my mares. Some will be as big as Blue but others will be far bigger still than the horses we have bred up to now. Our warriors are bigger than Franks. We wear mail. It is a good combination."

"It is one thing to have the horse and the mail but they need to be trained too. We both know that you are the best man to do that."

"And I am getting no younger." He pointed to his sons. Gilles rode with me but there were two others, Erik Gillesson and Bagsecg Gillesson. "They are the future."

"Then I shall give them a fief each."

Gilles said, "I thank you for the honour, lord, but I would like to serve you a little while longer and learn from you. When we met with Mauger he confided in me that he had learned from watching you. I have seen much already and we have yet to fight."

"Then when you are ready you shall have one but your other sons, Erik and Bagsecg shall both have a fief now. When I leave, we will ride north of the river. There are some fine lands there. I have silver from the King, Erik. I will buy the horses your sons need to begin their herds. They can pay me with a tenth of the foals that they train. A man can never have too many horses."

Bagsecg and Erik were good men. Bagsecg was the eldest. I had fought alongside him and knew him to be puissant. He had a wife and two sons. Erik was also married but he had no children. We left their wives at home when we rode north. All of us were keenly aware that rebellion had taken the lords of the farms I would give to them. There were two which I thought were suitable. They had been the closest ones to Rouen which had been attacked. As such, I had emptied both manors of all who had rebelled. They were like settlements of ghosts. Montville and Quincampoix were just five miles apart and ten miles north of Rouen. I had been seeking two trustworthy lords to begin the work of settling them and Erik and Bagsecg were perfect. Montville was a better site for a stronghold while Quincampoix had the best land for horses. Both would need to be rebuilt but the two older sons of Erik Gillesson liked what they saw. I promised to send men to help them build. We had slaves we had taken in raids. They laboured improving roads and working on our churches. They could help build defences.

The two brothers returned with me to Rouen. I had Father Harold give them some of King Charles' silver and we discussed how they would defend the land to the north of Rouen. When they left, I was in a better frame of mind. The rebellion had cost me the lives of many warriors and their families. I had felt guilty that I had not watched over them. I would not make the same mistake again.

Leif and Robert were growing into fine young men who would be great warriors. They had some skills. If they were destined to be my bodyguards and, eventually, to be lords then they needed much work. Sven Blue Cheek would have been the perfect warrior to train them but he was in the Otherworld. Egil Flame Bearer would do a good job. Their first training took place in my outer bailey. The rich men of the town who had aspirations for their sons to be lords sent them to Egil. He was paid to train them. They were shown how to fight the Viking way. That meant using a shield as a weapon as well as your sword. It meant learning how to lock your shield with your neighbour and fight as a single line. Using my oathsworn they were shown how to fight in a double line with spears sticking over their shoulders. They even had to face a mock attack from my oathsworn warriors. That was the hardest lesson of all.

Gilles Leifsson then gave them harder lessons in riding and fighting at the same time. He was the best judge of horses and he picked, for them, the gentlest of horses for their first foray into the art of using stiraps and a long spear. Even though he was patient there were many bruises and falls. I was not concerned about the rich young men and I concentrated on Leif and Robert. Both struggled at first. There was much to think about. They had to hold a shield and the reins of their horse. They had to guide their horse with their knees. They had to learn how to use the saddle with the high cantle and their stiraps to enable them to punch with their spears. For the first week or so of the training that was all that was managed. When Gilles was happy that they could sit in a saddle and move the horse forwards and backwards he progressed to showing them how to strike at an object. He devised a swinging piece of wood the same size as a shield and had them ride at it. He had cunningly made it at shoulder height. When they missed it and almost all of them did miss the first few strikes, then the wood smacked them in the shoulder. Once they could hit it more times than they missed he showed them how to punch with the shield.

They thought they were horsemen until we began the lessons in using a sword to strike. This time we used turnips. Some Franks practised with melons. Gilles chose the harder turnip for a skull did not slice open like a melon. It was hard like a turnip and offered resistance. Some fell as their arms jarred against the turnip and the wooden pole. They had to be taught how to time and angle their swing. Their final lesson was with the animal heads. We brought animal heads from the abattoir. This would be a more realistic test. The eyes of the dead animal stared as the riders charged. When they struck there was a little blood and the sensation of slicing through flesh before grating and grinding on bone. It taught them what it would feel like when they rode to war. When they had all achieved it, I wandered amongst them and showed them the damage to their blades.

"When you fight in a battle the keen edge lasts but a few blows and then you are using an iron bar. Each time you charge you kill with your spear. You keep the spear as long as you can." I laughed, "Unless, like me, you have a long sword. After the sword has dulled it ceases to be an edged weapon. Use it to break skulls and bones. That is why we wear caps beneath our coifs and helmets. The wisest expense you will ever make is to buy a good sword, good mail and the best helmet you can afford." I pointed to the half dozen rich young men. "You six do not have the advantage of Robert and Leif. I will have my weaponsmith, the best in Normandy, make their weapons. You will not have that benefit. Choose wisely.

By the time the two had had such basic training, we began to plan the raid on Caletum. One of the reasons I had delayed the raid was the preparation. Leif, my captain and navigator, had gone with one of the knarr captains who traded with Lundenwic and Bruggas. He had sailed along the coast. When he had been in the two ports he had paid for maps. He used King Charles' silver. I know the King thought I would use it for rich jewels and golden ornaments. That was not my way. When he returned the two of us pored over the charts. I could see that Caletum had not developed into a port. It was a village made up of huts, fishing boats and Olaf Olafsson's hall. It would involve much work. Mont St. Michel was a monastery built on a rock in the sea. It was formidable. Caletum was a low-lying island in the middle of swamps and shallows. It was equally formidable. There was a way in. The fishing boats which were based on Caletum had a safe channel. Although they were not marked on the map, Erik had been able to see the ships as they returned to the shore. He knew where the channels lay. There was neither jetty nor quay. The fishing boats were just grounded on the beach. That suited us for it would identify the place we would land. The channel we would have to negotiate also dictated our manner of attack. We would have to step the mast and row in. We could not rely on the wind. If we grounded then all would be lost. When we were confident with the plan then Leif sailed to Caen to speak with Sámr and his captain. We would not alert Olaf as to our intentions. Sámr and I would meet at sea. There was a tiny village called Witsant just ten miles south of Caletum. We would have to step the masts before then.

Father Harold knew of my plans. I knew I could trust him. Like Padraig before him, he was a pragmatic man. I did more good than harm. He could, sometimes, be the voice of reason I needed. He did not understand me as Padraig had done but I listened to him for he made sense.

"Lord, when you capture this traitor what will you do with him?"

I looked at him as though he was an imbecile, "I will kill him!"

"Lord, you cannot do that." I did not argue. I would let him give me his reasons and then tell him he was wrong. "You rule a land which is Christian. There are more of Frankish blood in your land than Norse." I nodded. He was right. "The rest of Frankia and the Empire look to you and wait for you to be a barbarian. King Charles is your friend but acts such as the maiming of rebels just make you look like a wild animal. You cannot just kill him."

"Then what should I do with him? Pat him on the hand and say do not do it again?"

"No, lord. You put him on trial. Choose lords to be his jury. Let them hear the evidence and then, when he is found guilty, you decree his punishment."

"Is that not the same as killing him out of hand?"

"No lord, for you have used the law. You need laws. This land needs fairness. Men will suffer much as long as they know that there is a system in place to protect them from wrongdoing."

I laughed, "Father Harold, you are a clever and devious man. This is your way of having laws written."

He smiled, "We can write them and phrase them properly if you come up with the laws you would like in place." He hesitated, "You cannot use the blood eagle."

My eyes narrowed, "Why not?"

His eyes and his voice implored me to hear him. "You need justice to be seen to be done. It will encourage men to obey your laws."

"Believe me, watching a man have his back laid open and his lungs pulled out will deter wrongdoing."

"It will be public. You want your people to see you as fair." He pointed to my sword. "You and your son are known as Long Sword. Let that be the instrument of death. Take the head of the offender. If you wish to deter others then the head could be displayed on the gates. That would serve as a better deterrent."

He had given me ideas but I would not give him the satisfaction of agreeing too quickly. "I will draw up my laws and then tell you what the punishment will be."

The laws took longer to formulate than I had thought. I finished them just weeks before the raid. I would not be taking my young horsemen with me. This was a raid that needed Vikings. Egil Flame Bearer chose the men. He wanted men who could row and men who knew how to fight. Some were old warriors who now served in my garrison. Others were warriors who had chosen to farm. Egil knew them all. He had fought alongside them. I approved of every single one he chose. The other advantage we had was silence. These were not young warriors who would boast, over beer, of the planned raid. Ships came and went every day from my port. Count Arnulf and Olaf would have spies. The word was spread that I would visit my son. His wife was with child again and this would seem an appropriate time to visit. It was deceit but it might confuse a spy.

We left at night. Erik knew my river well. We did not row all the way. We used the current and the wind. We reached the mouth before dawn and we awaited Sámr. Erik had his compass and hourglass out. We would not leave the sight of land but a good navigator kept an accurate record of the sun and his position. The cloud-flecked sky made it harder for him to do so but he was patient. I looked at the skies. They threatened rain. That would not harm us for we had sealskin capes. My eyes were drawn to the west. I would not have many adventures left but one I had wanted was to sail across the Unending Sea. Since I had been to the bottom of the ocean and returned alive, I had felt an affinity with the sea. What lay to the west? Perhaps, when I died, my spirit would go across the seas and see.

Robert and Leif had not been at sea before. Now, as the swell from the west made us rise and fall, I saw them turning a little green. I gave them sage advice. "Fix your eye on some point on the horizon. Many men have emptied their stomachs on their first voyage but it does not endear you to the crew. They have to clean it."

I saw them nod and stare, as I did, to the west.

"Drekar to the south!"

The crew were all experienced and did not become alarmed. Sámr's ship hove into view and I said, "Leif, lower the sail, let us be about our business."

We could have left from Djupr. That would have been a short journey of no more than a few hours. However, Mauger had not commanded the port for long enough to be sure of all those who lived within its walls. A rider could reach Olaf before we would. I did not want the slippery snake to be alarmed. We kept the coast a smudge to the east. A sharp-eyed watcher might notice two ships sailing north but they would not be able to identify them. Erik checked the sun each hour and made adjustments. These were familiar waters. When he had sailed in the knarr to scout out the route he had identified features. To us, it was a smudge but he and his ship's boys knew exactly where we were.

"Lord, we have made better time than I expected. We will soon be close to Witsant. We do not wish to be seen."

"Then shorten sail." As his boys shortened sail I shouted, "We eat and then prepare for war."

Sámr reacted to our movement and he shortened his sail too. As the afternoon wore on and the sun began to set, we headed towards the coast. I was not a bad navigator but I was not in the same class as Leif. The ship's boy shouted, "Breakers to steer board!"

"Down sail! Prepare to step the mast. Rowers, take your oars."

I turned to my two boys, Robert and Leif, "Come, stepping a mast needs as many hands as possible. We have been passengers long enough."

In the time it took to take down the sail the rowers had their oars placed by their chests and then the whole crew lowered the mast and yard. They were laid on the mast fish. As they took their oars, I began a chant. It would not be sung for long but it would get us into the rhythm. I was not sure how many more voyages I would enjoy and so I chose a saga about me.

Ragnvald Ragnvaldson was cursed from his birth
Through his dark life he was a curse to the earth
A brother nearly drowned and father stabbed
The fortunes of the clan ever ebbed
The Norns they wove and Hrólfr lived
From the dark waters he survived.
Göngu-Hrólfr Rognvaldson he became

A giant of a man with a mighty name
Göngu-Hrólfr Rognvaldson with the Longsword
Göngu-Hrólfr Rognvaldson with his Longsword
When the brothers met by Rouen's walls
Warriors emptied from warrior halls
Then Ragnvald Ragnvaldson became the snake
Letting others' shields the chances take
Arne the Breton Slayer used a knife in the back
Longsword he beat that treacherous attack
When the snake it tired and dropped its guard
Then Longsword struck swift and hard
Göngu-Hrólfr Rognvaldson with the Longsword
Göngu-Hrólfr Rognvaldson with his Longsword
And with that sword he took the hand
That killed his father and his land
With no sword the snake was doomed
To rot with Hel in darkness entombed
When the head was struck and the brother died
The battle ended and the clan all cried
Göngu-Hrólfr Rognvaldson with the Longsword
Göngu-Hrólfr Rognvaldson with his Longsword
Göngu-Hrólfr Rognvaldson with the Longsword
Göngu-Hrólfr Rognvaldson with his Longsword

By the time we had finished, we were clear of the shore and heading north. We had a light hung from the stern and I saw Sámr just three lengths behind us. We now had just a few miles to row and then we would wreak our revenge on those who had rebelled. We would kill those who had betrayed us and killed their brothers.

I left my captain to steer the drekar and I went to the prow. The wind had swung since we had stepped the mast. Before it had been from the south and east and now it was from the east. It would continue its turn until it was northeasterly. It brought the smells of the land. We were just half a mile from the shore and a mixture of animal and human dung mixed with wood smoke drifted on the breeze. I stood at the prow and patted the dragonhead. *'Fafnir'* might be a dwarf but she had never let us down. I peered ahead. One of the ship's boys moved to the larboard side.

Erik was steering us towards the north. We would approach Caletum from the west. In the distance, I saw a flicker of light. Experience told me what that was. I said, to Folki, the ship's boy, "Do you know what that light is, Folki?"

"An aelfe, lord?"

I laughed, "No, Folki, it is a hut. Someone came out of the door and then closed it. We are close. Tell the captain that the village is just ahead. He should head a few points to the west."

"Aye lord."

The boy would remember this conversation when I was long dead and he was a man. It would be a comfort to me in the Otherworld knowing that I was still in men's thoughts. I waited until the houses began to take shape as darker shadows and Erik took us further west. Folki returned and I nodded to him as I went for my sword. I would not need my helmet nor shield. If Olaf and his men wore mail I would be surprised. I would try to take as many of the rebels back as prisoners. I wanted to make a demonstration of them for the rest of my land but I would not risk my men. Olaf, I would take myself.

As I walked down the centre of the drekar I saw that my men were mailed and ready. They were still rowing but it was not a hard pull. The wind was actually helping us now as it pushed us in the direction we wished to sail. Erik used the wind to push us a good half a mile from the western side of the settlement. Men could escape across the marshes and mudflats but it would be a risk. I had men ready with bows to chase them if they chose that route. They would not be able to move quickly.

Erik said, "Prepare to come about." It was a warning for the ship's boys perched precariously on the yard and the sides as well as for the rowers. They would have to work against the wind. The wind would take our words and the noise of the oars west. Sámr turned his drekar as we did. We would both reach land together. Sixty men would swarm ashore. The younger men would race through the village to cut off any escape. Most of those in this fishing village were either fishermen or were refugees from Normandy. Both would dread a Viking raid. Time was I would have been the first ashore. With my long legs, I could often leap three paces or so from the side. Now I was an old man and I would let younger and fitter men land first. With my sword now at my waist, I made my way back to the prow and pulled myself up by the forestay. The crew still rowed.

We were thirty paces from the beach when we were seen. I saw a woman, she had been outside making water and, as she turned, she saw us. Her cry, "Vikings!" would have an instantaneous effect. Men would rise and grab their weapons. Women would seek their children and, no doubt, what little treasure they had. They would get as far away from the Vikings as they could. It would be in vain. I had planned for flight.

"In oars!" The two commands came almost at the same time.

I saw the fishing boats on the beach. If they sought to use them to escape they would not be able to. Sámr's drekar actually crushed one of them as he misjudged the landing. Erik slid us gently onto the sand and shingle beach. My men poured over the side and splashed in the water. I jumped and landed on the sand. The tide was on the way out and I sank up to my ankles in the waterlogged sand. With my mail on I was heavy. I drew Long Sword and strode after my men. I shouted, "Olaf Olafsson, draw your weapon for I come for you!"

I wanted all to know who came for them. If they had honour, they would fight me and try to kill me. Erik Egilsson and Robert son of Henry were right behind me. They had their shields and swords. This would be their first opportunity to put to the test the skills taught by Egil. Ahead of me, the slaughter had begun. I heard the clash of steel on steel and the cries of men dying. The screams and panicked shouts of the women and the children filled the air. There was increasing light as doors were opened and the darkened village was lit by the light of fires burning within. People fled clutching their treasures. I saw two dead warriors as I moved towards the distant hall. Both had been men who had deserted me. They had died too quickly!

I heard a shout from ahead, "Shield wall!"

They were preparing to defend against us. What I did not know was exactly how many men were with Olaf. Eight lords had deserted me and they had taken some oathsworn with them. I had no doubt that there would also be Flemish warriors. I was more than confident about the outcome but a shield wall would mean there was less likelihood of prisoners. When you were fighting with someone armed in a similar way then you could take no chances.

I heard Sámr's voice, "Form line! The Duke comes!" His words told me that escape across the marshes and salt flats was now impossible.

I said, without turning around, "You two just watch my back. These men are dangerous." I raised my sword above my head so that all could

119

see it, especially Olaf and the men behind his hurriedly formed shield wall.

As I neared the hall, I saw that men had already fallen. Olaf had forty men in two lines before his hall. They had shields and helmets but I only saw two with mail. Some were Frisians and there were at least two Flemish warriors. The rest were men who had fought alongside me.

Sámr and my men had left a gap for me in the middle.

I pointed the sword at Olaf who was in the centre of his line, "Punishment and retribution are now coming, Olaf Olafsson, your father will be in Valhalla and his head will be hung. He will be wishing that he had strangled the babe that was born rather than he becomes a traitor."

"These are just words, old man! I am a Christian and my father died a pagan. He will be in hell and soon I shall send you there to join him." The words were bravado. I saw the piss puddling at his feet. He was scared. I had promised the blood eagle. His words were to make his men fight for him.

I held my sword over my right shoulder, "Enough words! Now is the time for blood! Now is the time for death!" Without waiting for my shield wall, I stepped forward. I swung my sword. There were none next to me for I had taken them by surprise. It allowed me a better swing. We had been ten paces apart. In the time it took me to take four of my strides I was swinging my sword at the shield wall. The edge hit Sven Green Eye even as his spear hit my chest. There was power behind my blow for my sword severed his neck. As he fell, he knocked into Olaf and his spear just touched my mail. The fall saved Olaf for Long Sword missed his chest by a handspan.

Then my men hit them. My sudden attack had disrupted the rebel line. I back swung my sword and it smashed through Olaf's spear halfway down. He had an open face helmet and I saw fear in his eyes. His spear had been as long as my sword. Now he would have to face my sword. His was a dagger in comparison. With my sword raised again, I brought it down towards his head. I turned the blade in the air so that it was flat. I hit his helmet square on. I had told Robert and Erik that a dull sword was like an iron bar. That was what I used. I struck the helmet to the side of the reinforced strip. The metal dented and still, my sword descended. It drove the helmet down and covered his eyes. The blow was not finished and it bent the helmet even more. When his legs buckled and he fell then I knew I had won. He had lost consciousness. I whipped my sword sideways and it bit into the neck of the warrior, Ulf, who was fighting

Sámr. Ulf had been a good warrior. Had he been deceived by Olaf or had I misjudged him? Olaf's collapse marked the collapse of their resistance. The men who had deserted me refused to surrender. They knew they would die. The old religion was stronger than the Christian one. Many had mortal wounds but fought on and retained their swords. My men could not afford to show mercy. They hacked, chopped, slashed and stabbed until the last of the rebels lay in a heap of mangled and bloody body parts. They had died with honour. Their oathsworn stood behind them. This was not over yet.

Shouting, "Robert and Leif, hold the prisoner!" I waded into the huddle of men who formed a circle singing their death song. I had meant to take prisoners but when Fámr son of Siggi, one of my bravest men, died I swung my sword in a long sweep. It was the mightiest blow I had ever struck. The three men I hit wore just helmets without coifs. All three heads flew from their bodies. With them ended all resistance. Lord Henry, my murdered men and their families were avenged.

Chapter 10

We did not leave until the next day. We raised the mast and yards and then loaded the drekar with the treasure the traitors had taken. At low tide, we sent the women and children across the causeway to the mainland. We put the bodies of the dead inside Olaf's hall and then we destroyed the fishing boats, the hall and the huts with fire. King Charles might be unhappy but I would live with his displeasure. Olaf's son had died in the fighting but I allowed his wife to live. She went with the women and children back to Flanders. We left on the afternoon tide and black smoke followed us as the Flemish huts burned. The Count of Flanders would rebuild. The site was too good to abandon. Next time he would keep it for himself.

Olaf was aboard my ship. He had been tightly bound and guarded by Robert. He had not been gentle with the wounded traitor. Olaf had been responsible for the death of his family. As we sailed south the blood still trickled from Olaf's head and none made any effort to tend to the wound. I stood and looked down at him. "You are a lucky man, Olaf Olafsson."

He laughed, "Me? Lucky? You have a warped sense of humour, Göngu-Hrólfr Rognvaldson."

"I promised you the blood eagle but I was persuaded to give you a trial."

"A trial?" I saw the confusion on his face. He thought me a cruel man and he was trying to work out my cruelty.

"They say I should show that I am civilised. Apparently, in the civilised world, you try a man before his equals. In the world of the Frank, you have the opportunity to defend yourself. That was denied many of your victims but if I am to be seen as a civilised man then you must be tried. That will be your fate. You can defend yourself but the judgment of your innocence or guilt will be down to those who hear your words."

"And who will they be?"

"The same lords with whom you sat in the council of war. The lords of Normandy will pass judgement."

He hung his head, "Then I am a dead man!"

"True, but your death will be a civilised one and you can confess to a priest. The world will see that the Duke of Normandy is now civilised."

His eyes flashed angrily at me, "You are nothing more than a count!"

I shrugged, "I rule a Dukedom and my loyal men call me Duke. What a traitor calls me does not matter to me!"

The squall which descended upon us halfway home seemed to be a judgement from the Allfather. It did not discomfort us much but Olaf Olafsson, with hands and feet bound, was rolled around my deck. Robert watched him to make sure that he did not slip overboard. He had to be returned to Rouen. His condition was immaterial. He looked as though he had been in a battle with ten men. His nose was broken and he lost teeth. I had no doubt that Father Harold would blame me but I was innocent. This was divine punishment.

When Sámr left us at the estuary mouth we began the tortuous journey upstream to Rouen. It was raining and the wind and tide were against us, but I viewed the two banks of the river as though for the first time. I knew that this might well be the last time I sailed home in a drekar and I could not help but remember the times we had raided here from the Haugr when this had been Frankia. I could hear the ghosts of the past speaking to me. I had fought many battles along this river. I had sacked churches where now I built them. I had taken slaves where now I received homage. The Norns had spun a seriously complicated web and I was at the heart of it. My grandfather's visit with the Dragonheart to the cave on Syllingar had set in motion events that could not be stopped. The rebellion had been a test. It was a test of me and my men. I had to change the way I ruled. My land was now more than the island my grandfather had first ruled. It was more than the Cotentin. It was Normandy and now Brittany. I knew now that my land was stronger and that there would be no further revolts. Our strongholds were better defended with ditches and palisades. Our warriors were better. We had more horsemen and better-armed warriors. If I went to the Otherworld before I reached Rouen it would not change what was. William had a child and another was on the way. When we held the trial, I would use it as an opportunity to let my lords know my wishes. The trial was also necessary. It would be a marker for the rest of the rulers in this part of the world that the Normans knew how to rule.

Father Harold frowned when he saw the bloody, bound prisoner. I did not bother to explain. "Have him locked in a cell. You may tend to his wounds if you wish. It is no matter. They are not life-threatening. It will take a week to gather my lords. Until then he gets small beer and bread. Anything more would be a waste. If he wishes to confess then you may arrange it. Egil, see to his guards. I want good men. One is in the cell with him at all times. His hands will remain bound even when he eats."

"Aye lord. he will be there for the trial."

I sent a rider to my son as well as to my lords. It was not important to have Gandálfr there or even Bergil but it was vital that my son attend the gathering. The lords who lived close arrived first. Mauger and Sámr took three days to reach me. My son took six. The night before the trial I held a feast. I had spoken with William before we ate so that he knew what I had planned. The last such meeting had been attended by Olaf Olafsson. I had him brought to be paraded before the lords prior to the meal. My three priest clerks were also in attendance. I had told them that they would scribe what was said and make copies for each of my lords. "Tomorrow, Olaf Olafsson, these lords will determine your fate. I will have no say in the matter. Whatever they say will be the judgement."

I saw him looking at the hardened faces. He had fought alongside many of them. He had thought to deceive them. He had sought to rule them. As he looked into their faces, he saw that they would find him guilty. What he did not know was the punishment. How would I kill him? Olaf was broken. He shambled off led by Robert and Leif. They would be his gaolers while we feasted.

When they had left us, I spoke. I measured my words now. Father Harold and his clerks would write down what I said. It was there for William after I had gone. I was making Norman history. "Tomorrow is the start of a new age here in this land of Normandy. We will rule by law. What I do, so do you. We can still hold a Thing to decide what must be done by the clan but in your own fief, you are the law. All punishments must be public ones. Sentences must be passed and be passed in open court so that all can see that our law is fair. Tomorrow we will all see how our new law works. No longer will two warriors disagree and fight. That makes for blood feuds. The court at Rouen will judge in disputes between my lords."

Bjorn the Brave looked worried. He was a good warrior and, on the battlefield, a clever general, but in other matters, he doubted himself, "That is a great responsibility, lord. What if we make a wrong judgement?"

I looked into his eyes, "You are a warrior and you live with that."

Sámr said, "Bjorn, I am not worried. It is what we have always done but it was not written down. Duke Robert, are there laws which are written down?"

I nodded, "Over the next year I will work with Father Harold and we will formulate the laws of Normandy. Any of you may pass comment on them. One year from now we shall meet again and hold a Thing. If we decide these laws are good then they will be adopted and then all of us," I stressed the word '*us*', "will be subject to them."

I saw in their faces the weight of their new roles sinking in. They were no longer the freebooting raiders who might plunder a neighbour's cattle. They could not just take what they thought was rightfully theirs. There would still be disputes but they would be settled differently in the future. There were many warriors, now long dead, who would not have accepted such rules and strictures. We had changed since we were the Clan of the Raven's Wing. The murder of our father and my exile in Norway had ensured that.

"Before we eat and," I grinned, "drink. I have one more serious item to tell you about. I am old and old men die." I heard murmurs from them. "I have lived long enough. When the traitor is sentenced tomorrow, I will be content. My son has a daughter. Who knows, soon he may have a son. I want all of you to swear on your swords that when I am gone that my son, William Longsword, will rule this land no matter what the Franks may say. More than that, when my son dies, if he has no male heir, then you will support his daughter Mathilde. She can be advised by a council of lords but the blood of Hrólfr the Horseman must rule this land. It was so prophesied by Skuld and if the blood of my grandfather does not course through the veins of the Duke or Duchess of Normandy then disaster will strike." My blasphemy had the three priests reaching for their crosses. Father Harold was already unhappy that my men would not be swearing on a Bible. I wanted the oath to be kept. I saw that my men took in the ramifications of my words. They knew what it meant to cross a Norn. They would not risk it. For all of us, Christianity was a new tunic we wore and if it was lost, we would not worry over much.

"Take out your swords." It sounded like wind whistling through trees as the blades were drawn. Each held the hilt before them. It looked a little like a cross. I hoped that would assuage the priests but, in all honesty, I did not care. They all shouted, "We so swear!" They kissed the hilts of their weapons. I saw that act gave satisfaction to the priests for, to them the sword was a cross. What they did not see was the fact that most of my lords, especially the older ones gripped the blades so tightly that they cut themselves. It was deliberate. Blood ran down the blades. It made it a blood oath and blood on the blade guaranteed they would keep it. With that business out of the way we drank and we ate. I spoke with my son. He was now changing. Marriage and the County of Brittany had done that. He was ready for my mantle and we spoke throughout the feast. Others drank the Viking way. I drank the old man's way. Neither my son nor I were drunk and much was decided.

The trial was held in my stronghold. We gathered in my Great Hall. I had invited the men of Rouen to attend, I wanted justice to be seen to be done. I had my throne. It did not need to be raised. William's was next to me. The lords who would judge completed the other sides of the square. The men of Rouen could stand and watch. Olaf was brought before us. Egil's guards placed him in the centre of what we now called, the court. He had been dressed and groomed. His bonds had been cut. He had been fed and given wine. I sat on my throne and William sat to my right. My lords sat on chairs around Olaf who stood facing me. My scribes were seated behind me. They could hear my words but they were discreetly seated out of sight.

"Olaf Olafsson, you are charged with treason. You did conspire with Normandy's enemies to take our land from us. You had fellow lords and oar brothers were slain. You had their families slaughtered. You failed to keep the oath you swore to me as Lord of Normandy! The charges are treason, murder and the breaking of an oath. What have you to say in your defence?"

Perhaps it was the wine we had given him after water for so long or it may have been some last vestige of the former Olaf but he was belligerent. "Göngu-Hrólfr Rognvaldson, you can put mail on a pig but it is still a pig. You are too uncouth to be lord of Normandy!" He glared at the lords around him. "All Vikings are barbarians. Until you become civilised then no man will take any of your family seriously. I do not regret what I did. My only regret is that I failed. I should have heeded the advice of others and had you and your bastard assassinated. It is what

126

you do with a mad dog. You end its life. Had I done that then I would be seated upon that throne and I would be the Count of Normandy!"

My son began to move and I said, "Hold. I am the judge here. Olaf Olafsson, these words come from you? They are not words put in your mouth by another?"

"These are my words."

"Then, lords of Normandy, what is your verdict? You may talk amongst yourselves and Sámr Oakheart can give me your judgement."

They did not take long. Sámr allowed them time to speak and then he walked the line. They had each been given a white pebble and a black pebble. They dropped one pebble into the bowl Sámr carried around. He came to me and showed me the bowl. It was filled with black pebbles. "He is guilty, Duke Robert."

I could see that there were no white pebbles but my priests could not see. The men of Rouen could not see. I had to ask the question. "Were there any dissenters?"

"No, Duke Robert."

I turned to look over my shoulder to Father Harold, "Write that down. It is important."

He nodded.

"Olaf Olafsson, you are guilty of the charges. The punishment is death. You called us uncivilised. If we were then my choice of punishment would be the blood eagle. You will not have that punishment not least for that is reserved for brave warriors and that is not you! Sámr Oakheart and Bergil Fast Blade, take the prisoner to the outer bailey. He will be executed in public for we have nothing to hide."

William carried Long Sword. Robert had sharpened it so that it could be used to shave. I had had a wooden block placed in the bailey. Olaf was carried there. My lords hurried out so that they could have a good view. The gates to my stronghold were open and some of those who had not been in the Hall began to come in when Olaf was taken to the block. Sámr and Bergil put his head across the block. As I neared them, I heard Sámr lean in and say, "I would stay as still as you can, Olaf. It will be quicker for you." It was spoken out of kindness. If he moved or struggled then I might not take his head. He would still die but it would be a slower death.

The imminence of his death seemed to startle him, "A priest! I need a priest!"

I had expected as much and I waved Father Harold forward. He knelt and listened as Olaf spoke. The delay allowed the bailey to fill up. Fathers put sons on their shoulders so that they could see better. I knew when the priest had finished for he made the sign of the cross. He stood and nodded at me. Olaf Olafsson was confessed. He had had absolution. In his mind, he would go to heaven. The heaven to which he went would not have either his father or any of the other warriors of the clan. He was welcome to it. I took the sword from William. Olaf had his head turned to look at me. It was a courageous thing to do. I raised the sword and, as I did so, he closed his eyes. It was a reflex. I brought the blade down and struck cleanly. The head fell and blood spurted. There was a moment's silence and then a cheer. Olaf was the only man I executed. From that day, so long as I lived, all my laws were obeyed. Olaf Olafsson had managed to do one thing right in his life.

A year to the day after the trial, the laws I had written were ratified by a Thing. The year had been the most peaceful year I could remember. We had no wars. We were not attacked nor invaded. The harvest was a good one. King Charles married and my son had another daughter, Gefn. The only black cloud was that I was ill for a month in Þorri. It was the winter sickness. I was hot and sweaty. I sneezed and I coughed. I would not have been worried except for the fact that this had never happened to me before. It was a sign of old age. I had now seen more than seventy summers! I feared that my time on this earth was drawing to a close. I threw myself into making Normandy as strong as it could be. I used the money from taxes to strengthen our ability to defend ourselves. Our men were better armed and mounted. Our strongholds, we now called them castles, were improved. All in all, I was pleased. When, almost a year after our Thing, I was summoned to Paris to meet with the King I wondered what it meant.

I went with my horsemen and Robert and Leif. Both were now young men. They were armed and mailed much as my horsemen. We had more young men for when they were trained by Erik all of them wished to serve with me. I rode with forty men to Paris. The days when I might be ambushed were long gone. When I reached King Charles' palace, I discovered the reason I had been summoned. His wife, Queen Eadgifu, had given birth to a son, Louis.

I was brought, alone, to the Great Hall. The King and Queen, along with the babe were there. The Archbishop of Paris was also present. It was the King who spoke, "Count Robert, I have a son. I would have you swear that you will do all in your power to see that he attains the throne of the West Franks."

It was unfair of the King to spring it upon me. I looked from him to the child. All babies looked the same to me but the older I grew the more sentimental I was. I realised that I would not have to do that which I promised. I had but a few years left to me. The King was hale and hearty and so I dropped to one knee, "I so swear."

The relief was so obvious on the King's face that I wondered if I had made a mistake.

He led me away and we went to a small ante-chamber, "You cannot know what a relief it is to have a son."

"You are safe now then, Highness?"

He shook his head, "Safer, that is all. The fact that you are my supporter is equally important to me. My enemies are circling like carrion around a dying animal. What you may not know is that earlier this year I was imprisoned by my nobles. It was only the intervention of the Bishop of Rheims that secured my release. I have few supporters. The birth of Louis buys me time." He poured me some wine and raised his goblet. "To Robert of Normandy! You are a rock. When you swore the oath to me you were a barbarian and now, even King Edward of Wessex acknowledges that there is a rule of law in your land. What could have been seen as an act of violence was changed to one of justice when you captured your traitor. That was well done. I knew that you were a clever man and you have proved it to the other kings."

I nodded and sipped the wine. It was a good wine. "It is important that you know of my oaths, King Charles. While you live, I will not attack your land. When you die, I will do all in my power to see that Louis attains the throne."

"Good."

"But know that those oaths die with my death. My son has not sworn them. I am an honest man and I keep my word but you need to know exactly what that means."

He looked surprised, not disappointed, just surprised, "You need not have told me that but it speaks well of you that you did. I know what the oath means. Despite your age you still seem, to me at least, to be in good health. I hope we both emerge from the next few years with our oaths intact. Now that I have a son I can begin to make my land safer. I have heard of a Magyar army that is rampaging the lands to the east of me.

Perhaps that threat will unite my lords. I had hoped the birth of Louis would do that but it seems I was wrong."

We spoke at length about the King's enemies. I learned that King Edward of England was unwell. That also worried King Charles for two of King Edward's sons, Athelstan and Elfweard were being touted by different factions as the next king. It seemed to me that our way of passing the crown to the firstborn seemed a better way.

The next year saw me determined to visit as many of my lords as I could. I also spent longer periods with my son and his now three daughters. He was still hopeful that he would have a son. I was not convinced. Perhaps his wife, Sprota, had been cursed. There were such women who only had girls. King Charles' first wife had been one such. I was now glad that I had put in place an oath that would outlive me. My men began to die. It was not in battle. Like me they were old. Some had been wounded so many times that it was inevitable that they should die before me. Gandálfr had the winter sickness but did not recover. Haraldr grew thin and coughed up blood. He died. The most grievous loss was Erik Gillesson. He died when he was in a stall with a horse. For some reason, the horse went mad and he was trampled to death. The horse was put down. My men knew what had caused it. It was the Norns. I wept when we buried him. Now there was just Sámr, Bjorn the Brave and Bergil Fast Blade who were memories from my past. The rest of my warriors would be waiting for me in Valhalla but it seemed I was still being spared. There were still things I needed to do.

Erik's son, Bagsecg, returned to Montfort. He would continue to produce horses and men for Normandy but it was not the same. I wondered why I was being kept alive. The Norns had not yet taken me but I could not see the reason.

It was not all sadness. Robert and Leif, son of Egil, now led my bodyguard and both had proved themselves to be good warriors. They had been trained by the best. Robert's start in life had been hard. Perhaps he had been forged like good steel. At Erik Gillesson's behest, we had begun to hold competitions at Montfort. It had begun after the Thing. It was designed for warriors to show their prowess. Using blunted lances and wooden swords lords competed with one another. It was a way of practising war without death being the result. It became an annual event at Heyannir. Robert and Leif, leading their team of warriors, won the prize for horsemen each year. My son, William, and his team won the shield wall competition. When Erik died, I asked his son, Bagsecg, to continue the tournament and to hold it in his father's honour. And so, without fighting, we practised for war and we were ready to fight. At heart, we were still Vikings, it was just that we wore a Frankish coat.

Chapter 11

War came when Louis was a little more than two. It was Hagano who caused the revolt. He had given away bishoprics belonging to Frankish nobles. The lords had had enough and this time they elected a new King. King Robert was Robert of Neustria. He had been plotting for some time with other lords and with the collusion of the King of the East Franks. The first I knew was when Bjorn the Brave sent a rider to Rouen. He told me that King Charles had been deposed and he and his court had fled to Évreux. He and his loyal lords now sheltered at the stronghold of Bjorn the Brave. The King had begged for me to come to his aid.

I was alone when the news arrived. I went to my study and looked at a map of Frankia. Was this the chance I had been waiting for? My oath was no longer valid. Charles was not king. I had sworn my oath to King Charles. His country would be in disarray and my army could seize huge chunks of land. We could even take Paris. I poured some wine and I reflected. Perhaps I was getting old or, more likely the spirits in the Otherworld spoke to me. I heard, in my head, Padraig's voice. In his own inimitable way, his voice calmly told me that I had sworn an oath to a man and not an office. The King and I had an understanding and I could not abandon him. I had sworn he would be King.

Stirred I went to Father Harold, "I need summons writing for my lords. We go to war."

"To war, lord?"

"King Charles has been deposed and we are honour bound to aid him. I want each of my lords to present themselves with half of their available men at Évreux."

"Half, lord?"

"I would not leave Normandy defenceless. That should be enough. I will use my bodyguards to send the missives. You have until they are saddled to write them. Have wax ready and I will use my seal!"

"Aye lord."

"Robert, Leif, summon my bodyguard!"

I suddenly realised that I felt energised in a way I had not felt for years. I now knew why the Norns had saved me for so long. I would be the barbarian who saved Frankia! I should have heard the Norns spinning but I did not.

I sent my bodyguard with the letters for my lords and then I summoned Egil. "I need half of the garrison to march to Évreux," I told him what had happened.

He nodded, "You are right to go to his aid, lord, and it is time we showed others that Normans can still fight. Since you defeated the Bretons, they think we have become soft."

"You know your son will be in the forefront?"

"He is a warrior and he has learned much. I could never fight from the back of a horse. I am pleased that he can." He laughed, "Aye and he can still fight on foot. He will be a better warrior than his father."

Egil and I went to study the maps. Both Neustria and Poitiers, not to mention Lothringia, were both far from Frankia. King Robert of the West Franks, as he now styled himself, would need time to gather an army. We were closer and my men could protect the King at Évreux. What King Robert would not do would be to try to cross Brittany. The last thing he would need would be an open war with me. Perhaps he hoped I would sit and watch. I had given my word and I would keep it.

I had given my riders more than one letter. The ones riding to the Flemish and Poitevin borders would be away for four days. The ones closest would arrive first. I marched with the men from Rouen and from Djupr and Caen. Between us, we had four hundred warriors. Bagsecg of Montfort and his horsemen would already be at Évreux. I knew that King Charles would have expected me to drop everything and run to his side but I had to plan. We had wagons filled with darts, stones, arrows and javelins. It would not slow us down as most of the army marched. We were not as slow as a Frankish army.

When we reached Évreux I was relieved to see that it had a huge armed camp surrounding it. There were men loyal to the King as well as his Lothringian warriors. Many of my men had already arrived and I saw that Bagsecg had taken charge of all of the horsemen. They would be our secret weapon in this war.

Bjorn was pleased to see me. He was not used to the company of kings. The King was with him and Count Fulbert who led the

Lothringian contingent. Hagano, the King's adviser, appeared to be absent.

"Count Robert, you came. I was not sure you would." The relief on the King's face was clear to be seen.

"I gave my word." I looked around. I could not see the main reason for the King's dilemma, "Where is Hagano?"

"I sent him north-west to gather more warriors and to bring them here."

"He has not returned yet?"

The frown showed me that the King was unhappy that he had not returned, "Hagano is a good man and he will bring warriors to us."

"And the Queen?"

"She took my son back to Wessex."

"She would have been safe in Rouen."

He smiled, "I know but she feared for our son. There is a channel between our enemies and her father. Her brothers will care for her." King Edward had recovered from his illness and now ruled England once more. "I am content for we can fight this foe without worrying about my family."

"And where are your enemies? Where is King Robert?"

Count Fulbert shrugged, "We think in Laon to the northeast of us."

Such poor intelligence was disappointing. "Why has he not advanced to Paris to occupy the palace and gain control of the capital?"

The King said, "I believe that he worries the citizens still support me. He has the support of the nobles but not the people."

"Then we have a chance. How many men do you command?"

The King looked nervously at Count Fulbert, "Count Robert, I am no soldier. Count Fulbert commands my men."

I did not know the Lothringian. I looked at him closely. What I saw I did not like. He did not look like a warrior. "Well, he does not command my men. I ask again. How many men do you have?"

The Count looked annoyed. "We have over two thousand men."

"And how many are warriors?"

"They can all fight."

"I did not ask that. I asked how many are warriors. I have left at home the farmers and those who have little experience of fighting. All of my men are seasoned warriors. When we are all mustered there will be fifteen hundred of us. Two hundred are the finest horsemen you will ever see. When we fight, the Normans will be under my command,"

"And the King will be under my protection." It sounded like petulance from Count Fulbert. The King would be safer if my men guarded him. I could hear the Norns spinning and I was powerless to do anything about it.

My son was the last to arrive. He came with just his bodyguards. More alarmingly neither Ragnar the Resolute nor Bergil Fast Blade was with him. He brought with him some disturbing news. "As soon as Robert found us, I sent out scouts. There is an army gathering at Poitiers." His eyes told me he had other news which was only for my ears. "I have gathered my men close to Andecavis. I will stop them from crossing the river."

Count Fulbert smiled, "So, Count Robert, you will not be bringing fifteen hundred men to the battle!"

"If there is an army which threatens my land from the south then I may not be bringing any men to this battle."

The smile was wiped from the Lothringian's face, "You cannot desert the King at this time! He needs you."

"I owe my allegiance first and foremost to the people of Brittany and Normandy. I will speak with my son privately and then give you my decision."

When we were alone William said, "There is a plot here, father. When Robert reached us with the news, I began a muster but I sent riders by secret ways to the south and east. I have explored the land there. I know the number of warriors who reside in the borderlands. Previously there were few of them. My riders reported that those numbers had trebled and we found spies and scouts all along our eastern border. We eliminated them."

"Then they were expecting me to send for you and they would have attacked as soon as you left. Clever. You did the right thing."

"And my scouts found evidence of Bretons in their ranks. They wore the sign of the Count of Cornouaille. We had heard rumours that he was gathering men in Poitou and this confirms it."

"Return to Andecavis and do what you must to protect our land. If you think you can take more, especially towns which bridge the river then do so."

He nodded, "You will not bring the rest of our men?"

"You are right William, there are plots and conspiracies. I asked myself why the army was gathering at Laon. If you wish to take Frankia then you need to take Paris and to hold it. If you are at Laon then Rouen is as close as Paris. King Robert, as he styles himself, is seeking Normandy as well as Frankia! We have to defeat this army, not for King Charles, but for Normandy."

"As ever I am in awe of your mind. You take care, father, I have need of you and your mind for many more years. I would like you to see my son born."

"Your wife is with child?"

"Aye and this time I am hopeful it will be a boy!" My son and his bodyguards left immediately.

When he discovered that my men and I were staying, Count Fulbert was less aggressive. The next day I was summoned to a meeting with the Count and the King. They had taken over Bjorn's hall. Men were still arriving, we could not leave just yet but Bjorn's resources were being stretched. There were lesser lords with the two leaders but they made way when I arrived and I sat next to the King. Count Fulbert had taken charge, that much was obvious. "We need to strike and take Paris, Count! We would have you use your horsemen to take and hold the bridges."

I shook my head, "I have too few. If you want me to take Paris then I will send for my ships. With my drekar, you do not need the bridges but taking Paris is the wrong strategy." I feared a conspiracy. If we headed to Paris then the army at Laon could attack Normandy.

The King frowned, "Then what is?"

"The army is to the north of us. If we take Paris, they could cut us off. Their army would be free to besiege us there and take my land."

Count Fulbert sneered, "Then this is all about you, Count Robert."

"I admit that I fear for my land. An army in the south and an army in the north could spell the end of Normandy. However, there is another reason. Robert of Neustria is in the north and if we eliminate him then the King's crown and throne are safe."

"And if we march north and he evades us and takes Paris?"

I smiled, "Then I bring my ships and we did as we did a few years ago, we take Paris." I was looking at the King as I spoke. I was reminding him that I had yet to let him down. I willed him to take my side over Count Fulbert's.

He nodded, "It is a good plan, Count Fulbert, and it takes us closer to Lothringia. There must be more loyal warriors there than you have brought."

That thought had crossed my mind. The three contingents, Norman, Frank and Lothringian were about equal in number. The Count frowned and then nodded, "If Count Robert will not do as I ask then we will have to adopt his plan. However, King Charles, you will be under my protection!"

With the cast of the die so the future of Frankia was decided. We left seven days later when the last of my men and the last Frankish warriors loyal to the King arrived. We headed north. Bagsecg and his men led. They scouted the roads and kept us warned of danger. The Count of Lothringia insisted that we be the van. Again, that suited my men for it meant we were not eating other's dust but I was also wary. It was our head that was poking above the parapet.

One of my most dependable warriors was Sven Mighty Arm. He held the fief of Gisors for me. It had a good stronghold above the river and, as we rode by his walls, one of Bagsecg's riders, Charles of Montfort, galloped in. Sven and I were discussing his home and how it could be defended. "Lord," the rider pointed northeast, "Lord Bagsecg is suspicious of the wood south of Bieuvais."

I turned to Sven who nodded, "Aye lord, the next few miles are the border. There are Franks who live there. From what I have heard they are loyal to Robert of Neustria. They were unhappy when King Charles gave the local abbey to Hagano."

Hagano was King Charles' bane. I had a decision to make. It was risky but I had learned that taking risks often paid off. "Charles of Montfort, ride back to Bagsecg. We will be bait. Tell him to secrete his horsemen until we are attacked. I want him to envelop our enemies with his horsemen."

I looked at Sven, "Sven, your local knowledge can make the difference here."

"There is a wooded area just south of Bieuvais. The road passes through it. If I wished to harm an invading army I would ambush there."

I looked at Charles of Montfort, "So tell Count Bagsecg our plan."

"Aye lord."

He rode off and I said to Robert, "Have the horn sounded for my leaders." The army kept moving as Sámr, Bjorn, Harold, Mauger and the others arrived. I quickly told them about our plan. "I want the men with bows in the centre of the column. They will be flanked by our mailed men. Have them all carry their shields on the outside. The Franks may be piss poor archers but let us not make it easy for them. We hold until Bagsecg attacks and you wait for my command to retaliate."

Sámr pointed south. The Lothringians and loyal Franks were three-quarters of a mile behind. "Do we warn them?"

"There is little point in alarming King Charles. He is not a man of war." I had learned that two years earlier the Magyars had invaded his eastern lands. Had that been me, I would have led an army and defeated them. King Charles had asked his nobles to help and they had refused. The Magyars had devasted several fiefs. It had been expensive. King Charles needed Count Fulbert to lead his men. I think it was at that moment that I knew King Charles was doomed. A king had to lead his men in battle. It would not change what we were about for I was defending Normandy. Robert of Neustria was every bit as much my enemy as King Charles'.

My bodyguard heard my words. Robert rode on one side of me and Leif the other. My shield was about my back and they held their shields so that they could protect me. Leif, who slipped his shield onto his right arm said, "Count, don your helmet."

I shook my head, "I need to see,"

"The helmet just has a nasal, lord, you can see. My father told me to watch over you and keep you safe. Don your helmet, please!" His voice was commanding. He was no longer the deferential youth who had first followed me. He was my oathsworn and he was doing his duty.

I saw Robert nodding. Sámr laughed, "You had best do it, lord. These two are strong enough to put it in place for you and besides, they are right! You and I have old ears and eyes. We do not watch for enemies, they do!"

He was right but I did not enjoy being spoken to as though I was incompetent. I donned my helmet. It was a tight fit for I had my arming cap and a coif. My weaponsmith had fitted an aventail to the back so that the back of my neck had two layers of mail and then the top of my byrnie protecting my neck. All of this took place as we plodded along the road. Blue was finding this easy for he was walking at the pace of men on foot. As I looked at my bodyguard, I saw why Leif had been so insistent. Thanks to Blue's size and my body the top half of my body and head were well above my guards. I was an easy target.

We travelled another mile and I saw the wood ahead. It spread out for many miles to the east and west. Ahead, beyond the wood, I saw the distant town of Bieuvais. Even if there was no ambush, we still had to either reduce Bieuvais or negotiate its surrender. We had taken this route because Creil, to the south, was a stronger enemy bastion. Bieuvais was just a small stronghold. However, we could ill afford to lose any men. We were heading towards the heartland of our enemies.

The ambush, when it came, proved that Leif's advice had been sound. Two arrows rattled off my helmet. They made my ears ring but otherwise did not discomfort me over much. I shouted, "Shields!" Leif held up his shield and moved his horse closer to mine. Robert did the same on the other side. I felt arrows hitting my back. I was a big target.

Robert said, urgently, "Lord dismount! You are too easy a target."

He was right and much as it galled me to do so I dismounted. I owed it to the men who protected me. As I stepped between Blue and Robert's horse, arrows thudded into my cantle and saddle. Then I heard Sámr shout, "Release." Our archers were good. They were also angered for their Count had been attacked. It sounded like a flock of birds rising into the sky as our arrows fell amongst the ambushers. I heard horns on both sides as Bagsecg and his men sprang their own attack. My bodyguards did not move as Sámr and Bjorn led our men into the woods to destroy the would-be attackers.

By the time Count Fulbert and the King reached us the ambushers had been slain and our men were stripping the bodies of valuables. The look of distaste on the Lothringian's face was confirmation that the man was unused to warfare. Taking from the dead was a common practice amongst warriors. The coming battle did not bode well. King Charles said, "How did you know?"

"I have good scouts." I pointed to the distant town. "And the lord of Bieuvais, is he an ally?"

The King shook his head, "I gave their abbey away and they were not happy."

"Then let me approach first. Perhaps the threat of a Norman attack might make their allegiance to the new king waver."

It may have been a combination of their failed attack or it might have been my presence which decided them but the gates were open and the lords and his men had fled. Being the first in meant we reached the hall before the Lothringians and the Franks. They had delayed their advance, I suspect it was to ensure that they suffered no harm and, perhaps, to give the chance of those in the town hurting us! Whatever the reason, we profited from my decision to lead. The general populace bowed and scraped as we entered. They feared me. It was not just in material such as treasure and food, I also learned where the enemy warriors were gathering, Soissons. By the time the King and Count had arrived, we had

139

eaten and I had questioned the burghers to find out as much as I could about the likely site of the battle.

After they had eaten, I sat with the King and his advisers. The King looked pleased, "We have done well. You have done well, Count. If all the opposition is like that, I will soon recover my lands."

The King was naïve. "King Charles, this was nothing like the real battle will be. This was a gamble that they could hurt our vanguard. It might have been they hoped to kill you in the first encounter and then the threat would be gone."

"Kill me?"

"You have been deposed, King Charles. We accord you the title but they will not. There is no sin in killing a former king." I realised he had not understood that. Regicide was a crime but with a new King of the West Franks, Charles was just an ordinary man. "I have heard that they gather at somewhere called Soissons. From what I can gather it is fifty miles from here and there is an old hill fort. They will undoubtedly use that to stop us."

The King nodded, "I remember it. There is another threat, Count. Before we reach Soissons, we have to pass through Compiègne. That is where one of my forebears, Louis, was deposed."

I shook my head. "They will not attack us there. We will be able to rest there. While we do, I will send my men to scout out the dispositions of the enemy."

Count Fulbert shook his head, "Taking charge again, Count?"

I smiled, "I am happy to take suggestions, Count Fulbert, but as you did not seem to know either the battlefield or the size of the enemy then I suggest you leave your posturing for a later time. I am a warrior and I have no time for politicians! I have known you but a short time and yet I recognise you for what you are, a politician and a second rate one at that."

His face became effused and red, "I do not need to take such insults."

I smiled, "I am afraid you do for the alternative is for me to take my men back to my own lands. Of course, on the way, we would ravage the land for we are, after all, barbarians."

It was a threat that could not be ignored. The King held up his hands, "Peace, Count Fulbert. Until we are at Soissons, we are all in the dark and the Count has shown that his men are more than capable of scouting out the enemy for us."

The Count stood, "Very well but I will join my men. I find the air here difficult to breathe."

I growled, "Be careful how you insult me, Count. If I come after you there will be little left for your men to bury."

He made to reply but I saw fear in his eyes. I might be old but my reputation told him that he would come off worse.

King Charles shook his head, "Robert, why must you be so aggressive?"

I turned, "King Charles, why do you have such poor choice of advisers? Hagano and now Fulbert? It is no wonder you are in this parlous position. I would have sent to my father in law, King Edward. The men of Wessex know their business. They could have kept you on the throne."

"I tried but Robert of Neustria is also an ally of King Edward."

I laughed, "Then the ones who will benefit will be the Saxons. Believe me, King, one day they will rule your land!" I saw that my words had come as a surprise to him.

Compiègne was the largest town we had seen. There was a palace there but no opposition. The burghers were hospitable but guarded in their welcome. They wanted their town left whole. They would not offend the Vikings. One advantage of our slow progress and our one victory was that some lords had managed to rejoin King Charles. They swelled our numbers but I was not confident of their ability to fight. Hagano brought two thousand men. Count Fulbert, on the other hand, was delighted for the contingent he would command was now more than five times the size of mine. I had also gained men as some lords who had missed the muster joined me. I sent out Bagsecg and his men to scout. Now that Hagano had joined Count Fulbert and the King I was ostracised. It was as though they did not need me. Once again, we had made ourselves comfortable and had the best quarters. None of my men would leave this part of Frankia poor.

Bagsecg and his men took three days to scout out the enemy positions. His news was not good. "Apart from this King Robert they have the Duke of Burgundy, Hugh, Duke of Paris, and Gilbert, the son of the Duke of Lorraine. They have more than sixteen thousand men."

Sámr nodded, "We have been outnumbered before."

I nodded, "Aye but not with such poor allies. Give me some good news."

"Would that I could, my lord. It looks to me like their best warriors will be gathered about the hill fort. The standard of Robert of Neustria is there along with the standard of Lorraine and Burgundy."

"Horses?"

"Their mounted men guard the southern flank of the hill fort. The rest of the army is to the north."

"Thank you."

Sámr asked, "We still fight?"

"I told the King we would but this news may make him reconsider."

When I entered the feasting hall it was as though we had won already. Hagano was nothing if not optimistic. The wine had flowed. All conversation stopped as I entered. They were about to have a sobering awakening when I gave my news.

I waited until I had their attention. "The scouts have returned. There are more than sixteen thousand men opposing us. You face Franks, as well as the men of Lorraine and Burgundy." I gave them all the news at once, including the dispositions. I used the chess pieces which were on the table to show them, graphically, the size of the problem.

They stood and studied it. Ideas were thrown back and forth. I could see that they did not want to attack. I wondered if peace would be made and we could return home. That would suit us. I would have fulfilled my oath to the King and we could make war, once more, on our neighbours. Of course, it might be better if those neighbours were weakened by war but we would grow and they would diminish no matter what happened.

Hagano was back and even Count Fulbert deferred to him. He spoke and I saw that gullible King Charles still believed the man who had lost him his kingdom. "I can see a way to defeat them, Highness. We know that their horsemen are to the south and the strength is on the hill. I say we use our best warriors, the Count of Normandy's horsemen, to neutralize the Neustrian horse. Then if the Norman's advance can attract the attention of Robert of Neustria, we can attack their weaker right flank and wheel around to take them in the rear."

It was masterful. All of the losses would be Norman and the victory would go to Hagano and Fulbert.

Count Fulbert smiled at me, "And that would suit you, Robert of Normandy, for you would be leading your own men."

"And taking the losses!"

"Are you afraid?" He had become bold and overconfident now that Hagano had returned.

I drew Long Sword and laid it on the table, demolishing the chess pieces, "Count Fulbert, I have had enough of you. Apologize or draw your sword and we settle this here and now!"

The Count physically recoiled, "I meant nothing! I apologize! Let us not fight amongst ourselves. That is what the enemy wants!"

Sheathing my sword, I said, "I came to honour my oath. I can see it is a waste of time. I will return to Normandy. Fight this war yourself." It was not petulance. I meant it at the time.

I saw fear on the faces of all. The King shook his head, "Clear the room. I would speak with Count Robert alone!" In all the time I knew him it was the most decisive act I remember him taking. They obeyed the King and shuffled out. When we were alone he pleaded with me, "Robert, I need you."

I shook my head, "These men are cowards and not to be trusted. If you listen to them you might lose your life as well as your crown."

"And that is why I am happier if you attack Robert of Neustria. You are the only one who can defeat him." He saw my cynical look, "This is not flattery, Robert. You have never lost a battle. The one Viking we all feared was Rollo. Robert of Neustria will be terrified of you. Yes, you will face more than half the enemy army but that gives my other lords the chance to win the battle. I know that your men are worth four of any other contingent in my army." I was not convinced and my face showed it. "I give you the title of Duke and I will pay five thousand pounds in silver for your men."

It was not the silver which convinced me, it was the title, "And the title goes to my son when I die?"

"Of course."

"In front of your lords?" He nodded. "I am still not confident but I will do as you ask. I do it for you, King Charles, and not these faint-hearted follies who call themselves lords."

He called in his lords and told them that I had agreed and that my reward was Duke of Normandy. Their faces showed their distaste and contempt for both me and King Charles. It was not the best way to prepare for a battle. I should have had him give me the title in writing. Later there would be men who said he did not give me the title but as his successor denied me the title the point is moot. I sent the treasure back to Rouen along with a letter for my son. If I perished, and it was likely I would, then I wanted William to have the silver and the title.

With the news delivered, the silver and the letter sent on their way, we prepared for battle. Secretly Hagano, Fulbert and the other lords hoped I would die along with all of my men. They believed that we would but that we would kill so many of the opposition that they would win. They were Christians. They did not hear the Norns spinning.

Chapter 12

We attacked two days later. The other leaders were happy for us to do so. In the short time, we were there, forty men deserted. None were my men. King Robert could squat upon his hill and watch our men seep away. We had to attack. Hagano and Fulbert organised what I thought of as the King's battle. I organised my own attack. My men were happy to be fighting uphill against overwhelming numbers. It was in their nature. When I told them of the silver we had been paid, they were even happier. I did not plan on throwing away the lives of my brave warriors. We were a diversion. I was confident in the ability of Bagsecg to drive the enemy horse from the field. My plan was simple. I would use my archers to disrupt the men who faced us. Bagsecg had told us that they would be crossbowmen. Our archers took pavise for protection. When they retreated, they would drop them and we would march across them. A pavise could not be carried. It was too big. It was braced with two lengths of wood. The enemy did not have as many mailed men as we did. King Robert had a hard core of veterans and the rest was made up of his lords and their villagers. We would advance steadily up the hill. This would buy King Charles' men as much time as possible to get into position to attack. We would employ the variation on the boar's snout formation. I would use my lords to each lead their own wedge. Each wedge and snout would be made up of hearth weru. The rest of the men would be in three ranks. They were good warriors and at least half were mailed but they were not the elite who would lead. Once they had made their first attack the archers and slingers would follow us up the hill and send their arrows over our heads.

The King and his advisers had asked us to begin the attack. I did not mind. It did not suit me to stand and wait to fight. We marched to our starting position beyond the range of crossbows and I had the horn sounded. Bagsecg and his horsemen charged towards the enemy horsemen. The Frankish horse had not expected an attack that had any kind of order. Barbarians fought without order. Erik Gillesson had learned the art of war from his father, Gilles. He, in turn, had learned from Alain of Auxerre. Bagsecg's men fought in regimented lines. The Franks took so long to face them that Bagsecg's men hit them while they were still forming. At the same time, my archers and slingers sent arrows and stones at the crossbowmen who were guilty of watching the fight to their left. The initiative went to my archers and slingers. The pavise prevented too many losses to my archers. When the crossbowmen fled my archers switched targets. The men of Lorraine took four flights and then began to advance towards us. They had little choice for those four flights slew many men and the warriors of Lorraine were wavering. Their Duke ordered their advance. It was our moment to strike. I had the horn sounded three times and my archers disengaged. We opened ranks for them and then, as they passed through, I began the chant. It was an old one. My grandfather had used it and it seemed appropriate.

The Clan of the Horse march to war
See their spears and hear them roar
The Clan of the Horse with bloody blades
Their roaring means you will be shades
Clan of the Horse Hrolf's best men
Clan of the Horse death comes again
Leading Vikings up the Frankish Water
They brought death they brought slaughter
Taking slaves, swords and gold
The Clan of the Horse were the most bold
Clan of the Horse Hrolf's best men
Clan of the Horse death comes again
Fear us Franks we are the best
Fighting us a fatal test
We come for land to make our own
To give young Vikings not yet grown
Clan of the Horse Hrolf's best men
Clan of the Horse death comes again
Clan of the Horse Hrolf's best men
Clan of the Horse death comes again

It helped us to march. I was protected by Robert and Leif. They were just behind me. The wedge to my right was led by Harold Mighty Fist and the one to my left by Sámr Oakheart. Bjorn was further right. The charging men of Lorraine could not stop. They careered into our line. I swung my sword and hacked through three spears and the belly of one man. Leif and Robert speared the other two and my sword swung again. More men were struck. My sword broke limbs as well as opening flesh and severing mail. The chant helped my rhythm. A Neustrian horn sounded and the survivors of their impromptu attack fell back. In the time it took to recall them a hundred men had fallen. It was not just our swords and spears which had harvested bodies, our archers and slingers had sent missiles over our heads. The enemy leaders should have pulled them back beyond the front line. Men who have been broken do not fight well. Instead, they tried to force them to turn and face us again. I saw their lords beating men into line. Their fear spread amongst the men who had yet to fight. The enemy line was falling back up the hill for we were steadily advancing. We were not moving quickly but steadily and inexorably. I watched them move back to another of the ancient grass-covered ramparts. We had gained a hundred paces of their defences. That was more than I had expected. We had two hundred paces now between us and an enemy

King Charles' horn sounded. The main part of King Charles' army was beginning its attack. We kept marching up the hill. We had the rhythm and we were able to stop singing. Instead, the men beat their shields with the shafts of their spears. The sound seemed to roll around the hillside and echo. It intimidated those we faced. The men of Burgundy and Lorraine had rarely faced Vikings. They had heard of us. The thought of berserkers filled them with fear. It had been many years since I had witnessed it but the idea of it was terrifying. Add to that the sight of an ancient giant who seemed immortal and the number of men who began to flee was understandable. We kept moving up the hill. Their crossbows were now behind their shields and they could not send their bolts at us. The ramparts and ditches had not been sharpened. They had not seeded them. Over the years they had become less of a defensive feature and they caused us little trouble We had more trouble negotiating the dead bodies.

We had our own battle to fight. The King and his men had the easier task and Bagsecg and his men were off chasing horsemen. We would fight any who were before us and try to get as far up the hill as we could.

I had no doubt that we would be stopped at some point. I risked glancing down the line. We still had all the wedges largely intact. I knew that some of those in the front rank would have fallen but their places would have been taken by others. Ahead of us, I saw that the men of Neustria were reforming their line. The fleeing men had taken others with them. Robert of Neustria was taking no chances. He was filling his front rank with mailed men. He was using his lords. He was gambling that his lords were better than the barbarian warriors who marched towards him. We would soon discover the truth of that. King Robert faced Harold Mighty Fist and his wedge. I know not if the King had chosen to move when he saw he faced me but my wedge was heading towards a Burgundian lord and his bodyguards. They held swords. They were long swords but not as long as the one I wielded. Arrows and stones flew from behind me. My men sent their missiles far enough ahead to miss us. They had the effect of making the enemy look to their defence rather than adding their weight to the line.

We had climbed a long way and our legs were tiring. My arms were not yet weary and I raised my sword above me. I brought it back until it touched the helmet of Hugo the son of the Corn Chandler. I let it rest there as we plodded the last few steps to the waiting Burgundians. I heard cries and the clash of steel as the rest of our line struck theirs. I think the Burgundians must have taken a step back. I brought my sword over my head from behind me. The advantage of such a stroke is that the warrior receiving the blow knows not where it will land. It could split his skull, hit his sword arm or his shield arm. As the Burgundian shield came up to his left, I switched my strike to his right. He made a belated attempt to block it with his sword but failed. My sword drove his mail links into his shoulder. The blade continued down, severing his arm. The men at his side tried to stab me with their own weapons. Their swords did not reach me for Leif and Robert thrust their spears into them and we had broken their front rank.

There were more ranks for us to deal with but the fact that they had put their best warriors in the front rank meant that the next ones we faced had weaker armour. As our wedge punched the hole deep into their line the bulk of my bodyguards laid about them and they carved a bloody line through the Burgundians. I heard a cheer from the side. The Neustrians had had a victory. It did not matter. We were winning this part of the battle. That was all a warrior could do. If we had lost the rest of the battle then, eventually we would be surrounded and slain but at that moment, with the top of the hill less than one hundred paces from us, the Normans were winning and that was all that counted.

They thrust their spears at me but I swung my sword and it splintered the shafts. The three men whose spears had just disappeared looked at me in horror. I reversed my swing and this time it was not wood I hewed but flesh. One had his arm half severed. Another had his guts laid open and the last his face torn open. As Leif and Robert stepped forward two of them perished and the third ran. Their only chance was to stop me but I was bigger than any other warrior and I was well mailed. My wedge and I were through two of the lines and the third awaited us. I saw that some of these were Franks. They wore leather mail and had oval shields. Again, three of them stabbed at me. I hit two of the spears but the third gouged a line across my cheek. As his bloody spear came away, he cheered. My sword ended the cheer when it bit into his neck. The blood spatter showered the other two and they ran.

Leif shouted, "Harold Mighty Fist has fallen. Robert of Neustria has slain him. There was nothing between us and the rear of the enemy line but I was honour bound to turn to my right. Harold Mighty Fist had been one of my lords. I shouted, "Sámr, continue the attack. I go to Harold Mighty Fist!"

"Do not worry, lord. I am getting into my rhythm."

As we swung to face the Neustrians, our wedge disintegrated. It had done its job. The bodyguards of Robert of Neustria swung around to face our threat. The years of training had paid off for even as I raised my sword for a scything swing both Robert and Leif had blocked the sword blows from Neustrian warriors and hacked, as Egil had taught them, across the unprotected thighs of these elite warriors. Their swords were well made and blood spurted. I brought my sword around. My height meant my normal swing was from on high down to low. Men expected a more horizontal strike from their enemies and their shields were, usually, slow to rise. The Neustrian lord I attacked was one such warrior. His shield barely rose as my sword chopped into his arm. Some of the men I led bore axes and they wreaked a terrible toll for they struck shields which were not as well made as ours. They shattered shields and broke limbs. I heard orders shouted as we carved our way through to Robert of Neustria.

Against the odds, we were winning. I did not know the price we had paid but we had almost captured the man who would take King Charles' throne. Then I heard a shout from ahead. It was the voice of Bjorn the

Brave, "Our horsemen come!" Then I thought the battle almost won. I heard the Norns spinning and I knew that I had to end this by taking or killing Robert of Neustria.

"Reform!"

If Bagsecg and his men were coming then they would be arriving from behind the Neustrians. We had to stop Robert of Neustria and his men from joining up with those fighting King Charles. We were a thin line between them. My depleted hearth weru formed up next to me. This sometimes happened in the most chaotic battle. Men stopped. They breathed and they sought new enemies. I spied Robert of Neustria. He wore a high domed helmet with a nasal. He had good mail and a long oval shield. His sword was a good one but not as long as mine. As I raised Long Sword, I saw the bloodied and hacked body of Harold Mighty Fist. He and his hearth weru had had a good death. I saw his sons, who had hurled stones in the battle of Paris, lying close by. They had died with their father. I felt strength rush into my tired arms. I owed it to the dead to end this well.

"Charge!"

I gave the order knowing that I led young warriors with quick reactions. My enemies did not expect an old man to move as quickly as I did. My long legs might have been ancient but they could still eat up the ground and they did. Even as the Neustrians tried to form another shield wall my sword swept across the thighs of the men before me. I killed none with the blow but three men had wounds which would result in their deaths. Leif, Robert and the rest of my young warriors tore into the men I had wounded and I shouldered the wounded men aside as I raced to face Robert of Neustria. The two of us found ourselves in a space vacated by men who had raced to fight my hearth weru and littered with the dead slain by my archers. His father had been my enemy and while I had never fought the man, we had been enemies for many years. He had killed my men and he did not fear me. He hefted his shield and stepped towards me. I did the unexpected. Raising my sword, I pivoted to swing around. My sword swung at shoulder height. The blade gathered momentum as I swung. If he had had quicker reactions, he could have tried to stab me in the back as I swung but my movement was unexpected. As it came around, I struck his shield. Few men could have withstood such a blow. The shield cracked, as did his arm and he tumbled backwards. He fell over the body of Harold Mighty Fist.

There are times for sword skills that impress other warriors and there are times for killing. This was a time for killing. As he lay, I swung my sword. The blade came down towards his prostrate body. He managed to bring his shattered shield across to protect himself. The blade smashed the already damaged shield in two. He cried out as the sword broke his arm and some of his ribs. He did not want to die and, as I raised my sword to end it, he rolled and tried to rise. His left arm hung uselessly by his side and I saw blood trickling from his mouth. His sword was still in his hand. I began my swing.

Raising his sword, he said, "You may have killed me, barbarian, but you have lost the war!"

My swing was begun and I took his head. Long Sword hacked through mail, flesh, muscle, ligament and bone. It severed the leather strap on his helmet and his helmet flew from his head. I reached down and picked up the head by the hair. I held it aloft and shouted, "Clan of the Horse!" There was a moment when all fighting stopped. The Neustrians and Franks who remained stared in horror at the head of their King. They had lost. The King was dead. The remaining warriors fled towards the north and east. We had won!

The words were hardly out of my mouth when Bagsecg led my horsemen towards me. I turned so that all could see that we had won. When I faced north, I saw that Robert of Neustria had not lied. Below me, I saw that the standards of Count Fulbert and King Charles were gone. The army was fleeing north. He was right. We had lost the battle. The enemy held the ground to the north and they outnumbered us. My victory was in vain, Harold Mighty Fist need not have died! There would be time for debate later. We were many miles from our home. I had to keep as many of our men alive as I could.

"Robert, have the horn sound fall back!"

Even as the notes echoed out, I knew that we could not take Harold Mighty Fist and the rest of the dead home. Their bodies would be despoiled and their weapons were taken. It could not be helped. They were in the Otherworld now and I hoped they would understand.

Bagsecg, his sword bloody, galloped up to me. I saw his two brothers lived too. He shook his head, "They knew what we intended, lord. As we chased their men from the field, we saw that there were another three thousand men hidden behind the hill. They attacked the King."

"Did he fall?"

"I know not. We disengaged and came to your aid."

He had made the correct decision. The King had lost but we had a chance to survive. I could still think and plan, "We head to Compiègne. We are too far from home to make the journey in one march. We rest and I can plan a way to get us home. I would have you cover our retreat. Have your brother Erik secure the town of Compiègne for us. They will not know the result of the battle yet." He nodded. "Do not waste your lives. If we reach Compiègne then you have done all that you could."

He grinned, "Do not worry, lord, I have just seen the mightiest warrior of this age fight as though he was a stripling boy. We can still do as you bid." He turned, "Horsemen of the Duke. Reform!"

The hill would help us. We could head down and away from the victorious armies of our enemies. The victors would still be stripping the bodies of valuables and celebrating the victory. Those who had fought with King Robert would be running until it was dark. Bagsecg and his men could sweep down and discourage pursuit. As I turned to watch my men begin to stream down the hill, I spied Bjorn and Sámr. They came towards me. Both walked although I saw that their swords were notched; their shields and mail were covered in blood.

"We head for Compiègne. It is a hard march but Bagsecg can watch our back."

"They died for nothing." Bjorn was looking at the bodies of Harold and his sons.

"They did not. They died with honour. This is not ended. I am no longer bound by an oath. King Charles is king no longer. We are unfettered. We can raid and begin to eat our way into the lands of the Franks. We can encourage more Vikings to come and help us raid. The Norns were spinning, Bjorn. We have not yet finished doing that which my grandfather began. Now let us march with order. We are Normans and not a rabble of Franks!"

We had twenty miles to go. For any other warriors who had just fought as we had then it would be almost impossible but we were different. With the wounded in the centre and our archers guarding our flanks we marched. We slung our shields upon our backs and we sheathed our swords. Those we had left on the battlefield would take some time to organize. We had to put as much daylight between us as we could.

Sámr Oakheart marched next to me, "I noticed that the wood of Compiègne is just twelve miles away. We could leave our archers there to discourage the enemy."

"If we reach the woods without being attacked then we will be safe. Our biggest advantage is that they are leaderless. The Duke of Burgundy was on the hill with Robert of Neustria. He is the heir. He fled. It is the men of Soissons I fear. Their Count knows this land. He was not on the hill. If he has horsemen then they might follow and attack us."

We walked in silence for a few miles. All of us were desperately thirsty and hungry. A battle dries the mouth. Retreat saps energy. Sámr said, "It was a great victory."

I shook my head, "If this was a victory then we would be on top of the hill stripping the dead of their mail and drinking their wine. We left the field with honour but it was not a victory. Look at our men."

He looked around and saw men with heads hung. He smiled, "Then let us raise their heads!" He began to sing.

Ragnvald Ragnvaldson was cursed from his birth
Through his dark life he was a curse to the earth
A brother nearly drowned and father stabbed
The fortunes of the clan ever ebbed
The Norns they wove and Hrólfr lived
From the dark waters he survived.
Göngu-Hrólfr Rognvaldson he became
A giant of a man with a mighty name
Göngu-Hrólfr Rognvaldson with the Longsword
Göngu-Hrólfr Rognvaldson with his Longsword
When the brothers met by Rouen's walls
Warriors emptied from warrior halls
Then Ragnvald Ragnvaldson became the snake
Letting others' shields the chances take
Arne the Breton Slayer used a knife in the back
Longsword he beat that treacherous attack
When the snake it tired and dropped its guard
Then Longsword struck swift and hard
Göngu-Hrólfr Rognvaldson with the Longsword
Göngu-Hrólfr Rognvaldson with his Longsword
And with that sword he took the hand
That killed his father and his land
With no sword the snake was doomed
To rot with Hel in darkness entombed
When the head was struck and the brother died
The battle ended and the clan all cried

Göngu-Hrólfr Rognvaldson with the Longsword
Göngu-Hrólfr Rognvaldson with his Longsword
Göngu-Hrólfr Rognvaldson with the Longsword
Göngu-Hrólfr Rognvaldson with his Longsword

Sámr was right to sing for every head was raised and smiles appeared. The words fed them. They were like a refreshing horn of ale on a hot day! It made us as one, once more. The battle of Soissons would become a song we would sing in the future but for now, we would sing of the day my brother died and we began to become Normans.

It was dark when we reached Compiègne. I saw that some of those in the town had tried to prevent my horsemen from holding it. They now lay dead. Erik Leifsson said, "I am sorry lord, some escaped west. We did not have enough men to hold both gates."

I put my hand on his shoulder, "You did what I asked. Now we hold here!"

In fact, more than half of the town had fled. The lords and merchants had taken the few horses they had and left. The ones who remained were the ones who could not flee. Bagsecg and his men arrived. Their horses and they were weary. We set guards on the gates and we ate. It was a sombre feast. Four hundred and more of my men had perished. I could not remember a day since Paris when we had lost so many men. Yet I survived. My work was not yet done. What else remained for me to do?

I rose early and I went to find Bagsecg. We went to the stables. The horses had had grain and water. "Are there any which can be ridden this day?"

"How far?"

"Come, let us find Sámr." I led him from the stable to the walls. Sámr was on duty and we peered into the lightening sky to the east. "We were lucky, yesterday. Today we cannot rely on luck. They will organize and they will follow us. I am counting on the fact that they will need food. We have it here already. We can recover but, eventually, we will need to march home and they will attack us on the road. They see a wounded beast and they will be like carrion. They will pick us off until it is a skeleton which crawls into Rouen." Their faces told me that it was true. "What I propose is to send a couple of riders. We left half of our men at home. We have half of that half march towards us. We do not follow the road we took here. They will be expecting us and the men who fled will have barred Bieuvais. We head to the Seine which is just thirty miles from Bjorn's land. I would have drekar meet us at the river and the rest of Bjorn's men."

Sámr said, "Will Bjorn be happy about risking his family?"

"I hope so. Bagsecg, choose your best horses and men. It will take them a day to reach our nearest fief. There they will be able to take horses. We wait here for three days. I want us and our horses rested."

"You risk us becoming besieged." He was not complaining. He was stating a fact.

I nodded, "I am gambling but I believe that the Norns have spun. Had they wanted me dead I would lie on that hill with Harold Mighty Fist."

Bagsecg nodded, "I will send Erik and Gilles. They are the best, save me, and they know horses." He gave me a wan smile. And if the Duke is wrong and we do die here, at least the blood of my grandfather will not be lost."

The two of them headed out before dawn. They took four men with them and two spare horses. They were well-armed and Erik was confident they could steal or take more horses and reach the river quicker than we expected. We prepared for war. It was a gamble but I had seen nothing on the battlefield which frightened me. We had better horsemen, better mail and better weapons. My army also had something else which marked them as different, Robert Duke of Normandy!

Chapter 13

The enemy did not reach us until the late afternoon. I think they expected us to be long gone. They approached the gates bareheaded. It was the sign they wished to speak. I recognised the leader. It was Count Rudolf of Burgundy. "King Charles has been deposed. He is on his way to his prison already. I am the newly elected King of Western Franks. I demand that you open the gates and surrender."

If he had been elected then it was only by those who had fought alongside him. There were many other lords who would have a say in the matter and they might choose Rudolf or they might choose another. This was a bluff to make us surrender. I had no intention of doing so. I waited and then, putting my hands on my hips, began to laugh, "Why? We defeated your father in law yesterday. His head and body lie on the battlefield. We were weary after hewing so many heads and decided to stay here. We have good walls and we have plenty of food."

"You owe me allegiance for I am your liege lord."

"Have you been crowned? I think not. Have I said I will bow the knee to a Burgundian pup? No. I swore an oath to King Charles. I kept that oath. If you wish me to open the gates bring King Charles here and I will open them to the King. I will not open them to you."

"We outnumber you!"

"Yesterday you outnumbered us and we still won! This time you do not fight Magyars! You fight Normans. Now is there more or can I go and eat? I am hungry!"

I did not wait for a response, I strode away. King Charles had given me the title of Duke of Normandy. Rudolf and the others knew it but they would never accord me the title. Robert and Leif followed me, "Lord," asked Robert, "what will they do?"

"I know not but it makes no difference to us what they do. They can attack us; they can besiege us or they can leave. We have to wait until our ships reach the Seine. We eat, we rest and we recover. When the time is right, we fight our way out if we have to. Do not forget, Robert, that they fought a battle too. We lost many men but they lost all of their horses, many of their best warriors and they lost their leader. Rudolf says he is King of the West but I planted a seed of doubt in his mind. He has not been anointed." I pointed to the church we were passing, "He could have been anointed here if there was an archbishop, the holy oil and if we were not sitting here. He will have to go to Paris. He has been elected by those he fought alongside. What about those who did not fight? What about those in Paris? Is there another who could steal the crown from under his nose? We stick to my plan." I smiled, "Do you now regret following my banner?"

They both laughed and shook their heads.

We not only ate and rested, but we also looted. The lords who had fled had been too concerned with their lives. They had taken most of their treasure but left enough for all of my men to profit. My men slaughtered all of the animals which remained within the walls and we salted them. They would feed us on the road. We would have no time to forage. The enemy thought we were beaten. They did not attack and kept but a loose watch around the walls. There were no siege lines. When, a day after our meeting, the standard of Burgundy left I knew that Rudolf had headed south to Paris. He would be crowned and secure the throne.

After three days I felt confident enough to suggest that we leave. I gathered my leaders. We would march together but in warbands. If we were attacked, and I fully expected at least one attack, then we would be able to defend ourselves more easily. Bagsecg and his men, now on grain-fed and rested horses, would be our screen. They would give us a warning of an attack. We had forty-eight miles to go and I planned on doing that in one march. We would take rests but we would not camp and we would not sleep. Even if my fleet did not reach us, I would be happier fighting with a river at my back. Each warband would carry its own food and drink. We would be self-sufficient. Sámr would lead the army, or what remained of it. Bjorn the Brave would be the rearguard. Bagsecg divided his horsemen into four and they boxed us in. We left an hour before dawn. We gave no warning.

Sámr's men slipped out in the dark and their knives ended the lives of the watchers to the west. The attack yielded us six horses which we gratefully took. Bagsecg's men, a quarter of them, left first and they walked their horses down the road. The last to leave would be the rest of the horsemen. I had contemplated firing the town but realised that would just alert the enemy and yield us nothing.

By the time dawn broke, we were five miles down the road. I had the largest warband. There were sixty men with me, fifteen of them were hearth weru. My horsemen were now with Bagsecg. At noon one of Bagsecg's men rode up to report that the rearguard had ambushed the pursuing men of Soissons. They knew we had escaped them and now they would hunt us. Our horsemen walked as much as they rode. We had to conserve the horses for the long journey home. As I walked Blue, I began to feel light-headed. I put it down to the excitement of escape. The Norns were spinning.

It was in the evening when the illness which would plague me for my remaining time in this world, struck. I felt dizzy and I thought it was a lack of food. I called a halt. I put my hand on my water bottle. My fingers would not grip. I felt the same as I had when I had sunk beneath the waves off the coast of Cent. It was as though my body was no longer mine. As I bent, I felt a flash in my head. It seemed that the side of my head was burning and I could hear nothing. I tried to grip my fingers but they would not obey me. I raised my head which felt as though it belonged to another. I saw faces looking at me. I did not know any of them. Had I been taken to another world? What was happening? I tried to speak but no words would form. Had aelfes taken me? Had I slipped into the spirit world? They spoke to me but I heard no words. I closed my eyes. I was Göngu-Hrólfr Rognvaldson! I was the Duke of Normandy. In my head, I could hear my voice. "Grandfather, help me! I know not what this is. How can I fight it?" When I opened them, I saw that my men had returned. I saw Sámr Oakheart, Bjorn the Brave, Robert, Leif, all of them. I smiled. It was in relief.

Sámr and Bjorn ran to my side. "Robert get your lord some ale. Lord, sit."

"I am fine Sámr. I was just a little dizzy."

Bjorn shook his head, "You could not hear our words. The side of your face looked like it had slipped. You frightened us. We have marched too far. We will camp here for the night."

Robert had brought ale. I drank half of the skin. I saw a piece of bread in Leif's hand. I gestured for it. I ate. As soon as the bread went down my throat I felt better. I heard Bagsecg say, "I will send to our men and have them meet us this side of the river!"

"No!" My voice was louder than I had intended.

"But lord, you are unwell."

"I have no wound and I am still Duke. You follow my orders. We have almost reached the river. A night march will bring us close enough to smell the water. My son needs the men who follow us. It matters not if I die. Normandy is all!" My face dared them to argue. I softened my voice. I had been frightened and they were terrified. "You have all trusted me and followed me for many years. Continue to do so." They were unhappy about it but they obeyed my orders. When we left to continue our march, I noticed that they were all so close to me that, had I had another incident I would not have been able to fall.

We were just four miles from the river when trouble found us. All were exhausted but I had been right. We could smell the river. It was the third hour of the day and we had walked further than any warband I could remember. I was proud of them. We were, however, caught. We were trapped by our enemies. Bagsecg's men reported two armies. One was marching west, along the river from Paris, and the other was following us down the road. Bagsecg said, "Lord, we will charge them and buy us time. You might reach the river."

I think they thought I was having another attack for I did not answer. My mind was working.

"Lord? Are you well?"

"Yes, Sámr. Have our ten best axemen hew down the biggest trees and block the road. Bagsecg, send your men to the river. Find our ships. I want every archer to run to the river! They are to prepare defences. We will also run."

"Lord, you are unwell! You cannot run!"

"No Bjorn! I am not. Obey me!" The horsemen and the archers took off and disappeared down the road. I pointed south. "I will stay here with my bodyguard and the axemen. Sámr, take the rest. You are all faster than I am. Prepare defences. If we are to die let us make them bleed." I was not yet ready to die. The attack in the night had merely made me realise that I had little time left in this world. If I was marked for death I would not go meekly. I would fight death as I had fought my enemies. As they left, albeit reluctantly, I pointed to the trees, "Go, Robert, take our men. Help the axemen. They can go through the woods but they will be slowed up. Use anything as a barrier." I smiled at him, "This rest will do me good!"

My men worked frantically and soon the first tree came down. When it did it accelerated the fall of the others for there were more axemen now chopping fewer tees. Robert and my men were helping by jamming fallen branches between them when the six enemy scouts rode down the road. My young warriors were on the other side of the barrier. This would be the first time they had fought when I was not there to command them. I was proud of them. Rather than allowing the scouts to run off the fifteen of them charged the six scouts. It took the Franks by surprise. Five were hacked from their horses but the sixth turned and started to gallop off. Leif took a Frankish sword and threw it, like a throwing knife. The Norns spun or the gods guided his hand, I know not which but the sword struck him in the back. They grabbed the reins of the horses and led them through the woods. I shouted, "Leave the trees. That will have to do. It will slow them down. Now we run."

Robert ran to me leading two horses. They were small. "And you ride lord!"

"My feet will dangle and the horse will not last long!"

"Lord, do not argue. Mount. Let us worry about the horses."

When I sat on the back of the horse my feet reached the ground. I lifted them behind me and Robert slapped the horse. It could not gallop but it moved as fast as the young warriors who ran next to us leading the other five horses in case I needed them. It was an undignified way to ride but I had to confess that had I tried to run then we would have been caught. The horse collapsed just half a mile from where I saw the shields of my men. I ran the last half mile.

Sámr smiled, as they parted to let me through. There was a double line of men and, behind them were archers. There was a beach just fifty paces from us. If our ships arrived, we could board them easily. "That was a sight to behold, lord."

I grunted, "And the drekar?"

"No sign of them yet, Duke The scouts say Rudolf leads the men from Paris. They are a mile away. Bjorn the Brave and his war band wait with archers. Bagsecg has secreted his men in the woods. They cannot use their horses to attack but the warriors can attack on foot."

Was it going to end here on the river I had raided for so many years before I was given Normandy? Despite the attack in the night, I did not believe so. I donned my helmet and drew Long Sword. When we had been in Compiegne, I had had it sharpened. I was ready to sell my failing body dearly. I heard the battle to my right. I could see nothing for Sámr had chosen a place we could defend using the trees and the undergrowth. What had happened to our drekar? Since we had been away had someone taken advantage and attacked us? I had a sudden sickening thought that this was the opportunity Count Arnulf might have been waiting for. Then I was forced to stop my worrying. I heard hooves as the men of Neustria came galloping down the road.

Sámr took command, "Archers wait on my command." We had taken spears from Compiegne and they formed a hedgehog barrier. The riders reined in. Sámr waited until there were forty horsemen milling just a hundred and fifty paces from us. Their hesitation cost them dearly. Thirty arrows descended and then another thirty. By the time ninety arrows had been loosed, there were twenty-two empty saddles and the survivors rode north. The next time they came they would be prepared. They would march behind shields. They would have crossbows ready to send their bolts into my weary warriors. That was time for my ships to reach me.

One of Bjorn the Brave's sons ran up, "Lord, my father says they have increasing numbers."

I nodded, "Galmr, take your warband and aid Bjorn. If you have to then fall back to us. If we are marked to die this day, we will do it together."

William and Berenger Bjornson grinned. William said, "Not this day lord! We did not run this far to be butchered by Franks!"

I heard horns from ahead. Sámr began to reorganise the lines of men. A wall of shields appeared. They were Swabians. These were swordsmen and they were good. This time the arrows would have little effect. The Swabians were mailed and they had good helmets and shields. I shouted, "Save your arrows for flesh."

The small saplings which had been cut down and laid across the road were not there as a barrier, they were there as a trap. Sámr knew the difficulties of keeping a straight line while walking on logs. A man could slip or trip and bring down men who relied on a solid line to make their attack. I held my sword above my head. The spears of my men would distract the Swabians from the logs. As soon as they came in range I roared, "Clan of the Horse!" and I swung my sword. A line of thirty spears jabbed out and there were cries from our left as Bagsecg led his men to the attack. I was lucky, the Swabian whom I struck had just slipped. He had his arms spread as he tried to regain his balance. Long Sword tore through his mail and ripped open his chest. Our spears found faces and gaps. Blades and spears plunged through mail into flesh. Axes hewed men as easily as trees. Bagsecg's men achieved complete surprise. They fell like demons on the flanks of our enemies and the attack faltered. Inevitably, Bagsecg's men were forced back but we had blunted their attack.

"Bagsecg, fall back! You have done all that you needed to."

The enemy reformed. Sámr shook his head, "That trick will not work a second time."

I stuck my sword in the soft soil. "Then we will find another. Have the wounded taken to the beach."

John the son of the Miller had a badly cut arm. He shook his head, "I can still fight lord."

"Aye, and you can still obey orders. Have your wounds tended and if we need you, we will send for you."

As he was taken away Sámr said, "We have bred a new type of warrior lord. The jarl in our fjord would not recognise these young men who wear no beards and speak so strangely."

I laughed, "Aye, Sámr, we are the relics of the past. We have passed on what we know about war and this is good. Your sons are the same. We have done our job. Now it is time for our sons to take over."

"I know."

"They come again!"

I drew my sword from the soil and stood to face the next wave of attackers. I saw that this time, they were using the woods on the sides as cover and to spread their attack. They were no longer using the road. They would not risk an attack by Bagsecg and his men. I was glad I had withdrawn them. Of course, it meant that we would be attacked from the side as well as from the north. This time they ran and held their shields above them. They were watching their footing. Some of our spears had been shattered and the enemy would get closer to us this time. It could not be helped. These were a mixture of warriors. There were a handful of Swabians wielding their swords and there were the men of Lorraine and Burgundians too. Each followed their own lord. These men had volunteered. With a new king on the throne, a heroic gesture and the head of the Count of Normandy could go a long way to securing an important fief.

I still knew how to time my swing and I began swinging when the enemy warriors were three paces from us. This might be my last fight and there was no point in holding back. I put every ounce of strength into the swing. The blow went from high to low. My sword hit one man in the neck and, as the swing continued, hit the jaw of the man behind. He just walked into Long Sword and the sword sliced through his mouth. His hands dropped his weapon as he put them to his slashed face and Robert rammed his spear into his chest. I reversed my swing and brought my sword up. It hacked through the arm of a man holding a pole weapon. Leif had an easy kill for the man was now weaponless. In the centre, we were winning. On the flanks, I heard closer fought combat as my less experienced warriors engaged our enemies. The sounds of fighting to our right grew louder as William, Berenger and Bjorn were forced back. It was a measured retreat. It was not like the battle of Soissons where the Neustrians had dropped weapons and fled.

Sámr shouted, "We need to fall back, lord."

He was right and I gave the command, "Step back!" The command was understood by all. We all stepped back on our right legs. None fell and when the enemy rushed at us, they slipped, tripped and sprawled on their own dead. I used my sword to stab down, through the helmet and into the skull of a prostrate Swabian and then, withdrawing Long Sword, stepped back. We moved back ten paces and lost not a man! There were now many wounded on the beach. Petr, who was my best archer, shouted, "Lord, we are running out of arrows."

"Then take the weapons from the dead and join the shield wall. We are Normans and we do not surrender."

Sámr turned and held out his arm, "It has been an honour to follow you, Göngu-Hrólfr Rognvaldson. We will meet again in Valhalla!"

I clasped his arm but shook my head, "Do not be in a hurry to get there, Sámr Oakheart. They have lost more men than we have. While we live then there is hope."

Mauger laughed, "Aye lord, I have much still to do in Djupr. This little war has been an inconvenience. Let us send them back to Neustria and we can make our strongholds stronger!" With men like that fighting behind me, we could not lose.

Ahead of us horns sounded and the enemy rushed towards us. I raised my sword. My shoulders ached. I was feeling my age. Robert and Leif still stood close by me. If I lived, I would make them lords. They deserved nothing less. Then I heard a sound in the distance that filled me with hope. I heard a cheer from downriver. That was Bagsecg. Then I heard a murmur which grew to a chant.

> *Skuld the Dark sails on shadows wings*
> *Skuld the Dark is a ship that sings*
> *With soft, gentle voice of a powerful witch*
> *Her keel will glide through Frankia's ditch*

With flowing hair and fiery breath
Skuld the Dark will bring forth death
Though small in size her heart is great
The Norn who decides on man's final fate
Skuld the Dark sails on shadows wings
Skuld the Dark is a sorcerous ship that sweetly sings
Skuld the Dark sails on shadows wings
Skuld the Dark is a sorcerous ship that sweetly sings
Skuld the Dark sails on shadows wings
Skuld the Dark is a sorcerous ship that sweetly sings
The witch's reach is long and her eyes can see through mist
Her teeth are sharp and grind your bones to grist
With soft, gentle voice of a powerful witch
Her keel will glide through Frankia's ditch
With flowing hair and fiery breath
Skuld the Dark will bring forth death
Though small in size her heart is great
The Norn who decides on man's final fate
Skuld the Dark sails on shadows wings
Skuld the Dark is a sorcerous ship that sweetly sings
Skuld the Dark sails on shadows wings
Skuld the Dark is a sorcerous ship that sweetly sings
The witch's reach is long and her eyes can see through mist
Her teeth are sharp and grind your bones to grist

It was the sound of men rowing up the river! Erik Leifsson was coming with my drekar. Would he reach us in time? "Our ships are here! We hold on for a short while! Have courage, Clan of the Horse!" My men gave an almighty cheer and then the enemy hit us. I was swinging my sword when they were three paces away. I did not have many swings left in me. My sword still managed to knock one warrior into the path of another and Sámr and Robert skewered the two men. Another tripped over the body of a fallen Burgundian and I laid his back open. My fingers suddenly failed me and I could not grip my sword with two hands. My right hand did not feel like my own. As my sword dropped, I ripped my seax from my scabbard. If I had to fight one handed then I would so. Suddenly arrows flew from behind us and began to descend into the enemy. One lunged at me. His sword struck my mail. I could not move my right side and I felt the sword slice into my flesh. I had strength in my left hand and I ripped my seax across his throat and then I felt my face burning again. All sound disappeared. I opened my mouth to scream but no sound came out. I was dying, I was going to Valhalla and I gripped my seax with all the strength I had left. My right leg gave way and I felt the weight of my mail pull me to the ground. I could not stop it. It felt like the time I had fallen from the drekar. I was drowning but I was not in the water. I saw faces around me. Robert, Sámr and Bjorn were speaking with me but I heard not a word. I tried to speak but I could not and then I felt blackness begin to creep, slowly across my eyes. All was black.

Chapter 14

I dreamed.

I saw my grandmother. She was with Hrólfr the Horseman. They were both smiling at me. Their faces disappeared and I saw my father. He rose from the sea. His face was covered in blood and he was wounded but he, too, smiled at me. Was this Valhalla? It could not be for my grandmother was a Frank and not a warrior. Perhaps women did go to Valhalla. Warriors would need women. Then I realised that she was not a Viking either. She had been a good woman and she would be in the White Christ's heaven. I saw my grandfather's mouth moving. I could not hear him. I had taken my affliction to the Otherworld. Then I heard his familiar voice. "It is not your time. Wake. It is not your time. You must wake. This is not your time. You must move!"

I tried to stir and then the voice changed and became Sámr's, "He moves! He is waking!"

I opened my eyes and saw I was in my chamber in Rouen. I moved my right hand. The affliction had gone. I could move my limbs. I could hear. I tried to speak, "How long?" I had a voice. Was I healed?

Father Harold came into view and there was another dressed in priestly robes. Father Harold spoke, "Lie still, my lord. You have lain like this for two days. We thought you dead."

The other priest sniffed and said, confidently, "I did not think he was dead!" His hand suddenly descended and he used his finger and thumb to open my eye wide. He peered into it. He seemed satisfied with what he saw and he nodded, "Count Robert."

"Duke." I forced the word through dried and cracked lips.

He sighed, "Titles! Duke Robert, I am Doctor Erasmus. I am Greek. I was on my way back from Jorvik when you were brought in. I think I might have saved your life."

"Then I thank you. What was it that tried to kill me? Was it a wound?"

"The wound in your side is nothing. If you want to know what was trying to kill you it is your body. I have not cured you. One day you will suffer another such attack and it may be fatal." He looked at me, "Your face burned? You could not move? You could neither hear nor speak?"

"Aye, how did you know? Are you a galdramenn?"

He looked at Father Harold who smiled, "A witch."

He snorted, "I am a man of science. I have seen your condition in others. There is no cure. You will have more such attacks until you have one which will end your life. You need more rest than I think you have been taking. You cannot go to war again. Your men say that you have seen more than seventy summers?"

"I believe so."

"Then God has granted you extra years. Use them to enjoy life. You are a rich man. Live like one." He stood. "And now I must board the ship."

"Have you been paid?"

He nodded, "Of course! A king's ransom." He smiled, "I am worth it!"

With that, he left. I liked him. He was arrogant but he was honest and seemed to know his business. He had known what only I truly knew. I was dying. I suppose I had known it. I would not live the life of a rich man. I was still Duke of Normandy and I had a Dukedom to rule. I sat up. "So, Sámr, what happened after I fell?"

"With the crews of the drekar, we drove the enemy from the field. We made a longphort and Bagsecg and his horsemen drove their captured horses across the river. We took the treasure and the mail from the dead and we returned here."

"And why do you remain? Caen needs you."

He shook his head, "My oldest friend almost died. The doctor is right. There are more important things in this life than war. I will hand Caen over to my son. He is ready for power. He will rule well and if he will not then you and I will be dead soon enough. We have done all that we should have done. Our time has gone and the world we made will be shaped by those we fathered. I will ride home and then return in a month. That will give you the time to rest." He turned to Father Harold. "Until his son returns, I empower you, Father Harold, to restrict what the Duke does."

I saw that Father Harold did not relish the responsibility of trying to make me behave but he nodded. When Sámr had gone I turned to Father

Harold. "I have had a warning, and I will not be a burden. I do need to see Robert and Leif."

"Of course, lord. They have been camped outside your chamber since you returned."

When they came in, I saw the look of apprehension on their faces. Robert forced a smile, "You live!"

"Aye, and I thank you for what you did on the campaign. How many of our men remain?"

Leif pointed to Robert, "Just us two, lord. The rest died well."

I shook my head, "And they should not have died! We needed young men like that to rule this land. I am now disbanding the hearth weru. I go to war no longer."

The look on their faces was pitiful, "You rid yourself of us, lord?"

I smiled, "No, Robert, I promote you. Harold Mighty Fist and his sons died. You shall have his fief, Robert, and you Leif will be the commander of Rouen. Your father, like me, needs to take life easier now. Well, what say you?"

"Duke!" Leif dropped to his knees and took my hand in his. "It is an honour. How can we thank you?"

"By doing what you have these last few years. Instead of looking after a cantankerous old man, look after Normandy."

When they had left me, I asked, "And has there been any word from my son?"

"Rumours only, lord. There have been battles. He has not requested more men and I can only assume that he has been successful. Doctor Erasmus told me about this illness, lord. It is fatal. You could die tomorrow."

"Or I could live another ten years?"

"That is so."

"Then I must live my life. I will not put men in danger because of my illness. I will not go to war. If an enemy comes to Rouen then I will die with a sword in my hand but I will, in the fullness of time, make my son Duke of Normandy."

"Lord, you are Count."

I smiled, "Before the battle, King Charles gave me and my son the title in perpetuity. He did not write it down but there are others who know I was given the title. We will use it. The days of bowing the knee to Paris are gone, Father Harold. If young Louis attains the throne then it may well be that Normandy acknowledges him as liege lord but he is a child and in England. The next few years will see how my son can rule. I will watch. I will advise. My days as a warlord are over."

He left me. The admission was as much for me as for him. If this ailment took my power of movement and thought from me then I would risk no man's life. I needed my son and I needed him in Rouen. I had to begin to train him. Each day that was granted to me would be like the first day of my life. I had died once before but I had been young. Now, if I died, there would be no return.

The next day I awoke and almost cheered. Each night, when I went to bed, I would wonder if this was my last day. I took to sleeping with a seax next to me but I could not guarantee that my hand would be on the hilt when I died. I sat and wrote a letter to William. I could write, albeit badly. I did not want to dictate to Father Harold. I wanted my son to know the truth. I wanted him to hear my words as though we were in the same room. It took all day but I was happy with the result. I sealed it and asked Leif to find me a trustworthy rider. I then went to walk my streets. I had neglected this city for so long. I had taken it for granted. Now I looked at it with fresh eyes. My grandfather had dreamed of such a home. For my father, the Haugr was as grand a place as he had ever lived in. Rouen made the Haugr look like a pig sty. I had two Dukedoms and one of the finest cities in the civilised world. I would enjoy it.

Each day I walked a different part and spoke to the people. Oft times it was old warriors but, increasingly, it was with folk I did not know. At first, they were wary for I was their lord and master. They could suffer if they offended me but, I know not why, they warmed to me. Some even looked forward to my peregrinations. They spoke to me of their families and their occupations. They talked to me about their successes and failures. The fact that I was their lord and they were able to speak to me seemed to make them closer to me. Had I missed an opportunity? I had been Lord of Rouen for many years and this was the first time that I had bothered to talk to them. I spoke with the widows of men who had died fighting for me. Many of their husbands had fought alongside me. No one had told me that they had died. They were not lords. They were men who stood in the shield wall. I had been too busy looking outward. It was time to look into my land.

There were changes to me. I no longer wore my mail and Long Sword hung above the fire in the Great Hall. Doctor Erasmus had told Father Harold that I needed to change the way I lived. I had to walk more. That suited me. I walked my town. He told me to eat more fish. That was easy and I would walk, each day, to the fish quay to buy fresh fish. I was told to drink more wine and less ale. That was also a simple change. Less ale meant I did not need to get up so many times during the night. As the months passed, while I waited for word from my son, I began to feel better. I still had occasional spells when my right hand tingled and the side of my head felt as though I had leaned against a chimney but they diminished as time went on.

For the first week, Leif Egilsson had followed me about the town until I had faced him, "Leif, if I need a bodyguard in my own town then all that I have done thus far is a waste and I deserve to be slain. You now guard something greater than this ancient and decrepit body, you guard my town. You worry about the town and I will worry about death."

Sámr had returned and he spent a month with me before he was satisfied enough to return to Caen and his son. "It is good, lord, to hand over to my son. I can look at him and see how he does things differently to me. I may not like the way he does everything but then he is half Norse and half Breton. He is a different beast to me. I grew up in a fjord in Norway. We eked out a living and lived in wooden houses. I think I would have died there some time ago had you not been fished from the water and brought, by Sven Blue Cheek, to change our lives forever. I often think about those we left there. Your descent to the depths changed our world." He had left but promised to return regularly. Like me, he was now enjoying a simpler life. He appreciated taking the time to talk to people and to look at simple things like sunsets.

I also made changes to my home. I had lived, largely, alone and in a world of men. When Sámr and his wife, Birgitta, had visited, she had told me how austere it was. I had rooms built to accommodate guests. I had women from the town make tapestries to hang on the walls and I made the new rooms homely.

Almost half a year had passed by the time William returned. He came with his wife and daughters. He now had four. I had not seen him for so long that he was almost a stranger to me. Bergil and Bjorn the Brave also accompanied him although they were without their wives. I greeted them in my Great Hall. The three men stared at me and examined me closely. They knew of my ailment. I knew that they were looking for an outward sign of the disease people called Duke's Bane.

I first greeted my granddaughters. I barely knew them. "I am your grandfather. Do not be put off by my fierce face and the fact that I am a giant. I am a friendly giant and I hope, if your father stays here a while, that we can get to know each other. I should dearly like that." It was too early to expect smiles and I saw apprehension. It would be a challenge. This would be a different battle but I would win it. I did not have years stretching out before me and I wanted the girls to remember me. The eldest, Mathilde, was the one who met my stare. She did not smile but looked at me as though she was studying me. "Father Harold will take you to your quarters. I hope you like them, Sprota. If you do not then I beg you to tell me. I will make them the way that you wish."

The old Duke must have terrified my son's wife for the words of the reborn Duke made tears spring into her eyes and she rushed to me to hug me. Her head barely reached my chest, "They say you are so fierce and I confess I was afeard to come here. You are now the gentlest of men. We will stay as long as you need, Duke Robert."

"No titles here Sprota. The only title I wish to be accorded is, grandfather."

When Sprota and the girls had gone I sent for wine. I knew the three men wished to know about me but I needed news from the south. I became businesslike, "So, William, how goes it in the south?"

"You are well?"

"We can come to such insignificant matters later. I will be better when I know of Brittany and the people there."

He sighed and sipped his wine, "I was unhappy that I had to take so many men from you and when we heard of Soissons then I almost broke off my war to return to you."

"It was the Norns, William. We had our victory. The defeat was King Charles'. He chose his leaders badly and he followed their advice. The result is he now languishes in prison."

William nodded, "The Neustrians and their allies had planned well. They thought to draw us off so that the Count of Cornouaille could retake his land. We barely had enough men to hold them but we did. We needed Lord Bagsecg and his horsemen." He smiled. "You needed them more. When time allows, I will speak with Lord Bagsecg. I need horsemen and horses."

"He and his sons will train your men. It worked for me."

"Aye, it did. When we came north, we saw the fiefs with the new lords. Those young men of Rouen are not Vikings but they are Normans! It took some time for us to rid our borders of the threat and then we besieged Andecavis. It was not that we sought more territory but Andecavis guards the entry to Brittany. We captured it and I placed Rolf, son of Gandálfr in command. He is a good warrior and helped us take the town. I have spent the last months scouring the land for rebels. I would have come sooner but Father Harold's letters told us that you were healing."

Bergil nodded, "Aye, lord, now that we have given you our news what of yours?"

I sighed and told them. I did not tell them dramatically. I gave them the facts. I had not told all in my letter and they had heard rumours only. I described the events after the battle and then concluded, "So, Doctor Erasmus has given me the sentence. It is death. We know not when it will come. I would make you Duke of Normandy, William. The sooner we do that the better."

He shook his head, "I do not shirk the task. I know I will be Duke of Normandy one day but your enemies are still in awe of you. Their eyes are on you. While that is so then I can travel Normandy and speak with men like Mauger and Arne in the north. I can visit Bagsecg and our other lords in the east. I have learned much about Brittany. I need to know all that there is about Normandy. Bergil will return home and watch the south. With your permission, my family will stay here in Rouen and I will spend time travelling. I also need to travel to Wessex."

"Wessex? Why?"

"The Norns have spun. We do not raid with our ships. We fight on land and our enemies are to landward. King Charles gave you the title of Duke. His son is in England. I would go and speak with the Queen and with her father, King Edward. I want an alliance with Wessex. It is the most powerful kingdom in the land they now call England. I have learned that diplomacy can win wars. With Wessex as an ally then the men of Flanders will be less of a threat."

I smiled and raised my goblet, "You have grown wise, my son."

"Because I have learned from a great teacher, you. When I return and I have done all that I intend then I will take on the mantle of Duke. We will hold the ceremony here in Rouen."

"You know that outside of these lands they still call me Count?"

"Aye, just as they think of us as Vikings. As you showed at Soissons, we are not, we are Normans."

Bergil and William stayed a week. I learned more about the battles in the south and why my son was suspicious of the men of Flanders. They had captured some Flemish mercenaries fighting for the Count of Cornouaille. It was from them that they learned of Count Arnulf and his ambitions. Our northern border was a weakness. Then they left and I got to know my granddaughters.

I could never get their names right. I wondered if this was my ailment. When I had had my first attack, I had not recognised Sámr, Mauger and the others. The grandchildren did not mind and the ones who could speak teased me about it. I bounced them on my knees. I gave the older ones horse rides on my back. I told them stories. Some were made up but others were real. I told them of my grandfather and father. The story which fascinated them the most was the tale of my sinking beneath the waves. The younger ones were still little more than toddlers but they could understand my words. Mathilde, the eldest, was quite a sensitive child. When I had the youngest on my knees, she would stand behind me and stroke my hair. When she thought I had had enough of the smaller ones she would whisk them away so that I could have quiet.

One night, when her mother and the servants had taken the others to bed, she sneaked into the study I used. I liked to go there at night and carve chess pieces. I had made half the set already. I was using walrus tusks. I liked the feel of the smooth bone and it coloured easily. I had begun making them when I had first visited the market and I had found the act of carving, soothing. Soon I would be ready to stain one half with cochineal. Once I would have used that to stain my eyes and terrify my enemies. Now I stained chess pieces.

Mathilde crept in while I carved. She tried to sneak in but I knew she was there. She gave a gasp when I said, "Come, little one. What is it that you wish?" I put the knife and the half-carved queen on the table and held my arms for her. She scurried around and I lifted her on my knee. She laid her head on my chest. "Should you not be in bed?"

"I asked my mother if I could speak with you. She said I could."

"Then let us talk. Do you wish a story?"

"Perhaps but I have questions." I nodded. "My father says that you are dying."

"Aye child. I am the oldest man in this land. I should have died many times before. Perhaps I was kept alive so that I could see my granddaughters. If so then it is the greatest gift I could have been given."

"I do not want you to die."

I put my arm around her and squeezed. I said, in her ear, before I kissed her, "And I do not want to die. I had thought I would be ready but I am not. Life is precious. I have a family I need to get to know." This would be hard. I had been baptised but, in my heart, I still believed in the old ways. I could not make Mathilde doubt her faith. "You know there is a heaven?" She nodded. "Well, when I was growing up and before I was baptised, I believed in a slightly different heaven. It was one filled with warriors. This new heaven is better for when I die, I shall see my mother again and my foster mother. I believe that they have been watching over me. When I die, Mathilde daughter of William Longsword, then I will watch over you and your sisters."

"I would rather have you here. I would rather curl my fingers in your beard and hear you do funny voices. I would watch my sisters ride on your back and I would have nothing change."

I sighed, "As would I but that cannot be. We have to make the most of the time we have left."

"And when you are gone my father will rule?"

"Aye, he will be Duke of Normandy."

"And when he dies, I will be the Duchess and I will rule?"

She was clever and had thought things through well. "Would you like that?"

"I am not sure I could ever fight but if I had to then I would."

"If you had a brother then he would be Duke. It is not because you are a girl that this would be so but, as you said, you would have to fight. I have spent more than sixty years fighting."

"Did you have sisters?"

I nodded, "And I have not seen them for so long that I can barely remember their names or their faces."

She cuddled in, "I am sad, grandfather. You have had a hard life and God has not treated you well!"

I smiled as I saw her grip her crucifix, "We all have different lives. Make the best of what you are given Mathilde and live life to the full."

The door opened and I heard Sprota's voice, "Come child. You have bothered your grandfather enough."

I kissed the top of Mathilde's head, "There was no bother. Any time she wishes she can join me."

As she was taken away, I wondered at the change in me. There were people who were terrified of me still. What would they say if they saw the sentimental old man with tears coursing down his cheeks? The old man who would change everything just to have enough years left to see Mathilde become a woman.

Chapter 15

My son took more than three months to travel the land north of the river. He was no longer the young warrior who lived for raids, drinking and whoring. He had grown. Had that been my doing or a family? Was it inevitable? I had never had the opportunity for that. I had spent my formative years in the Haugr with my grandfather and then a brother's treachery had made me fight for life and a place in the world. In the end, I decided that it was the Norns.

"I will return to Nantes. William son of Æbbi will make a good lord for that town and Bergil can be Count of Brittany." He looked at me, "With your permission, of course."

I nodded, "You are, as far as I am concerned, the Duke of Normandy now. I hold the reins of power until you can mount the horse. It is a good decision Æbbi Bonecrusher was a loyal warrior. He will be happy that his son has turned out so well."

"It will take me some time to ensure that all is well in Brittany. You are happy to continue here?"

I smiled, "What you mean is do I think I will live long enough to hand over power?" He looked shocked. I shrugged, "That is out of my hands. The Norns spin. You must make the south secure. We have made the north a bastion. It was good that you gave Mauger power over the northern lords. He is no Olaf Olafsson and he will give us a warning of Flemish attacks. Go home and that will give Father Harold and I the chance to make this hall a home for you and your children."

He smiled, "And there will be another soon enough."

"Good, and this one may be a son although your girls are a delight. I shall miss them when you leave."

"And they, you."

He was right. The day they left all of them sobbed to stay. Mathilde gripped my hand and refused to go. I picked her up, "Mathilde, you are the eldest. You must set an example for your sisters. You will return here and then you shall see me every day. Know that I will miss you."

She nodded, "Can I ask a boon, grandfather?"

"Of course."

"Could I have a lock of your hair so that I can curl it in my fingers? It will remind me of you." She leaned in, "Bergljót, is not a Christian." Bergljót was an old Norse woman. Her husband, Arne Three Fingers had died in Paris. "She told me that there are women called volvas and they spin hair and cloth together. It keeps their men safe. I would keep the lock of hair safe and then you shall not die."

I did not think it worked like that but I was happy to accede to her request, "Of course." I put her down and, taking my seax cut a long curl of grey and brown hair. I handed it to her.

"Thank you, grandfather. Now I am content for I know I shall see you again."

They left. The Norns were spinning but Mathilde's words set in motion a series of thoughts. Mathilde seemed to understand me in the same way my grandfather had. Could his spirit be in her? When I died would my spirit return to one of her children? Perhaps the new babe in Sprota's belly. Then I realised that Mathilde was born many years after my grandfather had died in Wessex. Could it be that I had to die first? I was distracted as I walked around my town.

Everyone had met my grandchildren. I had walked around the town holding the hand of my two eldest granddaughters. The girls had been polite and they had charmed everyone. That was the topic of conversation, certainly from the women as I walked alone. The men, especially those who sailed had more serious news for me.

"The men of Flanders and Frisia grow bolder lord. Your river is safe but some knarr have been taken at the mouth of the river. Captains now sail with other ships for safety."

Until my son took over that was my responsibility. Time was I would have set sail in *'Fafnir'* and I would have rid the seas of the pirates. "I will deal with it. Thank you for the information. If there is further trouble do not be so slow to give it to me."

"I am sorry, lord, but you seemed so happy with the children that we did not wish to bring a black cloud into your life."

I went to the home of Erik Leifsson. He had a knarr which he used to trade but he was the best drekar captain I knew. He was in port and unloading his knarr. "Leif."

"Aye, lord."

"What have you heard of Flemish and Frisian pirates?"

He frowned, "I thought it a rumour. None have bothered me."

I pointed to the men unloading his knarr. They were all warriors. "With a crew like that it is not a surprise. There are easier targets than the knarr of Duke Robert's captain. I would like you to take my drekar to sea. I will find the crew. Sail the mouth of the estuary and take any Frisian or Flemish ship you find. We let them know that these waters are Norman!"

"Aye lord."

Men were more than happy to serve on the drekar. I paid them from the money we had been given by King Charles. I wondered how he was faring. He had not been the best King but he had been someone I could speak with. Had he remained in power then who knows how our lives might have been different? I told Father Harold to authorise the payment for the men. "How are our finances, Father Harold? Soon you will answer to my son and I would like to know, before I hand over power, that all is well."

"It is, lord. You have not taxed the people too hard and that encourages trade. With no Viking raids, there is an air of optimism. I was speaking with the Archbishop and he says it is not so in the land of the West Franks. Duke Rudolf, who now calls himself King Rudolf, does not live in his own land and he taxes them heavily. There are rumours that he risks revolt."

There would have been a time when I might have taken advantage of such unrest and attacked them. Perhaps my son would. This would be a perfect time to claim more land on our eastern borders.

"And do we know who King Rudolf's allies are?"

"The Count of Flanders and the Duke of Lorraine."

The attacks from the Flemish might be more sinister in nature. Perhaps they were trying to weaken us in the west and then attack from the east. My son had put defences in place which would make that highly unlikely to succeed.

When Erik returned, twelve days later, he was followed by a fleet of five drekar. They had no shields along their sides and I was unconcerned but I was still apprehensive. It took time for them to dock and I went to greet them. Egil and his son, with ten of the garrison, accompanied me.

I did not know the warrior who led them. Hagrold was a Norse Viking. He, however, knew me. Erik explained before I met with them, "Lord, we found Frisian and Flemish ships. They were west of Djupr and heading for Eu. Jarl Hagrold and his ships were engaged in a battle with them. We joined in. It seems the Jarl was on his way here. *Wyrd*, eh, lord?"

"*Wyrd* indeed."

I took the Jarl and his hearth weru to my Great Hall. The eyes of all of them were wide as they entered my home. I would have been the same when I had first come back from the land of ice and snow. They sat at my table and I saw his men rubbing the highly polished surface with their hands. They had ale but it was served in finely carved wooden beakers and not horns.

"I am grateful to you, Jarl Hagrold, for defeating my enemies."

"It was an honour but they were only Frisians and Flemish pirates. It is an honour to serve the last living legend."

I nodded, "You mean the Dragonheart?"

"You and he are often spoken of in the same breath."

"My grandfather knew him. He was a real legend. The sword that was touched by the gods... I should have liked to have held it."

"You are the reason we are here. We would like to emulate you."

"But Normandy is now taken. There are fiefs but you strike me as warriors and not farmers."

"No, Duke, you misunderstand us. We would not take what is yours. We would make, for ourselves, a home like yours but further south. We have heard that the land of Aquitaine is ripe for the taking."

I was relieved. "Aye it is and my son holds the land north of the river. If you sail south, to Nantes, then he would be able to advise you. You have families?"

"They are in the land of Northumbria. My cousin has land close to Jorvik. Since King Edward and his sons conquered that land it is not a place for Vikings. They will winter there while we sail south and gain a toehold. We hear that your grandfather began with just one island?"

"He did. Raven Wing Island. He used that to raid the mainland and then took the Haugr."

"He did so with just one drekar?"

"He did."

"Then we hope to take a larger piece of land. We have six hundred warriors. We brought just five of our ships. Another fifteen are in the mouth of the river."

"Then I wish you luck. When do you sail?"

"It is a long voyage up your river. We came merely to ask your permission. We will sail now."

After they had gone, I began to think, once more, about The Norns. They were spinning. My son had said he would be away for half a year. Hagrold and his men doubled the delay. William sent me a letter to tell me that he had stayed to ensure that our borders were safe and that the raiders did not become greedy and take what was ours. Hagrold was a man of his word and he did not. However, I remained alone at Rouen. I did not see my grandchildren. By the time my son did reach home, he had another daughter!

I had another attack. It was not as bad as the first one. I seemed to be frozen and could not move. I know not how long it lasted but I was alone and I faced up to the fact that I might be dying. I did not die but I decided that if I was to die, alone, in my bed, then I would be prepared. I took one of my old swords from my chest and laid it on the bed. I kept it in its scabbard but, from that night on, I slept with my hand on my sword. If I woke and could not move then at least I would die with a sword in my hand.

Over the next months, I grew accustomed to lying with my right hand on the hilt of the old sword. My servants were a little frightened the first few times they came to wake me and saw the sword but, soon, they forgot about it.

It was in the long nights of Mörsugur that I had another disturbed night's sleep. Egil and Leif had dined with me. My son had sent a letter apologising for his continued absence. He was about to sail to Wessex and speak with King Edward. To make up for it he had sent a barrel of his best wine and we had enjoyed it. Neither Egil nor Erik now stood a watch at night. A younger warrior, Stephen, who had fought well at the battle of the river, had been promoted to captain of the night guard. After Leif and Egil had left he escorted me to my chamber and ensured that there was a sentry outside the door. I prepared for bed and lay with my hand on my sword. What I did anticipate was a dream. When I had strong wine, and especially after speaking with old comrades, I tended to dream and to dream loudly. The sentries had all commented on the fact that I often shouted in my sleep.

I fell asleep quickly and I dreamed. It was an old and familiar dream. It was the day that my father died. I was on the drekar and I was young. I was not yet the warrior I would be.

I was standing on the gunwale looking out to sea when men came with swords and daggers. I jumped down and ran to the steering board. I noticed two things. Ragnvald was standing there with a bloody knife in his hand and my father's chest was covered in blood. His throat was bloody. I dropped to my knees and put my head to my father's mouth. He was not breathing. Ragnvald Hrolfsson was dead. I looked up and saw Ragnvald, my brother, lurching towards me with his bloody blade. As I raised my sword to kill him my life changed forever. I was struck in the back by a blade and a third Danish ship crashed into us. I found myself toppling over the side. The sheer strake was before me and I overbalanced. I was unable to stop myself. I tumbled overboard. My mail dragged me beneath the murky waters. I forced myself not to panic. I gripped my sword and kicked from the muddy bottom. I began to rise. I heard a cry as my head broke the surface.

I sat bolt upright in bed. I had had this dream many times but I had never heard a voice. The hilt of the sword was still in my hand. It was reassuring. I was about to turn over when I felt a change in the air. The door was opening. A sentry would never open the door. He would knock. The cry I had heard had not been in my dream. I slid the scabbard from the sword as I slipped off the bed. I grabbed my seax and I moved silently to the side. The door slowly opened. There should have been light from the torches in the passageway but there was none. I knew that the door was opening for I felt cold air. I stared at the door. I knew where it was. I saw shadows moving. I was in the shadows at the side of the room. Despite my size, I was invisible. These were killers who came to end my life and the shadows moved towards the bed. I could not tell how many men there were. I could have, perhaps, slipped out of the door and raised the alarm. That was not in my nature. Besides I knew not what mischief they had been up to. There were other guards and if they had all been slain then my best chance to survive was to surprise my would-be killers. I was a warrior, albeit an old one. I had to remember that I was not wielding Long Sword and I moved, silently, towards the men who were closing with my bed. I could now make out the men. There were five of them and they looked to have swords in their hands. When I was younger five would not have been a problem. I was old and I was ill. Would this be my last battle?

As soon as I saw their blades begin to descend, I struck. I brought my sword into the back of one killer while I stepped forward and ripped the seax into the side of another. The one whose spine I had struck screamed like a pig being castrated. The other three turned and, as they did so they whipped their weapons at the huge dark shadow that was me. I heard shouts from down the corridor. Help was on its way. The question was, would they be in time? I flicked my seax up at the sword which almost struck my middle and brought my sword down at the neck of the nearest would be killer. A sword was blindly thrust towards my middle. I tried to twist away but I could not avoid it. The blade sliced down my side. I saw, as I turned to face the last two killers, lights in the corridor and I heard feet pounding towards us. The light from the door illuminated me and the two remaining killers. They were both armed with swords and, even as I turned to face them, they both drew a dagger and advanced purposefully towards me. They were willing to die so long as they took me with them.

The door was flung open and Leif and Egil led my men into the room. The killers were brave men and they still tried to accomplish their mission. They ran at me. I was bleeding and I was old. Young Rollo would have thrown caution to the wind and charged them. Older, wiser Rollo, bleeding from his side, stepped back. I blocked one sword blow with my sword and the second with my seax. Two daggers drove towards my chest. They did not make it. Two blades emerged from their chests and they were thrown to the side. Men with torches ran in and the room became as bright as day. It was like a charnel house. The man I had stabbed in the side had bled to death. There was a puddle of blood as big as the man. The one I had almost severed was sprawled on my bed. I would need it cleaned well before I was able to sleep in it again.

Father Harold appeared in the doorway. He made the sign of the cross and then shouted, "Our lord is hurt! Fetch honey and vinegar."

One of the men who had been stabbed in the back tried to rise. Leif and his father, Egil Flame bearer, along with the two sentries they had brought began to hack and chop at the man. It was almost a berserker frenzy.

"Hold! He is dead! How is Stephen?"

Leif shook his head, "Stephen is dead as are two of the men at the river gates! You were lucky lord and we were less than vigilant."

I began to feel dizzy. Was I having another attack? Even though the bed was bloody, I had to sit upon it, "There will be time to learn lessons later. First, while my wound is tended, search for others. If five could enter then why not twenty?"

The drink must have still been affecting them. Realisation dawned, "Quick, my son. Organize the search. I will guard the Duke!"

Father Thomas arrived with the honey, bandages and vinegar. Father Harold said, "Lift your arms, lord, we will take this bloody shift from you. Father Thomas find a clean one from the chest." I saw him taking in the bodies and the blood. "You will have to sleep in the guest quarters until we can cleanse your room, lord."

I nodded, "I can always sleep in the warrior hall. There I would be safe."

Egil said, "Not so, lord, one of the new guards, Einar, is missing. I never like him. He had strange features. We will have to question all of them and find out if this treachery runs deep."

Once my shift was taken from me the wound could be examined. The assassins had used very sharp swords and the wound was deep. Luckily it had missed my ribs. The priest stitched it and then I was dressed. "Egil, your arm. Let us go down to the Great Hall. I will feel safer in a larger room."

It was dawn by the time Leif had completed his search. Another guard was found dead. His name was Ulf and he had been on watch with the missing Einar. They had been at the town gate. The killers had entered there. I knew not how or why the river gate guards had been killed.

"So, what do we know?"

"The five dead men all had Flemish coins. One of my men noticed them in the alehouse by the river. He thought they were crewmen from the Frisian ship which docked last night."

I looked at Richard, who gave the report, "And is the ship still in port?" Richard's face told me that he had not even thought about it. He ran off. "And how many men can we trust? I would have thought all of them but perhaps I was wrong."

"You are definitely wrong. I will rephrase the question. Egil who can we trust?"

He looked at his son, "The men I appointed."

I saw the disappointment in the face of Leif. His son nodded, "I will examine the heart of all of the men I chose."

Richard ran in, "The ship has left port. They are gone."

I shook my head, "They are not! There are loops in the river. Leif, take mounted men. You can catch them. It will take half a day to reach the sea. Ride as fast as you can and stop them. Bring them back alive if you can but do not let them reach the sea."

Leif nodded, "I will take my new men. That will be as good a test of their loyalty as any."

He left. "That is brave, not to say foolhardy, Egil."

"My son has made a mistake but I cannot believe he has misjudged the other twelve men he chose."

"Perhaps you are right."

"Lord, why do you not want them to reach the sea?"

"This is the work of Arnulf. I want him to wonder if his plan succeeded. No one must know of this."

"Lord, there are too many bodies to hide."

"Dismember the killers and throw their parts in the river. We spread the story that our guards got drunk and there was a fight. Have Father Harold make the servants swear to remain silent." I shook my head, "Had I not slept with my sword in my hand... perhaps this ailment was sent to save me and not to kill me." I finished the wine, "I need William here! I am too old for this. I was slow. Time was four would have been dead in the time it took to slay two."

"If you are old then what does that make us? No, Duke, you are still, Göngu-Hrólfr Rognvaldson. From now on we use chamberlains to sleep behind your door."

It was not until the next day when Leif arrived back. They had with them the broken body of a Flemish sea captain. Leif threw the man to the floor in my Great Hall. Egil had not left my side all day. "You were right Duke. We caught them at Le Trait. We made a raft of fishing boats. They fought hard but they died. Einar fought like a wild animal. Only the captain was saved. I lost six men. I trust the rest." It was a statement that brooked no argument and I nodded.

Egil asked, "And has he talked?"

"He has. He boasted how Count Arnulf and the King of the Franks were coming for your land. Your death was to provoke a rising similar to the one which cost so many of our men their lives."

I walked over to the man. I was about to lean over and grab him by the scruff of the neck when I thought better. I had thought him half dead but he was not. He lay with his arms close to his boots. A small bodkin appeared in his right hand and he lunged up at me. It was my height that saved me. He could not reach me. Leif's sword took his head.

"I am not fit for this task, lord. How did he get a weapon past us?

I picked up the bodkin, "Simple, this is a sailmaker's bodkin. You did not search his boots or it may have been in his belt. Short of stripping him naked, you would never have found it. The news you have discovered is timely. Send to Bagsecg. We need his men. Send a rider to Sámr. We need his ships to go to Djupr."

Father and son looked confused, "But why lord?"

"You told me his words. Now I know I was right not to let his ship escape. The Count of Flanders will already be marching into our land. He thinks me dead! He will count on confusion around Rouen. With half of our army in the south then he would be able to capture the north again. We need to get to Mauger and end this threat."

"You cannot lead, lord. You are wounded and you are still unwell."

"Then this will be the battle where I die with a sword in my hand. Far better than to die frozen to the spot and unable to move. At least this way I die like a warrior. We ride now!"

Chapter 16

I took Long Sword down from the wall. I donned my mail and I mounted Blue. When I had returned from Soissons, I had thought my days of fighting were over. I was wrong. Father Harold and Father Thomas tried to dissuade me from leaving, "Lord, you have a wound and you are not a well man! Your son has a large army. Let him come to meet this threat."

"And while we wait our enemies strike. I will go. I leave Egil and Leif with the garrison. You will be safe."

"It is you we think of, lord."

"I am unimportant. Watch my home for me."

When I reached the gates the men I would lead, all two hundred of them were waiting. Egil and Leif were also there. Egil shook his head, "We have let you down lord. I do not wonder that you cannot trust us to accompany you."

"Then you do not know me. I trust both of you and no blame is attached to either of you but I need Rouen protecting. Your men are all that stand between my town and our enemies. I will return but, if I do not then do not think badly of yourselves. I do not. I chose two good men and they have not let me down."

Robert had brought his men and he joined me halfway to Djupr. There were forty men with him. Half were mounted. I nodded to them, "That must have cost you money, Robert."

"My father died because his men were ill-equipped. I eat from wooden platters and beakers. We drink beer but I have men who ride to war and are well protected."

As we rode, I told him the size of the problem. He was clever and had learned much, riding with me. "We just need to hold them, lord. Your son will come and we have Djupr to fall back upon. The days of easy raids over the border are long gone."

"I hope you are right."

Hope rose as we neared Djupr. Lords joined me and our numbers were swollen until there were five hundred of us. Bagsecg and his two hundred horsemen would already be at Djupr and Mauger would be scouting out the enemy. I just feared that we were late. I was exhausted when we reached Djupr. My wound had wept and I felt dizzy. My head grew hot. I did not need an attack of my ailment here. I was reassured by the presence of Bagsecg and Mauger. Both appeared calm and in command of the situation.

"We have scouted, lord. The Franks and the Flemish have Eu besieged. My horsemen have begun to raid their supply lines. Our border strongholds have held and they are having to send supplies from Flanders."

Mauger nodded, "I have three hundred men ready to march, lord."

"And how many men do we face?"

"Two thousand."

"Then we do not move until Sámr arrives with the rest of our army. When we fight, we have to win the battle. At Soissons, we won but the army lost. We need to send them back across the border and to be licking their wounds."

"Aye, lord." Mauger looked concerned, "Are you well?" I smiled and he added, quickly, "You should not have rid yourself of your hearth weru!"

"I am flattered that Count Arnulf holds me in such high esteem. He must really fear me!"

They both laughed. Mauger said, "Of that, there is no doubt."

Bagsecg asked, "And your son, will he come?"

"I sent him word but he is in Aquitaine. We will assume that if he does come then he will be late. When Sámr brings his ships, we will hold a council of war."

Mauger said, "We could sit behind our walls until your son comes."

"And what of Gilles son of Faramir? Eu is not as strong a town as this. Do we allow our shield brothers to be sacrificed so that we will not?"

Bagsecg shook his head, "What Mauger means is you should sit behind your walls. We can face Arnulf and King Rudolf. He has now been elected as King."

"I thank you but I do not need to have nursemaids. This battle, Bagsecg, will be determined by a shield wall. You and your horsemen will continue to do as you have done. You will attack any of the men who are not in camp. You will cut them off from Flanders. We will starve them into submission. I have no intention of wasting the lives of any of our young men. We need Sámr and his men to swell our numbers. His ships will give the illusion of numbers. When they sail along the coast Count Arnulf will think we have double the numbers we actually do."

Even as we spoke nature was taking a hand in the battle. It began to rain. The roads in this part of the land were not the best. Water was the way they travelled. The enemy camp would become a more unpleasant place. Our men, the ones who camped outside Djupr's walls, also suffered but not as much for they were well fed. The low cloud also aided us when Sámr arrived. His fleet of ten ships was almost invisible as it edged into the harbour beneath a veil of cloud.

"I brought all the ships and men I had, Caen is safe enough from attack."

"Good. Then you have five hundred men?"

"Five hundred and twenty. I could have brought more but we did not have enough ships."

"That will do. Have your men brought ashore. We hold a council of war."

This would be my battle. I did not think I would fight. I was certain my men would not allow it but I would direct the fight and it would be my plan. I explained what we would do and how we would do it. My aim was not to defeat them. That would take a miracle. It was to deter them until William could arrive and make the border secure. I planned on sending the drekar, under sail and with shields along their sides to moor north of Eu. We would then march to Eu and face them ready for battle. While Bagsecg and his men intensified their attacks on the enemy's outposts we would advance on them. The damp and the rain meant we could not use our archers. They would have to attack as slingers. It would not be as effective but if we could not use archers then they could not use crossbows. It would become a straight battle between their men on foot and ours.

"Sámr, you will lead the attack. We do not use multiple wedges we use a boar's head with just two tusks. You lead one and Mauger the other. The battle horn will be with you. It will be your decision to fall back."

"And where will you be, lord?"

"I will be with my standard behind the wedge. I will find a place with height so that I can view the battlefield."

Mauger said, "There are few such places. Better we take a wagon. I will have four of my hearth weru guard you." He smiled, "You seem to have rid yourself of those sworn to protect you."

I shook my head and my voice was filled with sadness, "Most, I fear, are in the Otherworld." I nodded, "If that is all then we leave before dawn. I would travel the fifteen miles and reach them before the sun is up; if it rises at all. This blanket of cloud and rain looks set for some time."

As we ate that night, I was aware that I was fighting with a very small number of lords. I knew my son was making the south secure and putting a barrier of Vikings between our enemies and us but the north was where the real danger lay. Before I handed him the crown of Normandy, I would have to ensure that he lived in Rouen. Sámr had news of my son. "He has done well, lord. Hagrold is aggressive and has already taken large parts of the land around Limousin."

"Limousin? That is over a hundred miles south of the Loire."

"I told you he is aggressive. Your son protects his supply lines to his ships. Other Vikings arrived to follow the banner of Hagrold. I do not say he will make a land like Normandy but he will take some shifting. The lords of that land are unused to the way we fight."

Sámr saw my son's action as commendable. I did not. He was not losing men but he was just securing land for another clan. His place was here!

I did not mind being up early. Sleep was no longer a welcome occurrence. I went to bed each night, sword in hand, and I feared I might never wake up. I was the first awake. I was not even certain that I had slept. I roused Sámr, Robert, Mauger and the other lords who slept in the walls of the stronghold. I had fires lit and hot food prepared. I donned my mail. The stable master at Djupr had saddled Blue so that it was I led the army north through the drizzle and across the mud. The four hearth weru drove the wagon. It was filled with stones for the slings, darts and javelins. If the day went badly then it would become a fortress where we would make our last stand. The fact that an old and patently sick man led the army encouraged them to hurry and keep up with me. Sámr and my other leaders were also mounted and they were around me like a protective cloak. Bagsecg himself scouted the road ahead.

Blue plodded along easily. I was able to keep watch to the east. The sun took some time to rise and we were nearing the river and the enemy lines when it did so. Bagsecg rode back. "The enemy camp is just a mile ahead."

"Good. Thank you Bagsecg, now you can do what you do best, you can make the enemy fear your vaunted horsemen."

He nodded, "Aye, lord but stay safe eh? If anything happened to you while I was supposed to be protecting you then the spirits of my father and grandfather would never let me rest!"

My men were Christians but the pagan in them lurked just below the surface.

Sámr and my lords dismounted and began to array their men. The enemy camp would be blissfully unaware of our presence. As soon as Sámr marshalled the men into their lines then we would be heard but until then they would be rising and preparing fires. They would make water. They would prepare to attack Eu and its walls again. Bagsecg's scouts told us that Gilles, son of Faramir, had repelled six attacks. The enemy would think that the seventh might be the one to succeed.

As the wagon lumbered up, I heard horns in the enemy camp. Either we had been seen or this was the call to rise. Most of the darts, javelins and stones were distributed. We left a quarter in the wagon as a reserve. Sámr and Mauger began to form their wedges. The horses were tethered to a line between two trees and ten boys were set to watch the beasts. Once we saw the last rank form, my men manhandled the wagon to a place just behind them. We placed it on the road and chocked the front wheels. I clambered aboard with Mauger's four warriors. I could see the enemy camp for the sky was lighter. We had been seen. The horns had been a call to arms. From my elevated position, I could see the stronghold. The charred walls told me that the attackers had tried to use fire. The rains had put an end to that. Then I saw the sails of the drekar as they sailed north. Count Arnulf would wonder if they would disgorge men to attack his rear. Bagsecg's horsemen had already threatened his retreat.

I turned to the warrior next to me, "Unfurl the banner. Let them see who commands here." What little breeze there was came from the west and the flag fluttered behind me. Count Arnulf would know that I commanded. I was the bait that would, hopefully, draw them away from Eu. Sámr would judge his moment and we would begin a fighting retreat to Djupr.

As I had hoped the enemy did not wait for us to attack. King Rudolf had witnessed the effect of our men charging an enemy. The whole enemy line lumbered towards us. They had risen and we had been upon them. They had not eaten. Some would not have made water. They had armed in a hurry. There is a ritual to battle. Each piece of armour, the coif, the arming cap, the helmet, the sword, all play a part and there is an order to the donning of them. The men who attacked us would be wondering if all the straps were secure. Had they remembered all the weapons they liked to use? Doubt is a deadly enemy.

Sámr began a chant. It was to let the enemy know who commanded.

> *Göngu-Hrólfr Rognvaldson with the Longsword*
> *Göngu-Hrólfr Rognvaldson with his Longsword*
> *And with that sword, he took the hand*
> *That killed his father and his land*
> *With no sword, the snake was doomed*
> *To rot with Hel in dark entombed*
> *When the head was struck and the brother died*
> *The battle ended and the clan all cried*
> *Göngu-Hrólfr Rognvaldson with the Longsword*
> *Göngu-Hrólfr Rognvaldson with his Longsword*
> *Göngu-Hrólfr Rognvaldson with the Longsword*
> *Göngu-Hrólfr Rognvaldson with his Longsword*

As my men chanted, they banged their shields. Perhaps it was my imagination but I was sure the enemy line faltered when the chant began. Sámr's spear started our boar's head to march. The two lines would clash and Sámr wanted the weight of our mailed warriors and the two points to drive into the enemy lines. The archers and slingers raced around the sides and hurled their stones at the enemy. If only a quarter of their stones found a target they would be weakened. It sounded like hailstones as the specially chosen stones from Djupr's beach hit wood, helmets, mail and flesh. The cries, shouts and screams told me that they had hit. I saw some men fall and others reeled. The archers and slingers were reckless and waited until the last moment to run behind the safety of our boar's head.

The lines collided. Mauger and Sámr led their wedges to drive deep into the enemy lines. This was the first time I had been able to observe the effect. Sámr and Mauger were each protected by two warriors who were the best that we had. I saw Flemish warriors slain. Their bodies remained upright and the two wedges drove deep into the enemy lines. It was like the splitting of a log. The split became wider and I saw the enemy line buckle. The slingers and the archers ran around to the sides. The slingers hurled their stones and the archers threw darts and javelins. The enemy could only use their shields to protect from one side and men on the flanks began to die. The enemy line rippled.

The battle was going well but the rippled line meant that we had points of weakness and some Swabian warriors in the colours of King Rudolf suddenly broke through and came directly for me. It was a bold move for if the standard fell then the heart would go from my men. Although the breach was sealed ten men who had broken through raced towards me and my five guards. I grabbed a javelin and hurled it at the eager Swabian who closed with us. He was knocked back as the steelhead drove deep into his chest. I threw a second which hit one in the shoulder and then I drew Long Sword. My four guards had also thrown darts and javelins. Six men reached the wagon. I swung my sword in an arc. The Swabian whose sword swept towards me died before his sword was halfway to my legs. My sword split his head and half of his spine, One of Mauger's men was not so lucky and a long sword hacked through one of his legs. Even so, his dying fall was courageous. He threw his body onto his killer. The wagon proved to be a wise choice. My long arms and Long Sword, allied to the doughty defence slew the remaining Swabians. As I looked up, I saw that the battle was at a crucial stage. There were more of the enemy than remained to me. Just then a horn sounded from Eu and was answered by a horn from the east. Gilles, son of Faramir led his men from their stronghold and Bagsecg disobeyed my orders and brought his horsemen to charge the enemy. It was a decisive moment. Horns sounded and the enemy broke. They began to fall back. This was not a rout. It was a retreat. We had won and we had saved Eu.

Chapter 17

Leaving the wounded and a third of our men to repair Eu the rest of my paltry army followed the enemy host as it headed north. The rain slowed both of us but we found wounded and dying warriors who had been abandoned. They were given a warrior's death. We stopped at the river which marked the border. I saw Count Arnulf and King Rudolf; both looked the worse for the journey. We were four hundred paces apart but I saw the fist of the King of the Franks raised at me. He was just another in a long line of enemies. "Now, let us return home. Sámr, if you take charge of the bulk of the army, I will ride with Bagsecg and the men of Rouen. I am getting too old for this."

Mauger shook his head sadly, "And yet you still accounted for more men than my hearth weru. The world will not see the likes of you again, Duke Robert."

It was a long three days to reach Rouen. All of us, men and beasts were weary. Bagsecg spent the night with us in Rouen. He had a long journey ahead of him. My priest clerks, Leif and Egil looked anxiously at me as I entered my hall.

"The enemy is defeated and our land is safe. Any word from my son?"

"He is ten days away. He brings his family and he is travelling at their speed."

At least he was coming. "Leif, have my mail cleaned and my sword sharpened." I did not think I would need it again, I was wrong.

Father Harold asked, "And did you suffer another attack, lord?"

"No. I was saved from that embarrassment. Have a bath filled for me. I can feel the damp and the wet makes all of my joints ache. Winter draws closer."

I felt better as I luxuriated in a hot bath before a roaring fire. My servants brought me a treat, buttered ale and honey infused with a red-hot poker. I could only drink one or two but one or two were perfection.

We had arrived back in the early afternoon which meant that by the time I emerged from my bath and was dried and dressed it was time to eat. These days were lonelier at meal times. Egil ate with his family and I made do with Father Harold. He always annoyed me the way he would pray before he ate anything. I didn't need to but I always waited for him to finish no matter how appetising the food. That evening he seemed to make an effort for his prayers were cursory.

"When your son arrives will you make him Count of Normandy?"

"No." Father Harold looked shocked. It was just my little joke, "I will make him Duke of Normandy."

"But only the King can award that title."

"And the King did. King Charles gave the title to me and my heirs in perpetuity. There were witnesses. They may be my enemies but they know the truth as do I. The attack by King Rudolf shows just how much he fears me. And he will learn to fear my son." I looked at the old priest. "Tell me, Father Harold, are we bad masters? Do we treat ordinary people and thralls badly?"

"No, lord, quite the contrary. You are remarkably fair but that does not matter. There are ways of doing things and you cannot change them."

I smiled, "I think we have already begun to do so. I will not see it in my lifetime but when Mathilde is a woman this land will be powerful."

I was relieved when my son and his family arrived. I would ensure that he did not leave again. It was Mathilde who greeted me with the most warmth. She threw her arms around me and hugged me, "You have been fighting again!"

"I am just trying to keep a land that is safe for your family. Now that you are here, I promise that I will wander no more. I will just become a fat old man who watches his granddaughters play."

Later that night I learned more about the war in the south. "Hagrold is a good warrior but he is reckless." I smiled and my son nodded, "I know, that charge could have been levelled at me once but no more. I had to stay to ensure that he had sound bases close to the river. He wishes to bring his men's families south. I waited until he had two towns he could defend. I am sorry, now, that I did so for you almost lost half of Normandy."

I shook my head, "I did not lose anything. A part was almost stolen but the work our lords did to strengthen their defences saved us. When they come to the cathedral you must thank them."

"Cathedral? Thank them how?"

"I am handing over power to you. This last battle was a too close run. Brittany is not as important as Normandy. Here we control both banks of the Seine and that means we control Paris. That is why Rudolf tried to take it from us. You ask how do you thank those who fought for us and remained loyal? Give them coin. The coffers are full and that is down to them. They deserve it."

"Will you be able to sit and do nothing?"

"Who says I will be doing nothing? I have granddaughters. One day you may have a son although I am increasingly of the opinion that such a thing will require my death."

He laughed, "You are joking." He looked at my face, "I can see that you are not. What makes you think so?"

"A feeling and the fact that it was Skuld who spoke to my grandfather. You were not born until my father and grandfather were dead."

"Then I want no son. I would rather keep the legend that is you, alive."

"I am old, William. The ailment cannot be cured." He drank deeply. "When I die you will have to be as cunning as I have been. All of our enemies conspire against us. I swore an oath to get Normandy. You hold Normandy now and Brittany. You need not swear an oath. What you do need to do is to have loyal lords about you. Sámr, Bjorn and Bagsecg will not be around forever. Choose wisely and bind them to you. You have daughters. You should choose husbands for them."

"Was that how you chose my mother?"

"She was Breton nobility and it did not hurt. The fact that she made the beast with two backs with the priest just shows that all marriages are a lottery. Now we need to invite the great and the good for the ceremony. Many will not attend and think it insults us. It does not. It merely tells you who are our enemies. When King Charles gave us this land it was to buy him time. He was weak and under attack. He thought to give us a tiny corner and when the time was right, he would take it back. He was wrong. You must hold on to this land."

It took six months for Father Harold and the Archbishop to plan and organize the crowning. There had been no crown and I had one made. I used a Saxon goldsmith who lived in Rouen. I think the man had done something wrong and been forced to flee. He came from Lundenwic and was a gifted craftsman. Normandy was a safe and enlightened place compared with many of the states close by. Certainly, we were stable and our victories meant that our warriors were feared as much, if not more, than the Vikings from whom we were descended.

During that time, I suffered no more attacks. I played with my granddaughters. I taught Mathilde and Adele how to play chess. I had finished the red and white chess set. They were both quick learners but Mathilde had the cleverer mind. Sprota had yet to give birth to a son. If she did not have one then, eventually, Mathilde would inherit the land from my son. My lords had sworn an oath to do so and when William was crowned then he would ask for the same oath. Unlike the Franks, my lords kept their oaths. Sprota was the one who organized me. I would happily have attended the ceremony with just my mail and cloak upon my back but she had ladies make me fine tunics. Bootmakers made me boots made from the finest leather. She had servants wash and trim my unruly hair and beard. I knew what she was doing, she was making me civilised. Inside I was not. Inside I was still the pagan but the outer layer, the one the world saw, now looked like a Frank, albeit a giant Frank.

Our status could be seen when the Kings, Princes and lords arrived. King Edward came. I might have been flattered had I not discovered that he was on his way to Paris to speak with King Rudolf. He was here to try to secure the release from prison of the ailing King Charles. Neither Count Arnulf nor King Rudolf attended but King Henry of the East Franks did. The Duke of Provence was another who attended as was the Duke of Aquitaine. The latter came with a definite purpose. He sought our intervention in the matter of Hagrold and his Vikings who had now claimed a large piece of land. Aquitaine was vast and the Vikings held a small parcel but the Duke wanted to know how to deal with them. My son and I offered our advice. It was sage and it was honest. We suggested that he do what King Charles had done with us. Make Hagrold the Count of the region and use him to protect his river. He listened but I do not think he heeded our advice.

The actual ceremony was created by the Archbishop and Father Harold. It was full of Christian references. There was much of it in Latin which few understood. There was a great deal of singing. There was also something we understood. There was symbolism. The inverted sword my son held looked like the crucifix and that was reinforced by the actual cross my son kissed. He knelt before the priests. That was designed to show that the church held the power. The Archbishop had, originally, wanted to place the crown on my son's head. That was the one part we changed. After he had blessed the crown, the Archbishop handed it to me and it was I who crowned my son. He stood for the actual crowning. The Archbishop could not have placed the crown on his head while he was standing! I could. The last part was also not in the Archbishop's plan. My lords spontaneously cheered and began chanting my son's name. I smiled at the frown on the Archbishop's face and the shocked looks of the foreign dignitaries.

The feast we held afterwards was all the work of Sprota. She had spared no expense. I had given her the keys to the treasury before William was crowned. Had I had a wife then she would have done so. Gisela was unlikely now to be married to me. She lived in England, and with King Charles in prison, the arrangement was null and void. I was pleased for the girl. She could find a proper husband now. At the feast, I was accorded as much attention and honour as my son. I felt guilty about that. This was his time. Mine was over. Mathilde had asked if she could sit next to me and I was quite taken with the way she watched over me. She worried about me. For my part, I enjoyed listening to her. She had wit for one so young and that, allied to the natural honesty of children, made me smile as she commented on the men she saw at the feast.

And then, almost as soon as it was here, the ceremony and the crowning were gone. The lords left and Rouen went back to its normal life. Except that life was now different. There was a Duke and a Duchess. The fact that only those in Normandy recognised the title was irrelevant. The Kings and lords who had witnessed the ceremony could not acknowledge him as Duke for we were still, legally, part of Frankia and the King of the Franks had not crowned my son. William and Sprota acted like a duke and his duchess. Sprota endowed an abbey. That was both significant and astute. It endeared us to the church. The Pope had not attended the crowning ceremony but one of his representatives did. My son and his wife had a short meeting with him and the abbey was the result. We had legitimacy. My son had spies and my border lords were vigilant. They reported that all of this did not sit well with King Rudolf and Count Arnulf. It weakened their position and strengthened my son's. Once they left the dignitaries might dispute the title but I cared not.

When the two left to visit my lords or to visit King Edward I was left with the elder daughters. It was a joy for me. I watched them grow and I watched them change. Each day that I woke and I was still alive was one that was filled with laughter and questions. The girls wanted to know all about me. They had heard of The Haugr and my grandfather. They wished to know the truth from my lips. I did not do as the singers of songs did, I did not embellish the truth. I told them of the death of my father and the Danish drekar which had saved me from my brother's blade and sent me to the depths of the sea. Those first six months were a joy.

My son returned from the meeting with King Edward and he brought with him mixed news. We were seen as allies of the men of England and that was good. The meeting with King Rudolf had ended badly and King Edward's pleas for the release of King Charles had been in vain. As King Rudolf was an ally of Flanders then King Edward's alliance with Flanders also ended. The threat from the north diminished. My son was, however, approached by Athelstan while the two were hunting. Athelstan was not the elder of the King's sons but he wished to be the next king. King Edward was old. He asked my son to send killers to kill his brother, Elfweard. My son had refused, of course, but it was worrying. When William told me, I wondered at the ramifications. If Athelstan became king would he now view us as enemies?

And then, when my son told me that Sprota was with child again, came the news that Bjorn the Brave had died. He had not died in his bed. He had been murdered while out hunting. Those responsible had not been caught. That was disturbing. It came at the same time as the news that King Charles of the Franks had the wasting sickness. He would never see his family again and that made my own position even more precious. It was when Bergil Fast Blade was also ambushed and murdered that my son and I suspected a plot. I had known he was in danger. I had woken from my afternoon nap with a fearful image in my head of Bergil being butchered. When I told others of this, I saw the looks which implied I was losing my mind but Bergil and I had been oar brothers. Along with Sámr the three of us had been the heart of the clan when we had left Norway. He had died with a blade in his hand and he would be in Valhalla.

My son and I sat one night speaking of the defence of our land when the news came about Bergil's death. He and I had been as close as brothers. I had helped to give him a second life when his wife had run off. Bjorn's death had affected me, Bergil's devastated me. His son, Odo, brought us the news. The son looked just like his father except that he was clean-shaven. My son confirmed him as Count of Rennes. The death of Bergil had saddened us but it would not change the grip we had on Brittany.

"Bergil was a careful warrior. After Bjorn's death he kept good bodyguards about him and yet they were killed too!"

"Aye father. It worries me too. King Rudolf is too busy trying to deal with Hagrold in the south but Count Arnulf still desires the land around Djupr and Eu. These attacks in the south have all the hallmarks of one of his plots. He is a clever man."

I knew what I would do but I was no longer Duke. "You have a plan?"

He nodded, "Richard of Tours is half Breton and half Viking. He is clever. I will send him and two others to visit Lundenwic, Paris and Bruggas. Let us see if they can hear of any Flemish plot. When I was at King Edward's court I heard nothing but it is unlikely that the conspirators would have let word get to me."

It was a clever plan. By visiting the two larger kingdoms first they would hear of any whispers of killers. Bruggas was not the capital of Flanders but the port was at the centre of intrigue and gossip. More importantly, three men could blend in there. The other thing my son did was to warn all of the more senior lords who had fought against Arnulf and Rudolf to be on their guard. If Sámr fell to an assassin's blade too then I would take matters in my own hand. I would have a death with a sword in my hand and I would end the life of Count Arnulf. I should have listened more carefully. I might have heard The Norns spinning.

Sámr came to visit with me. We sat, as I thought, alone in my study and we drank wine. I saw how old he had become. Yet all those who had left Norway with us were now dead. It was no surprise. "If I am murdered too it will not change us, lord. My sons will still hold Caen and the fiefs close by. You and I might have been sprinkled with water but," he tapped his heart, "in here we are still warriors."

I laughed, "Aye, Sámr Oakheart. Only a galdramenn can look into our heads and our hearts and know the truth, When I am gone, I hope to be in Valhalla." I confided a worry. "I sleep, each night, with my sword in my hand but, during the day an attack such as I endured on the retreat from Soissons could come and deny me the opportunity to draw my sword."

"If I am close by, I will do so for you, old friend. I owe you that and more."

"Yet it is unlikely that you will be close." I shrugged, "We both know, unlike the followers of the White Christ, that such a decision is out of our hands. What will be, will be. I am content. I have my legacy. And, while I do not have a grandson, Mathilde more than makes up for that."

Sámr laughed, "Aye she is a delightful child. She is like a breath of fresh air and the way she watches over you... she is like a hearth weru!"

I never saw Sámr again. In many ways that did not matter. We had faced death together so many times that it was almost as though we were in each other's heads.

My son sent for me when Richard of Tours returned. With him came the news that Count Arnulf had hired mercenaries, Viking mercenaries. They came from the Land of the Wolf. Dragonheart had long been dead as had most of his men but they heard that there had been a falling out and much blood had been shed. The cult of the Ulfheonar had re-emerged. Those warriors had once been led by the Dragonheart himself. It was thought that it had died out with him. The great-grandson of the one they called Shape Shifter, had revived the cult. He had tried to take over the Land of the Wolf but a witch, from the cave of the Lough Rigg, had defeated him. The survivors had fled. An Ulfheonar can defeat all but a witch. They hired themselves out as killers. Now I understood how Bergil and Gandalf had been killed. Even I would struggle against a wolf warrior. We could, however, do something. My son sent riders to warn the lords of the danger. We now knew who we sought.

That night, as I sat and told Mathilde other stories from my youth, she asked me about the Norns. "Grandfather, you speak of these sisters as though they are real. Surely they are not."

I knew that I was stepping into dangerous territory. Sprota was a Christian. As much as she loved me, she would not be happy about pagan ideas and yet I owed Mathilde the truth. I would try to explain it in terms which she would understand. "My grandfather, when a young man, was sailing with a warrior called the Dragonheart. He was there when an island mysteriously appeared from the sea. He went below the earth and met a witch. She told him he would rule this land. He had never even seen it then. The Three Sisters are witches and they are the ones who decide what we do. They spin webs and spells which entangle men. There is a thread from the Dragonheart which links with my father. That thread now links the killers of Bergil Fast Blade to us. Father Harold could not explain it. There are many things we do not understand: how the White Christ turned water into wine." I shrugged, "I am old, Mathilde. Perhaps I am losing my mind but I see a pattern in all of this." I kissed her on the top of her head. "Do not let it give you bad dreams eh?"

She squeezed my hand, "You are not losing your mind, grandfather, and I will not have bad dreams but you have given me much to think on. That you believe this tells me that there might be some truth in it."

She was a clever girl and she could read. She also knew how to ask questions and listen for the answer. The two do not always go hand in hand. She spent the next month or so speaking with Father Harold and Father Thomas. She had a tutor, too. My son had hired a Greek and Atticus was a clever young man who answered her honestly.

She only had a month to learn all that she could for Sprota's baby was due. There was an air of expectancy about my hall. That, I think, was down to me. I had told others that I thought it was a boy. I had not told them the reason. It was about that time that I began to feel unwell. I put it down to excitement and the fact that the last month had been so enjoyable for me. I was no longer Duke of Normandy. I lived for myself. I went about Rouen without a care in the world. Often it was with Mathilde's hand in mine and there was no better place in the world.

The midwives and the women seemed to have determined that the babe would be born in the next couple of days. How they knew that I had no idea. My son would not be present. The story of the curse of the priest, although it sounded pagan, was strong enough to deter any man from being present. My son and I got drunk. I had not done so for a long time. Not long before I had had enough and retired to bed, I was certain that I saw Mathilde watching me. I thought no more about it but the Norns were spinning. I woke feeling better than I had for a long time. I rose and was greeted by women racing around my hall like chickens without heads.

I spied William, "It is the baby, father, it is due. It seems you were wrong. This will be a girl. You still live."

I laughed, "And right pleased am I for if the new granddaughter is anything like Mathilde then she will be a joy."

"I will go and see when the baby is due. Sprota has done this so many times that it should be quicker this time."

My head began to buzz. I put it down to the Norns and their webs; I walked towards the table where the food and ale were laid. I saw Mathilde looking at me. She was stood before the fire and Long Sword. Father Harold was busy in the hall, he knew that when the baby was born there would be much to do. It was as I walked towards the table that I started to lose control. First, I felt a fire in my head. I knew what that meant. Then, my legs ceased to work effectively. I tried to move them but I felt myself falling. I tried to shout but no words came out. I tried to put my hand out to break my fall but my body would not obey. Only Mathilde reacted. I saw her mouth open but I heard not a word. I crumbled to the ground. I was dying. The first attack and the subsequent ones had been nothing like this. I heard whistling in my ears and my head felt like it would erupt from the top of my body. I could see Father Harold and others rushing around but I heard nothing. I would not go to Valhalla. There was no sword in my hand and I could not reach one. Then I saw Mathilde. It looked like she was screaming. Father Thomas and Atticus reacted. They went to the fire and lifted down Long Sword. Mathilde ran to me and cradled my head in her tiny hands. Tears coursed down her cheek. She held my head and kissed my cheek. I tried to smile and to tell her that all was well but I was frozen. Father Thomas placed the sword in my hand. I could not grip but my eyes told me that he was wrapping my fingers around the hilt. My eyes pleaded with Mathilde. I wanted to tell her that I loved her. I wanted to say so much but I was dying and all that she would have to remember me would be a frozen face and dying eyes. It was not enough. I had been cheated. The last thing I felt in this world was a solitary tear splashing on my cheek.

Mathilde and the room disappeared. I was in a dark tunnel. I was just grateful that I could move. I could walk and I could smell. I smelled ale and woodsmoke; I saw a light ahead and, happy that I was no longer frozen, I strode towards it. It was an open door. As I stepped into it, I saw Hrólfr the Horseman and my father. They embraced me.

My grandfather said, "You have done all that was asked of you. You are a hero of Valhalla."

My father said, "We have awaited your arrival. Welcome."

Then I saw Bergil and Sven Blue Cheek, I saw Gandálfr. And I saw Jarl Rognvald Eysteinsson. They were applauding. I entered a hall and I saw Odin. He raised a horn of ale and then shouted, "Welcome, Göngu-Hrólfr Rognvaldson. We have kept your place for you. The Norns toyed with you but you have served your clan well. Join the heroes and take a seat next to Jarl Dragonheart for you two deserve much honour." I saw the Dragonheart and knew that I truly was in Valhalla.

I had passed to the Otherworld. My work was done but I had so many unanswered questions that I thought to ask Odin if I could return.

My grandfather leaned in and said, "Here you can see our world. Here there are no secrets. Normandy is safe and it is in good hands."

Mathilde

Epilogue

I am the granddaughter of the Duke of Normandy. I was there when he died. I am a Christian and I believe in God but I also believe that I was born to watch over his last years. Once my father and mother moved back to Rouen, I spent every waking hour watching the Duke. I worked hard with my studies so that Atticus would allow me to sneak off and observe him. I feared for him. He would die. My father was resigned to that fact but I wanted to stop it. I was there when he spoke with Sámr and unburdened himself. I knew all. Had I not been there then he would not have died with a sword in his hand. He believed in Valhalla. I do not but I had to ensure that he had a sword in his hand. He believed in it and the father of Normandy was entitled to his beliefs. I was a young girl but my voice commanded men to obey and they did. I saw, despite the fact that he was dying, that my grandfather knew what I was doing. He was not dead when the sword was placed in his hands and I gripped his fingers more tightly around the hilt. And then he died. It was as though the world had lost something important. It felt as though it had changed. My grandfather had changed the world and now he was gone. I believed that then and I believe it now. The nunnery where I live is a place of God but deep within me, hidden from everyone else is the belief that my grandfather is in Odin's feasting hall with the rest of his Viking brothers. When I give my last confession, I will admit as much but until then it is my last secret.

When my father took over, the first thing he did was to hunt down the Ulfheonar. My father believed that it was their acts of assassination which had accelerated my grandfather's death. Perhaps it was true. It took half a year but the killers were found and given the blood eagle. They were not tried. They lived beyond the law. There was also something pagan about them. Men called them shapeshifters. The church could not explain them but my grandfather, before he died, had done so. They were to do with the old religion. The days of the Vikings were numbered but that did not mean that all that they believed in was false.

It was the day of my grandfather's death that gave me belief and knowledge. On that same day, my mother gave birth to Richard who would become Richard the Fearless. He would be the warrior who continued my grandfather's work. My father, treacherously murdered by Count Arnulf, would not. I saw then an order which I could not see in the work of Christ and the church. Added to that was the fact that King Charles also died on the same day as my grandfather then the world as I knew it changed. I could never marry. If I was to marry then I needed it to be a man like my grandfather and such a giant would never walk this earth again. If I could not have that which I wanted then I would have a life I chose. With a brother, my grandfather did not need me to wield a sword and lead Normandy. There was little left for a woman, save the church. I became a nun and dedicated myself to gaining power so that I could help my little brother and fulfil my grandfather's dream.

When we laid him in the tomb in Rouen cathedral, I was not the only one who wept. His oar brothers, Sámr, Mauger and Robert all became unmanned. Father Harold and his priest clerks mourned the man who had changed the face of Frankia. It was a sombre day. I just regretted that I had not said more to this man who was a giant both literally and metaphorically. I was a child but I was a clever child. I should have said something. I regretted that decision to the end of my days. I felt I had let him down somehow. Yet, even now, when I am old and grey, I still hear his voice in the night. I have felt his presence close by me my whole life. I take comfort that when I die our spirits might be reunited. I am proud that I was the daughter of one of the greatest warriors to have ever lived. Hrólfr, Rollo, Göngu-Hrólfr Rognvaldson, Robert of Normandy, all were the same man but to me, he was just grandfather and writing these words on the parchment brings tears to my eyes once more. I did not know him long enough and that is my curse.

The End

Norse Calendar

Gormánuður October 14th - November 13th
Ýlir November 14th - December 13th
Mörsugur December 14th - January 12th
Þorri - January 13th - February 11th
Gói - February 12th - March 13th
Einmánuður - March 14th - April 13th
Harpa April 14th - May 13th
Skerpla - May 14th - June 12th
Sólmánuður - June 13th - July 12th
Heyannir - July 13th - August 14th
Tvímánuður - August 15th - September 14th
Haustmánuður September 15th-October 13th

Glossary

Ækre -acre (Norse) The amount of land a pair of oxen could plough in one day

Addelam- Deal (Kent)

Afon Hafron- River Severn in Welsh

Aldarennaöy – Alderney (Channel Islands)

Alt Clut- Dumbarton Castle on the Clyde

Anmyen -Amiens

Andecavis- Angers in Anjou

Angia- Jersey (Channel Islands)

An Lysardh -The Lizard (Cornwall)

An Oriant- Lorient, Brittany

Æscesdūn – Ashdown (Berkshire)

Áth Truim- Trim, County Meath (Ireland)

Baille - a ward (an enclosed area inside a wall)

Balley Chashtal -Castleton (Isle of Man)

Bárekr's Haven – Barfleur, Normandy

Bebbanburgh- Bamburgh Castle, Northumbria. Also, known as Din Guardi in the ancient tongue

Beck- a stream

Bexelei – Bexhill on sea

Bieuvais-Beauvais

Blót – a blood sacrifice made by a jarl

Blue Sea/Middle Sea- The Mediterranean

Bondi- Viking farmers who fight

Bourde- Bordeaux

Bjarnarøy –Great Bernera (Bear Island)

Byrnie- a mail or leather shirt reaching down to the knees

Brvggas -Bruges

Caerlleon- Welsh for Chester

Caestir - Chester (old English)

Cantwareburh- Canterbury

Casnewydd –Newport, Wales

Cent- Kent

Cephas- Greek for Simon Peter (St. Peter)

Cetham -Chatham Kent

Chape- the tip of a scabbard

Charlemagne- Holy Roman Emperor at the end of the 8th and beginning of the 9th centuries

Cherestanc- Garstang (Lancashire)

Cippanhamm -Chippenham

Ċiriċeburh- Cherbourg

Condado Portucalense- the County of Portugal

Constrasta-Valença (Northern Portugal)
Corn Walum or Om Walum- Cornwall
Cissa-caestre -Chichester
Cymri- Welsh
Cymru- Wales
Cyninges-tūn – Coniston. It means the estate of the king (Cumbria)
Dùn Èideann –Edinburgh (Gaelic)
Din Guardi- Bamburgh castle
Drekar- a Dragon ship (a Viking warship)
Drokensford – Droxford
Duboglassio –Douglas, Isle of Man
Djupr -Dieppe
Dwfr- Dover
Dyrøy –Jura (Inner Hebrides)
Dyflin- Old Norse for Dublin
Ein-mánuðr- middle of March to the middle of April
Eopwinesfleot -Ebbsfleet
Eoforwic- Saxon for York
Fáfnir - a dwarf turned into a dragon (Norse mythology)
Faro Bregancio- Corunna (Spain)
Ferneberga -Farnborough (Hampshire)
Fey- having second sight
Firkin- a barrel containing eight gallons (usually beer)
Fret-a sea mist
Frankia- France and part of Germany
Fyrd-the Saxon levy
Gaill- Irish for foreigners
Galdramenn- wizard
Glaesum –amber
Gleawecastre- Gloucester
Gói- the end of February to the middle of March
Greenway- ancient roads- they used turf rather than stone
Grenewic- Greenwich
Gyllingas - Gillingham Kent
Haesta- Hastings
Haestingaceaster-Pevensey
Hastingas-Hastings
Hamafunta -Havant
Hamwic -Southampton
Hantone- Littlehampton
Haughs/ Haugr - small hills in Norse (As in Tarn Hows) or a hump- normally a mound of earth
Hearth-weru- Jarl's bodyguard/oathsworn

Heels- when a ship leans to one side under the pressure of the wind
Hel- Queen of, the Norse underworld.
Herkumbl- a mark on the front of a helmet denoting the clan of a Viking warrior
Here Wic- Harwich
Hetaereiarch – Byzantine general
Hí- Iona (Gaelic)
Hjáp - Shap- Cumbria (Norse for stone circle)
Hoggs or Hogging- when the pressure of the wind causes the stern or the bow to droop
Hrams-a – Ramsey, Isle of Man
Hrīs Wearp – Ruswarp (North Yorkshire)
Hrofecester-Rochester Kent
Hywel ap Rhodri Molwynog- King of Gwynedd 814-825
Icaunis- a British river god
Ishbiliyya- Seville
Issicauna- Gaulish for the lower Seine
Itouna- River Eden Cumbria
Jarl- Norse earl or lord
Joro-goddess of the earth
Jǫtunn -Norse god or goddess
Kartreidh -Carteret in Normandy
Kjerringa - Old Woman- the solid block in which the mast rested
Knarr- a merchant ship or a coastal vessel
Kyrtle-woven top
Laugardagr-Saturday (Norse for washing day)
Leathes Water- Thirlmere
Ljoðhús- Lewis
Legacaestir- Anglo Saxon for Chester
Liger- Loire
Lochlannach – Irish for Northerners (Vikings)
Lothuwistoft- Lowestoft
Louis the Pious- King of the Franks and son of Charlemagne
Lundenwic - London
Lincylene -Lincoln
Maen hir – standing stone (menhir)
Maeresea- River Mersey
Mammceaster- Manchester
Manau/Mann – The Isle of Man(n) (Saxon)
Marcia Hispanic- Spanish Marches (the land around Barcelona)
Mast fish- two large racks on a ship for the mast
Melita- Malta
Midden - a place where they dumped human waste
Miklagård - Constantinople

Leudes- Imperial officer (a local leader in the Carolingian Empire. They became Counts a century after this.)
Njörðr- God of the sea
Nithing- A man without honour (Saxon)
Odin- The "All Father" God of war, also associated with wisdom, poetry, and magic (The ruler of the gods).
Olissipo- Lisbon
Orkneyjar-Orkney
Portucale- Porto
Portesmūða -Portsmouth
Penrhudd – Penrith Cumbria
Pillars of Hercules- Straits of Gibraltar
Qādis- Cadiz
Ran- Goddess of the sea
Readingum -Reading Berks
Remisgat Ramsgate
Roof rock- slate
Rinaz –The Rhine
Sabrina- Latin and Celtic for the River Severn. Also, the name of a female Celtic deity
Saami- the people who live in what is now Northern Norway/Sweden
Saint Maclou- St Malo (France)
Sandwic- Sandwich (Kent)
Sarnia- Guernsey (Channel Islands)
St. Cybi- Holyhead
Sampiere -samphire (sea asparagus)
Scree- loose rocks in a glacial valley
Seax – short sword
Sheerstrake- the uppermost strake in the hull
Sheet- a rope fastened to the lower corner of a sail
Shroud- a rope from the masthead to the hull amidships
Skeggox – an axe with a shorter beard on one side of the blade
Sondwic-Sandwich
South Folk- Suffolk
Stad- Norse settlement
Stays- ropes running from the mast-head to the bow
Streanæshalc -Whitby
Stirap- stirrup
Strake- the wood on the side of a drekar
Suthriganaworc - Southwark (London)
Svearike -Sweden
Syllingar- Scilly Isles
Syllingar Insula- Scilly Isles

Tarn- small lake (Norse)
Temese- River Thames (also called the Tamese)
The Norns- The three sisters who weave webs of intrigue for men
Thing-Norse for a parliament or a debate (Tynwald)
Thor's day- Thursday
Threttanessa- a drekar with 13 oars on each side.
Thrall- slave
Tinea- Tyne
Tintaieol- Tintagel (Cornwall)
Trenail- a round wooden peg used to secure strakes
Tude- Tui in Northern Spain
Tynwald- the Parliament on the Isle of Man
Úlfarrberg- Helvellyn
Úlfarrland- Cumbria
Úlfarr- Wolf Warrior
Úlfarrston- Ulverston
Ullr-Norse God of Hunting
Ulfheonar-an elite Norse warrior who wore a wolf skin over his armour
Uuluuich- Dulwich
Valauna- Valognes (Normandy)
Vectis- The Isle of Wight
Veðrafjǫrðr -Waterford (Ireland)
Veisafjǫrðr- Wexford (Ireland)
Volva- a witch or healing woman in Norse culture
Waeclinga Straet- Watling Street (A5)
Windlesore-Windsor
Waite- a Viking word for farm
Werham -Wareham (Dorset)
Wintan-Caestre -Winchester
Wihtwara- Isle of White
Withy- the mechanism connecting the steering board to the ship
Woden's day- Wednesday
Wyddfa-Snowdon
Wyrd- Fate
Yard- a timber from which the sail is suspended on a drekar
Ynys Môn-Anglesey

Maps and Illustrations

The Norman dynasty

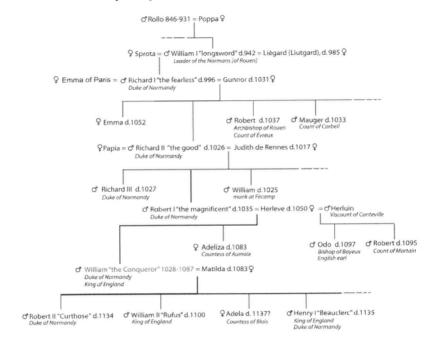

Courtesy of Wikipedia.

Historical note

My research encompasses not only books and the Internet but also TV. Time Team was a great source of information. I wish they would bring it back! I saw the wooden compass which my sailors use on the Dan Snow programme about the Vikings. Apparently, it was used in modern times to sail from Denmark to Edinburgh and was only a couple of points out. Similarly, the construction of the temporary hall was copied from the settlement of Leif Leifsson in Newfoundland.

Dates are very fluid in the sources which remain to us. Rollo's birth has been cited as any time from 840 to 846 and his son's death between 935 and 942. No two seemed to agree. I have used a consensus.

Stirrups began to be introduced in Europe during the 7th and 8th Centuries. By Charlemagne's time, they were widely used but only by nobles. It is said this was the true beginning of feudalism. Knights used stirrups. It marked the nobles as landowners who rode their horses and controlled large tracts of land. It was the Vikings who introduced them to England. It was only in the time of Canute the Great that they became widespread. The use of stirrups enabled a rider to strike someone on the ground from the back of a horse and facilitated the use of spears and later, lances.

The Vikings may seem cruel to us now. They enslaved women and children. Many of the women became their wives. The DNA of the people of Iceland shows that it was made up of a mixture of Norse and Danish males and Celtic females. These were the people who settled in Iceland, Greenland and Vinland. They did the same in England and, as we shall see, Normandy. Their influence was widespread. Genghis Khan and his Mongols did the same in the 13th century. It is said that a high proportion of European males have Mongol blood in them. The Romans did it with the Sabine tribe. They were different times and it would be wrong to judge them with our politically correct twenty-first-century eyes. This sort of behaviour still goes on in the world but with less justification.

At this time, there were no Viking kings. There were clans. Each clan had a hersir or Jarl. Clans were loyal to each other. A hersir was more of a landlocked Viking or a farmer while a Jarl usually had a ship(s) at his command. A hersir would command Bondi. They were the Norse equivalent of the fyrd although they were much better warriors. They would all have a helmet shield and a sword. Most would also have a spear. Hearth weru were the oathsworn or bodyguards for a jarl or, much later on, a king. Kings like Canute and Harald Hadrada were rare and they only emerged at the beginning of the tenth century.

I have used the names by which places were known in the medieval period wherever possible. Sometimes I have had to use the modern name. The Cotentin is an example. The Isle of Sheep is now called the Isle of Sheppey and lies on the Medway close to the Thames. The land of Kent was known as Cent in the early medieval period. Thanet or, Tanet as it was known in the Viking period was an island at this time. The sea was on two sides and the other two sides had swamps, bogs, mudflats and tidal streams. It protected Canterbury. The coast was different too. Richborough had been a major Roman port. It is now some way inland. Sandwich was a port. Other ports now lie under the sea. Vikings were not afraid to sail up very narrow rivers and to risk being stranded on mud. They were tough men and were capable of carrying or porting their ships as their Rus brothers did when travelling to Miklagård.

The Norns or the Weird Sisters.

"The Norns (Old Norse: norn, plural: nornir) in Norse mythology are female beings who rule the destiny of gods and men. They roughly correspond to other controllers of humans' destiny, the Fates, elsewhere in European mythology.

In Snorri Sturluson's interpretation of the Völuspá, Urðr (Wyrd), Verðandi and Skuld, the three most important of the Norns, come out from a hall standing at the Well of Urðr or Well of Fate. They draw water from the well and take sand that lies around it, which they pour over Yggdrasill so that its branches will not rot. These three Norns are described as powerful maiden giantesses (Jotuns) whose arrival from Jötunheimr ended the golden age of the gods. They may be the same as the maidens of Mögþrasir who are described in Vafþrúðnismál"

Source: Norns - https://en.wikipedia.org

Rollo

I have used the name Rollo even though that is the Latinisation of Hrolf. I did so for two reasons. We all know the first Duke of Normandy as Rollo and I wanted to avoid confusion with his grandfather. I realise that I have also caused enough of a problem with Ragnvald and Ragnvald the Breton Slayer.

Rollo is generally identified with one Viking in particular – a man of high social status mentioned in Icelandic sagas, which refer to him by the

Old Norse name Göngu-Hrólfr, meaning "Hrólfr the Walker". (Göngu-Hrólfr is also widely known by an Old Danish variant, Ganger-Hrolf.) The byname "Walker" is usually understood to suggest that Rollo was so physically imposing that he could not be carried by a horse and was obliged to travel on foot. Norman and other French sources do not use the name Hrólfr, and the identification of Rollo with Göngu-Hrólfr is based upon similarities between circumstances and actions ascribed to both figures.

He had children by at least three women. He abducted Popa or Poppa the daughter of the Count of Rennes or possibly the Count of Bayeux. It is not known if she was legitimate or illegitimate. He married Gisela the daughter (probably illegitimate) of King Charles of France. He also had another child. According to the medieval Irish text, '*An Banshenchas*' and Icelandic sources, another daughter, Cadlinar (Kaðlín; Kathleen) was born in Scotland (probably to a Scots mother) and married an Irish prince named Beollán mac Ciarmaic, later King of South Brega (Lagore). I have used the Norse name Kaðlín and made her a Scottish princess.

I apologise for the number of Franks called Charles. All of them existed and they had the soubriquets I gave them. None were flattering. The family of the King of the Bretons are also accurate. Godfrid, Duke of Frisia was a Viking and he was murdered. As insane as it sounds the King of the Franks gave his 5-year-old as Rollo's bride. As Rollo was almost sixty it does not sound right but they were different times.

The revolt in Normandy did happen. Rollo dealt with it harshly. Every male rebel was blinded and or had their feet or hands removed. They did not rebel again! The Battle of Soissons was a defeat for Charles but King Robert died in the battle. The battle of Eu was fought between King Rudolf and his Flemish allies against the Normans. They lost. Elfweard was murdered before he could become King of England. His brother did become a great King of England but many believed he had his brother assassinated. Count Arnulf had his vengeance and his killers ambushed and killed William Longsword just a few years after Göngu-Hrólfr Rognvaldson died. *Wyrd*'

This is the last book in the series. I originally planned a work which would take us to Hastings but that will be another series. I owed it to Göngu-Hrólfr Rognvaldson to end the book with his death. For those who have been on this journey, I hope you have enjoyed it. I enjoyed writing it.

Books used in the research

- British Museum - Vikings- Life and Legends
- Arthur and the Saxon Wars- David Nicolle (Osprey)
- Saxon, Norman and Viking Terence Wise (Osprey)
- The Vikings- Ian Heath (Osprey)
- Byzantine Armies 668-1118 - Ian Heath (Osprey)
- Romano-Byzantine Armies 4th- 9th Century - David Nicholle (Osprey)
- The Walls of Constantinople AD 324-1453 - Stephen Turnbull (Osprey)
- Viking Longship - Keith Durham (Osprey)
- The Vikings in England- Anglo-Danish Project
- The Varangian Guard- 988-1453 Raffael D'Amato
- Saxon Viking and Norman- Terence Wise
- The Walls of Constantinople AD 324-1453-Stephen Turnbull
- Byzantine Armies- 886-1118- Ian Heath
- The Age of Charlemagne-David Nicolle
- The Normans- David Nicolle
- Norman Knight AD 950-1204- Christopher Gravett
- The Norman Conquest of the North- William A Kappelle
- The Knight in History- Francis Gies
- The Norman Achievement- Richard F Cassady
- Knights- Constance Brittain Bouchard
- British Kings and Queens- Mike Ashley

Griff Hosker
March 2019

Other books by Griff Hosker

If you enjoyed reading this book, then why not read another one by the author?

Ancient History

The Sword of Cartimandua Series
(Germania and Britannia 50 A.D. – 128 A.D.)
Ulpius Felix- Roman Warrior (prequel)
The Sword of Cartimandua
The Horse Warriors
Invasion Caledonia
Roman Retreat
Revolt of the Red Witch
Druid's Gold
Trajan's Hunters
The Last Frontier
Hero of Rome
Roman Hawk
Roman Treachery
Roman Wall
Roman Courage

The Wolf Warrior series
(Britain in the late 6th Century)
Saxon Dawn
Saxon Revenge
Saxon England
Saxon Blood
Saxon Slayer
Saxon Slaughter
Saxon Bane
Saxon Fall: Rise of the Warlord
Saxon Throne
Saxon Sword

Medieval History

The Dragon Heart Series
Viking Slave
Viking Warrior
Viking Jarl
Viking Kingdom
Viking Wolf
Viking War
Viking Sword
Viking Wrath
Viking Raid
Viking Legend
Viking Vengeance
Viking Dragon
Viking Treasure
Viking Enemy
Viking Witch
Viking Blood
Viking Weregeld
Viking Storm
Viking Warband
Viking Shadow
Viking Legacy
Viking Clan
Viking Bravery

The Norman Genesis Series
Hrolf the Viking
Horseman
The Battle for a Home
Revenge of the Franks
The Land of the Northmen
Ragnvald Hrolfsson
Brothers in Blood
Lord of Rouen
Drekar in the Seine
Duke of Normandy
The Duke and the King

The Duke and the King

New World Series
Blood on the Blade
Across the Seas
The Savage Wilderness
The Bear and the Wolf
Erik the Navigator

The Vengeance Trail

The Danelaw Saga
The Dragon Sword

The Reconquista Chronicles
Castilian Knight
El Campeador
The Lord of Valencia

The Aelfraed Series
(Britain and Byzantium 1050 A.D. - 1085 A.D.)
Housecarl
Outlaw
Varangian

**The Anarchy Series England
1120-1180**
English Knight
Knight of the Empress
Northern Knight
Baron of the North
Earl
King Henry's Champion
The King is Dead
Warlord of the North
Enemy at the Gate
The Fallen Crown
Warlord's War
Kingmaker
Henry II

Crusader
The Welsh Marches
Irish War
Poisonous Plots
The Princes' Revolt
Earl Marshal

Border Knight
1182-1300
Sword for Hire
Return of the Knight
Baron's War
Magna Carta
Welsh Wars
Henry III
The Bloody Border
Baron's Crusade
Sentinel of the North
War in the West
Debt of Honour (May 2021)

Sir John Hawkwood Series
France and Italy 1339- 1387
Crécy: The Age of the Archer
Man at Arms
The White Company (July 2021)

Lord Edward's Archer
Lord Edward's Archer
King in Waiting
An Archer's Crusade
Targets of Treachery (Due out August 2021)

Struggle for a Crown
1360- 1485
Blood on the Crown
To Murder A King
The Throne
King Henry IV

The Duke and the King

The Road to Agincourt
St Crispin's Day
The Battle for France

Tales from the Sword I

Conquistador
England and America in the 16th Century
Conquistador (Coming in 2021)

Modern History

The Napoleonic Horseman Series
Chasseur à Cheval
Napoleon's Guard
British Light Dragoon
Soldier Spy
1808: The Road to Coruña
Talavera
The Lines of Torres Vedras
Bloody Badajoz
The Road to France
Waterloo (June 2021)

The Lucky Jack American Civil War series
Rebel Raiders
Confederate Rangers
The Road to Gettysburg

The British Ace Series
1914
1915 Fokker Scourge
1916 Angels over the Somme
1917 Eagles Fall
1918 We will remember them
From Arctic Snow to Desert Sand
Wings over Persia

Combined Operations series
1940-1945
Commando
Raider
Behind Enemy Lines
Dieppe
Toehold in Europe
Sword Beach
Breakout
The Battle for Antwerp
King Tiger
Beyond the Rhine
Korea
Korean Winter

Tales from the Sword Book 2

Other Books
Great Granny's Ghost (Aimed at 9-14-year-old young people)

For more information on all of the books then please visit the author's website at www.griffhosker.com where there is a link to contact him or visit his Facebook page: GriffHosker at Sword Books

Printed in Great Britain
by Amazon

63551454R00135